International Praise

"This tense psychological thriller from Holland's answer to Nicci French utilises a classic trouble-in-paradise set-up . . . What makes it so effective is the broader picture Maier paints of dislocated dreamers out of their depth, obliged to cede control over their lives."

—*The Guardian*

"Maier sketches characters that go beyond the standard thriller stereotypes."

—Barnes & Noble Review

"Maier manages to lead us away from the path we thought we were following and constructs an intriguing morality tale that is a bestseller across Europe."

—*Daily Mail*

"A sly, unusual thriller."

—Felony & Mayhem Press

"Excellent writing."

—*Literary Review*

"Terrific."

—*Sunday Times*

"Excellent little thriller. If you like your crime fiction suspenseful, erotically romantic, tense and pacy, this is definitely a book for you."

—Euro Crime

"Nova Lee Maier is a master of carefully devised plots, and she deserves an award for the final pages alone. But cleverest of all is the way she depicts her characters."

—*Knack*

"Smoothly written and brilliantly plotted."

—VN Thrillergids

"Nova Lee Maier clearly belongs to the writing elite in our country."

—*Algemeen Dagblad*

"If you can keep your reviewer's adrenaline pumping deep into the night, that is craftsmanship."

—*de Volkskrant*

CLOSE
TO
THE
CRADLE

CLOSE
TO
THE
CRADLE

A THRILLER

NOVA LEE MAIER

TRANSLATED BY ALEXANDER SMITH

amazoncrossing

Text copyright © 2014 by Esther Verhoef
Translation copyright © 2019 by Alexander Smith
All rights reserved.

No part of this book may be reproduced, or stored in a retrieval system, or transmitted in any form or by any means, electronic, mechanical, photocopying, recording, or otherwise, without express written permission of the publisher.

Previously published as *De Kraamhulp* by Ambo/Anthos in The Netherlands in 2014. Translated from Dutch by Alexander Smith. First published in English by AmazonCrossing in 2019.

Published by AmazonCrossing, Seattle

www.apub.com

Amazon, the Amazon logo, and AmazonCrossing are trademarks of Amazon.com, Inc., or its affiliates.

ISBN-13: 9781542044363
ISBN-10: 1542044367

Cover design by Shasti O'Leary Soudant

Printed in the United States of America

CLOSE
TO
THE
CRADLE

Day One

TUESDAY

"So this is where you live," whispered Miriam.

Her fingers were wrapped around the steering wheel of her Peugeot. They'd become slightly sweaty, and to her annoyance, she noticed that she'd started breathing faster. That was rare when she was on duty. Whatever happened, and however threatening the situation, she remained calm and professional, refusing to get carried away. She knew that she could always fall back on her training, experience, and colleagues.

But she wasn't on duty now.

She was on her own.

She leaned forward and looked up along the sleek façade of the apartment block. The glass glinted in the autumn sun. The building looked unwelcoming. As if the people who lived here considered themselves above the rest of the world. And in a literal sense, they were. The view from up there was bound to be breathtaking. You'd be able to see right across Rotterdam, the harbors, and the Maas.

How many floors did this building actually have? Miriam was forced to give up counting at twenty-five.

Somebody was honking angrily behind her. In the rearview mirror, she looked into the driver's flushed face. He raised his hands and gestured to her. Miriam resisted the temptation to get out, show him her police badge, and ask for his ID. After all, the man was right: she was holding up traffic.

She put the Peugeot into first gear.

Her carotid artery throbbed in her throat as she drove to the end of the narrow street.

❧

Hennequin turned onto Baljuwstraat. The sidewalks were lined with spindly little trees supported by stakes. All the houses looked the same: cubist, semidetached units with shared driveways and dark fired-brick walls. The glass in the large windows had a bluish tint, making it difficult to see inside.

Number 66 was halfway down the street. A plywood stork had been stuck into the gravel in the front garden, and a garland in the large living room window announced "It's a girl!"

The baby had been born in the hospital yesterday. If everything had gone smoothly, mother and child would have been discharged a few hours after delivery, but due to the very difficult labor, they'd been kept in till this morning.

Hennequin parked her car along the curb. She took her nursing bag from the back seat and walked up to the front door under the carport, which housed a gleaming Audi. She glanced inside: a clean, dark, sleek interior. No clutter. The car looked like it had just been driven off the lot. Below the license plate, the name of the leasing company was printed in small yellow letters.

She rang the bell and examined the lock on the front door. It didn't look too complicated, but it would probably be more convenient if she just had her own key. The family was unlikely to object. People who'd just had their first child were emotional, always a little off-kilter. Their whole life had been turned upside down by the arrival of a new human being. The maternity nurse was their confidante: a beacon of calm and wisdom in a new, unfamiliar situation. As a result, people quickly took her into their confidence. Hemorrhoids, vaginal stitches, family feuds, and other sensitive subjects were discussed quite openly with the maternity nurse—a complete stranger.

Recently, Dora had told Hennequin what she'd loved about this job, before she'd set up her own private maternity agency in her converted garage and started delegating to others. She'd said, "You meet families at the happiest, most intimate time of their lives. It's such compassionate work, so rewarding."

Hennequin saw it differently: the maternity nurse met people at the most vulnerable time of their lives, when they were least wary.

❦

Didi Vos was lying in the raised bed in the guest room. She could barely move. That had been the case for several months before the birth, but it was even worse now. Before, she'd been able to waddle along, constantly holding on to a wall or piece of furniture. It was often easier to go backward than forward. She could only move in straight lines; turning was impossible. Getting in and out of bed was an ordeal. She had to think about every step.

SPD—symphysis pubis dysfunction—had been the midwife's diagnosis, later confirmed by the gynecologist. She'd been referred to a physiotherapist, but his exercises hadn't done much good. Or any, in fact. Didi's pelvic bones had been weakened by pregnancy hormones, then pushed apart by the mass and weight of the baby. Every movement was agony. She broke into a sweat at the tiniest change in pressure. Lifting anything was out of the question. When she'd tried to put away a crate of beer that Oscar had left on the counter, she'd collapsed on the spot. It had taken her many painful minutes to pull herself back to her feet, surrounded by the crunching glass of the broken bottles.

"It'll get better on its own, after the birth," the physiotherapist had said.

But there was still no sign of that.

Perhaps it would never get better.

Didi had given birth with an epidural; the anesthetic had been injected through a tube inserted into her spine. The substance had numbed the nerves in her lower body. Unable to feel the labor pains, she'd just watched her stomach contract. It had been very strange, like looking at someone else's body. When the time came to start pushing, it was impossible. She couldn't control her muscles. She'd lost all feeling down there; everything was dead and numb. The gynecologist had reduced the anesthetic until the sharp pain came shooting back again. It felt like long claws were pulling her intestines and membranes apart inside her belly.

Yesterday, Didi had learned the meaning of the words "excruciating pain." Her carroty hair had been soaked with sweat, and her pale face had turned deep red. Feces had come out with the first contraction. No one had said anything, but she'd been able to smell it. Then she'd seen a nurse cleaning the plastic under her buttocks. Didi hadn't felt the cut. But she'd heard it. It sounded just like cutting open a cardboard box with a pair of scissors.

Oscar had stood at the foot of the bed, diagonally behind the gynecologist. She would never forget the look of horror on his face. And how he turned away.

❦

"I'm Oscar. Come in. Good to see you." The man opened the door wider for her.

She shook his hand. "Hennequin Smith."

Oscar looked at her in surprise. "Hennequin? That's an unusual name."

"I can thank my parents for it." She examined the father of the family. He didn't look bad. Tired, disheveled, but that was understandable for a man who'd just become a father. If she ignored the bags under his bloodshot eyes, he was holding up pretty well. Thirties, like her. Fairly tall, athletic, well proportioned, nice clothes—perhaps even a bit slick, the sales manager type. A perfect fit with his car.

She hung her jacket on the coatrack and went into the living room. It was spacious and modern. Everything was white, brown, or beige. When it came to interior design, the Stevens-Vos family didn't stray from the trends set by the big home furnishing chains. The outside was an exception. Through the sliding patio doors, Hennequin looked into the back garden, which was enclosed by a simple wooden fence. It appeared slightly unfinished, with grass and a few scrubby bushes. A two-story hutch had been built against the fence. "Jip & Janneke" was painted on the wood in elegant letters, and two lop-eared rabbits hopped back and forth behind the mesh.

Why on earth would grown-ups keep such creatures?

"Er, my wife is upstairs," she heard Oscar say.

Hennequin followed him up the hardwood staircase. Their footsteps sounded slightly hollow. Oscar led her into what seemed to be a seldom-used guest room. A white desk, laminate flooring. There was a single bed on risers by the window, with a triangular handgrip above it. A white figure with ginger hair was lying in the bed. All Dutch women received daily visits from a maternity nurse after giving birth, but this new mother clearly needed that support more than most: she looked pale and shivery, like a patient who'd been given only a few weeks to live.

That might not be so far from the truth, thought Hennequin.

Smiling broadly, she walked over to Didi.

❦

Didi took an instant liking to the maternity nurse. She looked a bit like she'd stepped out of *Real Housewives*, but she had a kind expression in her eyes. Her bleached-blonde hair was tied up in a loose bun on the back of her head. She was wearing a white nurse's uniform, with a pair of white sneakers at the end of her long legs.

"My name is Hennequin Smith." She looked at Didi sympathetically with strikingly green eyes and shook her hand. "I'm really sorry there was no one here to meet you when you arrived home this morning."

"Well, you're here now, aren't you?" said Oscar.

Hennequin nodded. "But even so, it's better if everything goes according to plan at such an exciting time."

"Dora said Jantine couldn't make it. Is she ill?"

"If only." Hennequin sat down on the edge of the bed. The mattress sagged under her weight.

A sharp stab of pain shot from Didi's pelvis through her entire body. She clenched her teeth and pressed her lips together.

Don't be pathetic.

Hennequin made a serious face. "Jantine had an accident. She fell down some stairs early this morning."

Didi raised her eyebrows. "Fell? Oh no. How is—"

"Fine. She broke her tailbone, but it could have been worse." Hennequin glanced at Oscar and then looked back at Didi. "Most accidents happen in the home."

"Yes, that's what they say."

Didi was suddenly overcome with tiredness. She'd barely slept in the hospital bed, feeling empty and alone without the reassuring wriggling of the baby, which had become so familiar in the past few months. Now, when she put her hands on her stomach, all she felt was a soft hollow behind the stretched skin and muscles. She hadn't been able to see her baby either, since she'd been placed in a little ward on the other side of the corridor with other newborns, where the nurses could keep a closer eye on her. Indy had been delivered by vacuum extraction. As a result, her little skull was pointy, and the skin was broken where the pressure had been applied.

Was that the baby she could hear crying again now? Indy had such a tiny voice. She sounded like a little lamb.

Hennequin stood up. The mattress sprang back, and the movement caused another stab of pain.

Didi resolved to ask the nurse—*Annelien?*—not to sit on the bed tomorrow. She was reluctant to mention it right now, on the first day, in case this beautiful, well-groomed woman might think she was a neurotic nag. But that was exactly how she felt. Neurotic. Empty. Tired.

Dead tired.

She watched Hennequin put her nursing bag on the desk and open it.

"Where's your baby?" said Hennequin.

"Next door," replied Oscar.

"OK, then. Let's have a look at her." Hennequin smiled as she took out a smaller bag and a folder. "I love babies."

❧

Miriam had undressed and gotten into bed. She'd closed the blinds and drawn the curtains. It was completely dark. The alarm clock was set for nine p.m. To make it through night shifts as a police officer, you had to get some sleep in the middle of the day before going to work, a method known as presleeping. That meant putting the phone on silent, disabling the doorbell, and trying your best to ignore outside noises.

Normally, Miriam had no trouble falling asleep. In preparation, she went to bed as late as possible the night before. But it wasn't helping today. She kept tossing and turning.

Since her brother had died six months ago, she hadn't had a moment's peace. *A fall down the stairs.* That had been the cause of death, according to the doctor. An accident in the home. Miriam had barely been able to believe it. Bart, dead, just like that? Bart, who'd slipped in his socks and fallen down the stairs of his Belgian mansion? Or had Hennequin Smith, that awful woman he'd married, had a hand in it? Miriam had hated her on sight.

Bart had met his wife on a business trip to the US. After returning to Belgium, they'd rushed into marriage. It had been a ridiculously expensive, over-the-top wedding at which Miriam had felt ill at ease. The bride in particular had given her the creeps. She wasn't sure why. The brunette was beautiful, clever, and cosmopolitan, and seemed to be genuinely in love with her brother.

Yet every time Miriam had watched her sister-in-law from a distance, it had made her hair stand on end. There was something not quite right about that woman.

Less than eighteen months after the wedding, Bart was dead.

"Professional bias," Rens had said, after listening patiently to her theory. He was the only colleague at the station still willing to listen when she wanted to talk about Bart's death and Hennequin's possible involvement in it. But like the others, he didn't follow her line of reasoning. "We see too much misery. People are strange creatures. You're still grieving; that's all." He'd put his arm around her and given her a friendly nudge in the ribs.

Professional bias. Maybe. She couldn't rule it out. She'd been with the police too long to be immune from it.

Yet there was such a thing as intuition.

Now that she'd tracked Hennequin down, she wanted to find out much more about her. But first, she really had to get some sleep, or she wouldn't be able to do her job tonight. Even on a quiet weeknight, she could expect to be called out to six or seven arrests. People wielding knives, car thieves, lunatics, men who couldn't keep their hands to themselves—night after night they were hauled off the streets, and Miriam had long stopped wondering where they kept coming from. She and her colleagues made the world a little safer.

But you couldn't even save your own brother.

Miriam rolled onto her side and pulled the covers angrily over her head.

❧

Daylight filtered in through the heavily patterned pink-and-blue curtains. The room smelled strongly of baby oil and brand-new furniture and fabric. There was a baby bath on a stand, and in the corner, a huge cuddly Miffy doll sat staring at the wooden floor. The wall was decorated with wooden hearts and stars, and a group of sappy-looking stuffed animals were lined up on top of the wardrobe.

Hennequin shoved a stack of forms under the changing mat on the pink chest of drawers. Over the next few days, she would have to use these forms to record important details concerning the baby's weight, bowel movements, and temperature.

She went over to the crib and glanced inside. Oscar came and stood beside her, still slightly uneasy in his new role as a dad and trying to appear nonchalant with his thumbs in his jean pockets. His face softened when he looked at his little daughter.

Hennequin could smell his masculine scent through the fragrance of the baby oil. She moved a little closer to him and peered at the child, who had a pointy head covered with bloody scabs and a tangle of red hair. Her skin was pale and wrinkled, as if she'd spent too long in the bath. The pink cotton bodysuit was a few sizes too big.

It was a mystery to her why people went gaga over babies. There was nothing cute about them. Babies were people who couldn't yet walk or talk, but their personalities, talents, and shortcomings were locked in their genes and would develop as they got older. Usually with disappointing results. The vast majority would grow up to be ordinary citizens, and that was how it was meant to be. Every society needed a large middle class to serve as a breeding ground for those who'd figured out how the game was played. Every general required platoons full of anonymous cannon fodder, and every church needed hordes of believers in order to accumulate wealth and power. Nowadays it was mainly the multinationals and media giants that fed on mindless consumers. TV shows, processed food, all-inclusive holidays. People lapped them all up, but these things didn't take away the frustration; they only made it worse. The frustration of being mediocre—in the end, mediocre was what almost everyone was destined to be.

Including Indy, the just under nine-pound shrimp who lay in her crib by the window and was the absolute center of Didi and Oscar's world.

Hennequin leaned over the crib. "What a beautiful child," she said in a soft voice. "I've seen hundreds of babies, but this one is particularly lovely."

"She takes after her father," said Oscar.

Hennequin glanced sideways and saw his eyes twinkle.

He gazed at her for a moment and then looked straight ahead again, slightly embarrassed.

"I have no doubt she does," she said, smiling.

❦

Miriam shifted into third gear. She was on her way to a parking lot just outside the city. A couple of Polish men had been caught emptying the diesel tank of a truck. Neither of them spoke any Dutch, and they were now waiting in separate police vehicles for Miriam to arrive. As chief duty officer, Miriam was summoned whenever suspects were arrested in order to authorize their detention for questioning on behalf of the public prosecutor. In her earpiece she heard a continuous stream of voices: partly coded messages from the control room and the station, brief conversations between colleagues who, like her, were driving around the area in marked vehicles. Years ago, shortly after she'd joined the police, she would listen intently to every message. Since then, she'd learned to filter them out and now only paid attention when, among the babble of words, she heard her call number or the first digits of the area she was patrolling. For Miriam, this one of the most appealing aspects of the job: you were never alone. You were part of something bigger, a close-knit group of people who were in contact with one another day and night.

But tonight, the communication equipment wasn't her only link to her colleagues.

"I went to her home this morning," she told Rens, who was sitting beside her, eating a sandwich. Normally, she was unaccompanied—a chief duty officer patrolled alone—but Rens was training to do the same job, and she'd been asked to show him the ropes.

"Whose home?"

"Hennequin Smith's. She lives right in the middle of Rotterdam, in a fancy apartment block."

"You mean that woman your brother married?"

Miriam nodded.

He gave her a searching look. "You can't let it go, can you?"

"I can't and I won't. I can't stop wondering. I just want to know what happened." *I want to know who she is.* She paused and then said more softly, "Don't you think it's strange that I haven't seen or heard from her since Bart died? After the funeral, Hennequin disappeared from the face of the earth."

"Well, I doubt you were her favorite sister-in-law," muttered Rens.

"True, but I was her only one." She glanced in his direction and then looked at the road again. "Do you think I'm getting carried away?"

"Not necessarily. But after that incident in Belgium, I think you'd better drop it until the dust settles. If you want to keep your job, at least."

Miriam clenched her jaw. In the week after Bart's death, she'd driven over to Belgium in a patrol car. A completely impulsive act. She'd done everything in her power to speak to the Belgian officers who'd been in Bart's mansion on the day of the accident and talked to his widow. She hadn't consulted her chief. Or anyone at all. She'd just driven there, blinded by grief. Afterward, she didn't understand how she could have acted so rashly. Her chief, Karel van der Steen, had put her on leave for a few weeks to come to her senses. "But don't you dare pull anything like that on me again, Miriam," he'd said. "Otherwise you can look for a new job."

Miriam drove the Volkswagen Touran into the parking lot. She saw a police van and another car covered with the same reflective blue-and-orange striped stickers as the Touran. Four uniformed colleagues stood talking in the dusk. Miriam had known them for years. Earlier this evening, she'd exchanged a few words with some of them during the briefing at the station. They narrowed their eyes against the glare of her headlights. Miriam positioned her car so that her lights illuminated the side of the van. She got out, leaving the engine running. Rens followed her.

She briefly spoke to the officers and then opened the side door of the van. The first suspect, dressed in jeans and a gray cardigan and handcuffed at the wrists, stared back at her. He could barely see her, half-blinded as he no doubt was by the headlights. His face was a picture of anger and frustration, but he kept his mouth shut. Probably from experience. Miriam knew that these kinds of thieves never gave up. They thought they had the right to earn a living this way. Getting caught was regarded merely as an annoying holdup. As soon as they got out of jail, it was back to business as usual.

In English, she told the young man that he'd been arrested for theft and would be taken to the police station to give a statement. Alternatively, if he wished to seek legal advice, he would have to wait in a cell overnight until a lawyer became available at nine a.m. Without hesitation, he opted for the latter and gave her the name of a lawyer, which she wrote in her notebook.

"Take him to the station." She shut the sliding door. "We'll deal with him in the morning." She turned around and opened the rear door of the squad car to reveal a nervous boy who, according to his ID, was only eighteen. He also chose to see a lawyer.

"They're all yours," she said after closing the door.

One of the officers started speaking into his walkie-talkie. He notified the control room of the arrests. If everything went as it should, the staff in the station's custody suite would also be informed of the Poles' imminent arrival via their own walkie-talkies.

Less than ten minutes later, Miriam pulled out of the parking lot. When she didn't have to process an arrest, as she had just now, or attend a crime scene, she preferred to drive around and keep an eye on what was happening in the area. Out here, an officer could make a difference. That was how her colleagues had spotted the diesel thieves, simply by being on patrol.

Miriam loved the night shift. There was something heroic about it. *Sleep tight; we'll keep watch.*

"How did you find her?" she heard Rens ask beside her.

"Through the grapevine."

"Come on, spit it out."

She said nothing.

He shook his head and looked out the window. It was half past eleven Tuesday night, and there wasn't much traffic. "So you're still investigating on the side."

"I just looked her up in the system," she said quietly.

"What are you going to do when Van der Steen finds out?"

She shrugged.

"I don't want you to get in trouble."

"I won't."

She raised her chin when she heard one of her units being summoned by Monique, a colleague on dispatch duty in the control room. A suspected arson attack on an industrial estate. One of the supposed culprits had been arrested and two had escaped. Monique gave a brief description of the men and asked the patrol cars to be on the lookout for them.

"Showtime," whispered Miriam. She braked abruptly and turned her car around.

"We'll be there in five minutes," added Rens, who'd heard the same message through his earpiece.

Miriam put her foot down. She switched on the blue light and sped through a virtually empty city.

❦

"Home sweet home," whispered Hennequin. She tapped the touch screen next to the front door, and her entire apartment was promptly bathed in soft light. Almost everything in her home was white, from the resin floor and the walls to the soaring ceiling. The same was true of the designer kitchen and most of the very expensive furniture, which had already been here when she moved in.

She'd only lived here for two months, but it felt like home. She'd grown to love the serenity of the interior and the constant, monotonous roar of the wind blowing around the tall building of glass and steel. It was a pity she couldn't get too attached to it.

She hung her jacket in the closet and pulled the pins out of her dark hair. Shaking it loose, she went into the bathroom, where she removed her makeup. In a box on a glass shelf, she saw her colored contact lenses. "Gemstone Green." She'd already taken them out this afternoon, as soon as she'd gotten home from her day with the Stevens-Vos family. Blue, green, or brown eyes; blonde or brown hair; long or short: it didn't require much effort to sow confusion.

Her penthouse took up one corner of the high-rise and was twice the size of the building's regular apartments. Two bedrooms, a sleek bathroom with a walk-in shower and whirlpool bath, an open designer kitchen, and a living room, all offering spectacular views over the city. That was the standout feature of her new home; the windows stretched from floor to ceiling and from wall to wall, in every room.

The interior was minimalist. There was a single low sofa and a dining table with Perspex chairs. A large gray rug and motorized curtains improved the acoustics. The only living thing other than herself within these four walls was an immense palm tree in a large pot in the corner, where the glass walls came together in a metal angle section. On the wall behind the kitchen island there was a print of a railway bridge. That was all there was to see, and all that Hennequin needed. Others might call the interior impersonal, or even cold. Hennequin found it calming.

She went into the bedroom, slid open the walk-in closet, and undressed. Taking a silk kimono from a hanger, she wrapped it around her body. She stretched until she heard her joints gently cracking. There was a tension in her body that wouldn't go away. She would have to call Mali again. A vigorous massage would do her good.

She walked barefoot into the living room, picked up the heavy remote control from the white laminate kitchen counter, and turned the music on. "Strangelove" by Depeche Mode. Brilliant. Eighties music was so underrated.

She got an opened bottle of Pouilly-Fumé out of the wine cooler, poured herself a glass, and immediately took a sip. She loved the way the liquid from the Loire Valley tingled on her tongue. In the bar of the five-star hotel where she'd just spent the evening, the wine had been as mediocre as the men.

She hummed along to the music, smiling at the lyrics. *Crimes. Sin.*

From the kitchen island, she looked across the living room and out through the window. Elongated clouds were racing across the dark-blue sky, their frayed edges illuminated by the moon. A sea of lights twinkled below, and in the distance the river glistened in the moonlight—a silvery ribbon that curved through the middle of the city.

Hennequin sat down on the leather couch and grabbed her iPad. She had an email from Dora. She could guess what it said: the agency still hadn't received all her documents. But Dora would have to wait. Hennequin had homework to do.

A few weeks ago, she'd downloaded a PDF entitled *Healthcare Protocols*. The 108-page manual turned out to be highly interesting reading. A sort of basic course in maternity care. She'd read through the text a few times and now knew it practically by heart. The knowledge she'd acquired had proved sufficient for her to bluff her way into the agency. But now it was time for a little extra training. She opened the *Breastfeeding Protocol* PDF and started reading.

❦

It was quiet and dark in the guest room. The recessed lights had been dimmed to the minimum.

"She's sleeping. I'm going to bed," said Oscar. "Is there enough milk in the fridge?"

"Hennequin prepared two bottles for the night. If that's not enough, I might have some in reserve here." Didi put her hands on her breasts and laughed nervously.

They'd become fuller in the past few months, but despite all that extra volume, they didn't seem to contain much milk. In the hospital, she'd managed to get a few drops out with a great deal of pain and effort. That was perfectly common, she'd been assured. Within a week, her milk production would be normal. But she had to keep pumping to stimulate milk flow.

Oscar had rented a breast pump—a buzzing, electric contraption—from the breastfeeding clinic. Didi thought it best if his involvement ended there. She didn't want to burden him any further. He was already so shaken up after the delivery. Fortunately, the maternity nurse was a gem. Earlier today, it had taken them a while to figure out exactly how to set up the pump. Once they'd gotten it working, Didi had found it painful, even on the lowest setting, but she hadn't let it show. A little bit of milk had come out of her breasts, and that was the most important thing.

Oscar pointed with his chin to Didi's iPhone. "Any minute now, I'll be out like a light. If you hear Indy crying, will you call and wake me up?"

She nodded. Indy was sleeping in her own room next door. And although, according to Oscar and Hennequin, the baby was perfectly happy there, Didi would've preferred to have her daughter with her at night. Snuggled up in her arms. But that wasn't possible. If she developed pain from the extra weight of the baby, she would barely be able to move. Hennequin had also advised her not to put the baby in a cradle beside her bed. After the difficult labor, mother and daughter needed plenty of rest.

Oscar planted a kiss on Didi's forehead. "Good night. See you in the morning."

No kiss on the mouth.

No hug.

She watched him walk out of the guest room and close the door behind him. Then she heard his footsteps on the laminate floor of the landing. She pressed her lips together and fought back tears.

Day Two

WEDNESDAY

Miriam put her service weapon and pepper spray in the safe and used her keycard to open the door to the stairwell. The parking garage was underneath the station. Her footsteps echoed between the concrete walls. It was six thirty a.m., but she didn't feel sleepy. Her body was still full of caffeine and adrenaline, like always after a night shift.

Being part of a team wasn't the only reason she couldn't wish for a better job than this. She loved the action, the variety. The rapid change of pace. Even on quiet evenings, the unit was almost constantly in demand. Violence, theft, drugs, guns—never a dull moment.

The lights of her blue Peugeot blinked when she unlocked the doors. She got in, started the engine, and drove up to the gate. It slid open before she had the chance to hold her keycard against the reader. She smiled. Annelies, a colleague who manned the sergeants' room, had seen her on one of the monitors and already pressed the button. The galvanized gate slid shut behind her. The barrier at the end of the complex also opened by itself. Miriam's walkie-talkie was in the cupboard at the station, so she flashed her lights and put her hand up to the camera to thank Annelies.

She drove out of the police complex and turned onto the public road. It was still dark, but that would start to change within an hour.

Miriam didn't want to go home yet. Without her colleagues' chatter in her ear and the steady stream of arrestees to deal with, she had only one thing on her mind: taking another look at that apartment block. There was a chance she might learn something.

❧

Hennequin listened to her voice mail. Somebody had tried to call her this morning—at quarter to seven. That shouldn't be allowed. She tapped her nails on the kitchen counter in annoyance.

Dora's voice sounded slightly distorted over the phone. "Hennequin? It's Dora, from the maternity agency. Er . . . I was wondering if you'd received my email about that paperwork?" She paused for a moment, almost as if she expected Hennequin to respond, then cleared her throat. "You won't forget about it, will you? Could you possibly bring it over today? It's not that I don't trust you, but if we have an inspection, it could get us into serious trouble. I have to abide by the rules, like everyone else."

"Of course you do," said Hennequin icily. "We all have to follow the rules, don't we?" She looked gloomily out over the city. A pale sun was shining. The ant people had now also come to life down below.

She put her phone on the counter and stretched. Half past seven. What a time to start the day. She would never get used to it; she preferred the evening and night. But it was for a good cause. She was eager to get back to work with the Stevens-Vos family and their dearly beloved shrimp.

Hennequin took her double espresso into the guest room that she used as an office. The curtains were closed, and that was how she liked them. There was no shortage of Peeping Toms in this city. She'd viewed dozens of high-rise apartments before deciding on this penthouse. During those viewings, she'd noticed something remarkable: every apartment had contained a telescope on a tripod. The telescopes weren't pointed at the stars or the horizon, but at the windows of neighboring buildings. All of them. Everybody was spying on everybody else. Hennequin had purchased one too, but it was still in its packaging. She knew other, more interesting—and so much more satisfying—methods to penetrate deep into other people's lives.

A couple of computers and several printers had been set up on a wide white desk. The devices made a soft humming sound. Her fingers found their way around one of the keyboards, and her hazel eyes flashed across the screen. She'd already prepared a few things, so there wasn't much work left to do. Less than fifteen minutes later, the printer spat out a sheet of A4 paper. It looked like a slightly sloppy color photocopy, exactly as intended. She grabbed the paper and examined it. "Diploma in Maternity Care" it read at the top in bold letters. Obtained eleven years ago by Mrs. Hennequin Smith, born in Haarlem. Date of birth, signature. Even the watermark of the original showed through a little. It looked great. Genuine. Besides, Dora was very trusting. She was unlikely to become suspicious.

Hennequin folded the sheet of paper and stuffed it into an envelope.

❦

The baby was crying. Didi had already called Oscar four times. She could hear his ringtone faintly through the walls, but he didn't answer. It was half past seven. Indy was supposed to have had her bottle at seven o'clock. And Didi needed the toilet.

She grabbed the handgrip above the bed and tried to sit up. It worked. Step one. Now she had to get her legs over the side. She gripped her knees for extra support. With jerky movements, she worked her way little by little to the edge of the bed until her feet were dangling in the air. That was step two. Now stand up. With extreme caution, she slid off the bed. Tears welled in her eyes, and sweat beaded on her face. She started to feel defiant. Why was this happening to her? It wasn't fair.

She'd always taken good care of her body. Exercised, eaten well. And now her body was letting her down, while all around her, women got through their pregnancies and deliveries without a hitch.

At work, one of the lawyers had called her attention seeking. Not to her face, of course, but behind her back. By that point, Didi had been in a wheelchair, unable to walk. She thought back to the countless people on the street and in the supermarket who'd ignored her and spoken only to Oscar. Talked straight over her head. As if her brain had stopped functioning along with her legs. On one occasion, in Ikea, she and Oscar had bumped into one of Oscar's colleagues, a pretty girl in a fitted blue dress. At first, she'd stared at them in shock, as if she could barely believe her eyes. She'd then quickly regained her composure and briefly made polite conversation. The next day she'd said to Oscar, "I didn't know your wife was disabled." The gossip had been going around the department. *His wife is disabled, and pregnant too.* Didi was fairly certain what their next thought had been: Surely he can do better? Oscar had said he'd found it funny. *Funny!*

She was on her feet. Finally.

Standing wasn't actually that bad. It was moving that hurt more than anything, such as lifting a foot or leg, which placed an unequal strain on her unstable pelvis. She dug her teeth into her lower lip and took a step. Too fast! An excruciating pain shot through her lower back and thighs like a lash. She froze.

Indy had stopped crying. Was Oscar with her?

Grim-faced, she began to shuffle backward, in a pathetic sort of moonwalk. This method was the least painful. Constantly leaning on the wall, she made it to the landing.

At that very moment, Oscar came out of the baby's room with Indy in his arms. His dark hair was slightly tousled, and he smiled at her. Her husband looked like a model on a poster. And she looked like a creature from Middle-earth.

"Sleep well?" he asked, kissing her on the cheek.

"Yes," she murmured, looking at the tiny tot he carried on his arm. Indy's eyes twinkled. Didi had read that babies of this age couldn't focus yet, but her daughter seemed to be looking her straight in the eye. That gaze went right through her. How beautiful she was. It was a miracle. Her child. *Their* child. She leaned over and planted a kiss on her little head. Indy smelled lovely, and her soft, fine hair tickled Didi's nose.

"Isn't she gorgeous?" she whispered.

"She certainly is. Good teamwork," said Oscar softly. "Is everything OK? Need any help?"

"No, thank you. I'll manage."

"In that case, I'll go and feed this little hell-raiser," he said, and went downstairs.

Didi opened the bathroom door. There was a water bottle for her to wash her stitches with after urinating and a pack of what looked like thick sanitary napkins. As she slowly lowered herself onto the toilet, she felt guilty about her dark thoughts earlier. *Think positive*, she told herself. She'd given birth to a beautiful and healthy child with soft hair and tiny fingers that already closed around her thumb when she gave her a bottle. What was more, she had a handsome, attentive husband with a responsible job who'd taken a whole week off work because he didn't want to miss this special time. Didi wasn't her old self physically nor emotionally, but that would get better eventually. She just had to get used to her new status. It still seemed unreal. Sometimes it felt as though she and Oscar weren't actually parents and were only pretending. But the child was real. Everything was going to be all right.

She grimaced and squeezed her eyes shut as she emptied her bladder and felt the burning in her stitches.

❧

Miriam had stopped her car in a loading bay. This gave her a good view of the futuristic building where Hennequin lived. She'd been here for almost an hour, but nothing out of the ordinary had happened. Picking at a hangnail, she looked at the building in annoyance. What was she waiting for? What did she expect to achieve? Perhaps Hennequin wasn't even at home. Or she was sleeping in. Or she left via a different exit. Maybe she was spending all day in bed. It wasn't as if she had to work. Miriam's brother had left almost his entire fortune to Hennequin Smith, totaling more than five million euros after the sale of the mansion in Brasschaat. But still. Stubbornly, Miriam kept staring at the building. She couldn't bring herself to drive home.

Not yet.

Her behavior wasn't normal; she knew that. This was bordering on obsessive. She was starting to show the same character traits she saw in the stalkers and psychopaths she loved to take off the streets. Nevertheless, this was not nearly as strange as what she'd done last week. She'd inherited only a small share of her brother's estate, but it had still been enough to pay off half her mortgage. With the rest, Miriam had wanted to do something for her brother.

Last week, after much hesitation and internet searching, she'd taken the plunge and contacted a private detective agency in Florida. A man with a drawling accent and the improbable name of Chucky Lee had listened to her story and then sent her an invoice for a retainer, which she'd dutifully paid. That was the last she'd heard from "Investi-Gators." Either Chucky was delving very deeply into Hennequin's past, or Miriam could kiss her money goodbye.

There was movement in the parking garage. A black Alfa Romeo emerged. It was driven by a woman with stylish, loosely upswept hair. She was alone.

A shiver went down Miriam's spine. Hennequin had bleached her hair, but she still had the same attractive, feminine figure. The Alfa turned right and drove down the street. Instinctively, Miriam started her car and joined the traffic.

❦

Indy was sleeping contentedly on Didi's arm, her eyes closed, her tiny fingers half-curled. Indy's nails were paper-thin, like scraps of parchment. Didi stroked them with her fingertip. How beautiful she was. Unearthly beautiful. This child was worth all the pain.

She was grateful for the midwife's suggestion to put a bed in the living room. Now she could watch TV and see what was going on in the street. The downside was that she had to come downstairs in the morning and go back upstairs at night. One step forward, two steps back. But she didn't mind. It was much more sociable.

Hennequin came into the room with two mugs of coffee. Didi accepted one. She turned her head away from the baby to take a sip.

"Dora told me it was a difficult delivery." Hennequin had fetched a dining chair and was now sitting beside her bed. Her smooth, tanned legs shone under the white cotton uniform. Didi still thought her maternity nurse resembled the women from *Real Housewives*, but she struggled to identify her slight, peculiar accent.

Didi nodded. "It started with the SPD. Or pelvic pain, as the midwife called it at first, but at that stage she didn't know how serious it was. I'd heard of it, but I don't know anyone who's had it. Do you?"

Hennequin stirred her coffee. "It's not very common, fortunately."

"The midwife assured me that it wouldn't necessarily cause problems with the delivery, but in the end, they had to send me to an obstetrician because I wasn't having any contractions."

"You were induced?"

Didi nodded again.

"Dora told me you had an epidural."

"I started having contractions, but I was barely dilated." Didi gave her a blow-by-blow account of the birth. Of how she had counted the minutes and ended up kneeling in front of the hospital bed, crying in pain. Only after enduring one excruciating contraction after another for a whole day and night with no sign of progress had she received an epidural. "Things went faster after that."

Indy had been born just after midnight. She was a big baby. That had also made the delivery more difficult than usual, according to the obstetrician. Didi was proud of Indy's size. Even though she'd been confined to a wheelchair, her child had lacked nothing inside her womb.

"Do you know why they decided on a vacuum extraction?"

Didi shook her head. "Not exactly. A lot of it passed me by. Too much, in fact."

"It sounds intense." Hennequin put her mug on the table beside the bed. "You poor thing. And to think that was your first experience of childbirth. Was Oscar there?"

Didi nodded again and her face clouded over. She really would have preferred it if Oscar had stayed at the head of the bed when Indy was born. It couldn't have been a pretty sight. The incision. *That sound.* The vacuum pump. She turned her head to one side and swallowed back tears.

"Oh dear," she heard Hennequin say. The maternity nurse put a hand on her forearm. "Was it that bad?"

Didi bit her lower lip and nodded again. She didn't want to cry.

"Why aren't you breastfeeding Indy?"

"I'm pumping milk for her."

"That's not the same as breastfeeding," said Hennequin sternly.

"It was a joint decision. This way, Indy isn't completely dependent on me, and her father can feed her sometimes, or the babysitter, a few months down the line." She looked at her baby. "Also, the nurse said my nipples were too flat, so it would be difficult for Indy to 'latch,' as she called it." She shrugged. "Bottle-feeding is simply more practical. I'll have to go back to work when my maternity leave is over."

"What do you do?"

"I'm a lawyer. I work full-time at a law firm." Lowering her voice, she added, "I don't want to be one of *those* mothers."

"What do you mean?"

"The kind of woman who turns into a mother hen as soon as she has a child. Before I got pregnant, Oscar and I often went out for drinks and to dance parties with friends, that sort of thing. We want to keep doing that."

Hennequin looked pensively at the bed. She said nothing, but it was obvious what she meant.

"The doctor said that the SPD is caused by the pregnancy hormones and will go away on its own. Very few women are left permanently disabled. A tiny percentage, he said."

Hennequin remained silent, then said thoughtfully, "It's good that they put it to patients that way. As a new mother, if you start stressing about things like that, it'll affect your milk production." She stood up. "Can I make you something to eat? A slice of toast or a fried egg, perhaps? Then I'll check your uterus and your stitches."

❧

Miriam looked at the recently built house. There was a wooden stork in the garden. According to the pink garland hanging in the window, the occupants had had a girl. Hennequin had parked her Alfa in pride of place in front of the house. A nice car, but not the sort you'd expect to be driven by a wealthy widow who lived in an exclusive skyscraper downtown. The biggest surprise had come when she'd seen Hennequin get out of the car carrying a nursing bag and wearing a white uniform. Was she a midwife? A health visitor? A maternity nurse? Miriam couldn't remember her brother's widow having any background in healthcare. She didn't strike her as the type. Far from it. She vaguely recalled Hennequin doing something with computers, although she didn't know exactly what. But then she couldn't remember much about her at all, since they'd barely ever spoken to each other. Yet even if

Hennequin did work in healthcare, she didn't need to anymore. She never had to work again in her life.

In her notebook, Miriam took down the address—Baljuwstraat 66—and the Alfa's license plate.

Then she stretched and yawned. She tucked her auburn hair behind her ears and glanced in the rearview mirror. The whites of her brown eyes were shot with red. It really was time to go home and get some sleep.

❧

It didn't look good, the sight she was presented with: slightly embarrassed, Didi parted her trembling knees. Bloody. Swollen. Threads from the stitches, some of which seemed to have come loose. It would never be the same again. Ruined. Hennequin was certain she would never let herself get pregnant. Ever. No way.

With a blank expression, she poked at the soft skin between Didi's pubic bone and navel. That was what the guide had said to do. She didn't know exactly what she was supposed to feel for, but this was probably close enough. In that soft mass she would apparently find something firmer: the uterus, which, all being well, would shrink a little every day until it reached its normal size. Growth was a sign of bleeding or some other problem. That would need to be checked out. Hennequin wondered what she would do if she did notice Didi's uterus getting bigger. Let it grow, probably. Until the woman burst.

Didi made a hissing sound, and her body stiffened.

Hennequin prodded again, a little harder this time.

"It hurts," whined Didi.

"I can't help it, sorry. Just grit your teeth." With two fingers, she poked the flabby belly once more. She could now clearly feel something hard inside and pressed it, felt the contours. She ignored Didi's trembling, her whispered "ouch." Yes, that hard thing was elongated and ended just below the navel.

"That's one down." Hennequin produced a faint smile and grabbed the thermometer. "Now lie still."

Didi hadn't looked at her since the start of the examination. She'd turned her head away and stared out the window through the sheer curtains, acting as if it had nothing to do with her, as if her lower body belonged to someone else. Hennequin could understand that only too well. There were long, narrow tears in the skin of her belly. Stretch marks. These too would never go away. Didi had paid a heavy price for the shrimp. But those sacrifices were peanuts compared with what was to come.

"Put those underpants back on." Hennequin nodded to the stretchy mesh underwear that Didi wore beneath her nightgown. She disinfected the thermometer and put it back in Didi's makeup bag. "I think you should take a shower soon."

Hennequin leaned over the dining table and noted her findings on the form from the maternity agency. Second day, second measurement. On another form she kept a record of the baby's weight and the daily number of wet and soiled diapers. The end result looked professional. It had to. A midwife would call in every two or three days after the birth. She hadn't seen anybody yesterday, so she was expecting a visit today.

"Shall I make you some coffee? Or a cup of tea?"

"Yes, tea please," said Didi. Her face showed that she was in pain. She was still trying to get the elastic pants back in place. Hennequin was not going to help her with that.

She went into the kitchen and filled a mug from the hot water dispenser. Opening the lid of a wooden tea box on the counter, she took out a bag and dunked it in. It was very quiet in the house this morning. The baby was sleeping, Didi wasn't very talkative, and Oscar had gone out. His wife had sent him to the supermarket to buy drinks for the guests who were expected starting tomorrow. He also had to stock up on rusks and sugar-coated aniseeds, the traditional food served to visitors of newborn babies. Didi had told Hennequin all about the personalized bags of luxury sweets she'd ordered as gifts for her guests. She'd asked Oscar to pick those up too. He'd immediately grabbed his coat and jumped into his Audi, relieved to get away for a while.

Didi's husband clearly hated being stuck at home. His natural habitat was the business world. He was accustomed to his hectic, high-powered job as a sales manager and was struggling to adjust to his supporting role within these four walls. Hennequin was sure that Oscar couldn't wait to get back to work and impress his colleagues with stories about becoming a father. The trainees and the saleswomen would probably hang on his every word.

But there was another reason he was so desperate to get out of the house: he was trying to avoid her. Oscar was doing his very best to be a good family man. He was determined not to foul his own nest.

It was sweet of him. Very sweet, but utterly futile.

She looked at the microwave, whose smooth surface served as a mirror, and undid the top button of her work blouse. Arching her back, she made a half turn and grinned at her reflection.

❦

Miriam parked between two cars with parking permits just like hers on their windshields. She got out and locked the Peugeot.

The prewar terrace had a motley selection of shops and restaurants on the ground floor topped by two stories of apartments. They were shaded by a row of large plane trees in a grass strip between the service road and the wide thoroughfare. The leaves were already starting to turn.

Miriam felt at home here. Her granddad had been born and raised in this neighborhood. He'd died some time ago, but had told her countless stories about his youth in this city, exciting tales about the war, sailors, the Surinamese and Chinese. Only later had Miriam realized that her granddad had probably embellished them slightly, but by then she'd already followed in his footsteps and joined the police force.

As Miriam crossed the service road, she greeted Daoud. The pizzeria owner was standing in his doorway, smoking a cigarette. Next door there was a furniture shop that held sales all year round and didn't open till one o'clock in the afternoon. The shop didn't look very inviting; to save energy, the owner only turned on the strip lights when customers came in. To the right of the furniture showroom was a small art gallery, a long, narrow space with a modern white interior. From the street you could see pictures hanging on the walls and colorful sculptures on plinths. The two tall windows directly above the gallery belonged to Miriam's apartment.

Miriam walked up to the blue painted door sandwiched between the furniture shop and the art gallery. Three doorbells had been screwed into the wood at the side: one for the gallery owner, who lived behind his shop; one for her; and one for the apartment on the top floor, which had been vacant for the past six months. Miriam climbed the narrow, dark staircase to the first floor.

She hung up her coat in her small hallway. It was dark inside. The curtains had been closed when she'd gone to work at half past nine last night. Miriam left them drawn since she would have to sleep again soon.

Her apartment was small but cozy. There was a seating area facing the street that opened onto the L-shaped kitchen with a breakfast bar at the back. Her bedroom and bathroom were next to the kitchen.

Out of habit, she turned on the TV and went into the kitchen to get a swing-top bottle of beer from the fridge. She opened the curtain slightly. The back of her apartment overlooked other, similar apartments with brick balconies and enclosed rear gardens with sheds. On some of the balconies, clothes were hanging out to dry. In the distance, she saw residential and commercial towers gleaming metallically in the pale autumn sun.

This neighborhood had once had a bad reputation, like so many in the centers of big cities, but in recent decades, the council had renovated many of the run-down homes. Now, the area was attracting more and more nice young people who'd outgrown their student housing or were moving in together. One of them was her downstairs neighbor, Boris Meijer, the gallery owner.

Outside business hours, he was often working down in his studio, a glass extension at the rear of his apartment. There was an easel next to his desk. From her kitchen she couldn't quite make out what he was working on, but she could see his solid shoulders moving as he painted, and his muscular neck supporting his striking, tilted head when he stepped back to look at his progress. He'd occasionally shown her some of his work. She liked it better than the paintings he sold in his gallery, but according to Boris, nothing he'd produced so far was worth exhibiting. Perhaps her opinion of Boris's work was colored by Boris himself.

He wasn't there today—or at least not painting in the studio.

She closed the curtain again, emptied her bottle of beer, and put it on the counter. This afternoon she would check the license plate of Hennequin's car and find out who lived in that house on Baljuwstraat. First, she had to try to get some sleep.

❦

Oscar came in with three full shopping bags. Hennequin took one and followed him into the kitchen.

"Are these all groceries?" She lifted the bag onto the counter and looked inside. Bread, milk, fruit.

"Yes. And gifts for visitors. My parents and sister are coming tomorrow." Oscar put the other two bags down. He looked at them rather uneasily, as if they were foreign objects and he had no idea what to do with them.

"Shall I unpack?"

"Um, yes, please." He ran his fingers through his dark hair and looked at her.

She opened the kitchen cupboards and put everything away. Oscar was still standing there. His eyes were burning holes in her back.

She turned to him. "Shall I pour you a drink?" she asked softly. "Make you something nice to eat?"

"It's OK. I can do it myself."

"But I'm happy to help." She smiled at him. That wasn't difficult. Didi had been lucky in love. Until now. "Ham and cheese omelet?"

He raised his eyebrows. From his surprised reaction, Hennequin could tell that it had probably been a while since anyone had cooked eggs for him. "Sounds good."

She put her hand briefly on his forearm. Lifting her eyes to him, she said softly, "A man needs meat and eggs, Oscar. This is a special time. You have to enjoy it. I'm happy to help."

❦

Miriam had barely slept. Normally she had little trouble shutting out the noise, but now every clink of the radiator startled her. Someone was sawing nearby. Irritated, she threw off the duvet. It was one o'clock, and she'd done nothing but toss and turn, thinking about Hennequin Smith, about Bart. Was she going crazy? Was she being paranoid? Even her parents hadn't questioned the cause of death. She would have to call or visit soon. Since they'd moved out of the city, she'd hardly seen them.

Shortly after Miriam had taken a permanent job with the police, her parents had made an incomprehensible change. They'd snapped up an old house in a hamlet near Grevelingen Lake in Zeeland with the intention of turning it into a bed-and-breakfast.

To Miriam and Bart, the news had come as a complete surprise. Their parents had no experience in hospitality—except as valued customers. But the house had since been renovated, and the bed-and-breakfast had built up a good reputation.

An hour's drive was hardly a trip around the world, but Miriam had still felt abandoned. Long before that, Bart had moved to Belgium. She was the only member of the family who'd stayed in the nest. And she certainly wasn't planning to leave. She belonged in this city. This was her home turf.

But now Hennequin had settled here too. What was she doing here? It almost felt like her brother's widow was laughing in her face. Baiting her.

❦

Hennequin stood in the kitchen, looking at the rabbit hutch against the fence in the garden. It had long wooden legs and two floors and was fronted with mesh panels. Jip and Janneke weren't impressed by all the luxury; they didn't even make use of the space. They sat motionless beside each other in the straw, with bulging eyes that looked anxiously out into the world, even when they were at rest. Their noses were the only thing that moved. That was how you could tell they were alive. Hennequin hadn't heard either Oscar or Didi mention the two rabbits. Perhaps, amid all the excitement, the new parents had forgotten they had pets locked in a hutch outside.

She entered the living room. Didi was in bed with her eyes closed. Oscar was at the dining table, eating his omelet while reading the newspaper on his tablet.

"Who do Jip and Janneke belong to?"

"They're Didi's," said Oscar.

"Is anyone looking after those rabbits at the moment?"

Didi opened her eyes and looked at Oscar in alarm. "I thought you were going to do that. Wasn't that what we'd agreed?"

"I *am* doing it," he muttered, and looked at Hennequin. "Perhaps just not as often as she'd like."

Didi's response was surprisingly fierce. "Why can't you get it through your head that those animals need feeding and looking after every day, not just once a week?"

"Rabbits can manage fine with a bit of straw and hay."

"They don't *eat* straw; straw is bedding. How many times do I have to tell you that?"

Hennequin looked from one to the other, as if she were following a ping-pong match.

Didi sought her gaze. "Is it bad, Hennequin? Does the hutch stink?"

Hennequin shrugged. "No idea. I haven't been outside. I was just wondering." She turned toward the kitchen. "I'll go and take a look at them. I don't mind cleaning the hutch out if necessary, but I'm allergic to rabbits, so somebody else will have to take them out and put them back in."

"Great," said Oscar. "I'll put them in a box in a minute."

Didi looked at her husband angrily. "Oscar, didn't you hear what she said? Hennequin is allergic. And I don't think caring for pets is the job of a maternity nurse."

"It's no trouble," said Hennequin sweetly.

"Now I'm worried. Os, would you please go and see if they're OK?"

Oscar stood up in annoyance. "Stop overreacting. Those animals are hardly going to be at death's door from one day to the next. But whatever, I'll go and check on them."

❦

If she really couldn't sleep, she might as well get out of bed. Miriam kicked off the covers and slipped into a tracksuit. She brushed her hair, which fell just over her shoulders in choppy layers, and gathered it into a ponytail. Quickly she applied mascara to her eyelashes and left it at that. She didn't need much makeup. Her dark eyes were expressive enough. But even if they hadn't been, it wouldn't have changed her routine. Miriam wasn't a girly girl. Never had been. She'd always preferred to play with boys rather than girls, and she'd rarely shared the same interests as her classmates. She was quite small and on the skinny side, and people often mistook her for a boy, especially in her teens when she still wore her hair short. Nobody made that error once her hormones kicked in and her body took on a rounder, more feminine shape. But she'd remained small and slim.

Miriam went into the living room and turned on the TV. In the kitchen, she made a cup of coffee. She listened with one ear to the news and soaked up the hustle and bustle passing by outside. The traffic droned, sputtered, and buzzed on the gray asphalt. At the back of the terrace, where the gardens were, it was very quiet. Rustic almost. That contrast had instantly drawn her to this apartment.

She could still remember telling Bart excitedly that she'd made an offer on it. He hadn't shared her enthusiasm. Quite the opposite. He didn't like the neighborhood, which baffled Miriam because his roots were here too. He'd warned her that it was too dangerous for a woman on her own. He wanted something better for his little sister and would've preferred Miriam to move out of the city, ideally to Hillegersberg or one of the surrounding villages. Bart's place in Brasschaat had had a swimming pool, security cameras, and electric gates. An impregnable fortress, fully walled in; you couldn't even see it from the road. Miriam had loved the house and its warm décor, but found all the security measures and isolation from the outside world rather uncharacteristic of her brother. It wouldn't surprise her if Hennequin Smith had had a big say in the choice.

It was ironic that he would die in that house, of all places. All that security hadn't been able to protect him. And neither had she.

Hennequin set the basket of clean laundry on the dining table. It was surrounded by leather-covered chairs on castors. Oscar had wheeled one of them to the bed. He was sitting beside his wife, one ankle on his knee and the baby in his arms. Hennequin's glance lingered briefly on Didi. In the gray afternoon light that filtered through the sheer curtains, she looked like a pale farmer's wife in a seventeenth-century painting. A diffuse shape.

"You have a slight American accent," remarked Oscar suddenly. "Are you American?"

She smiled. She could say yes, but she didn't. It was safer to stay closer to the truth. "I used to live and work in America. I'd almost forgotten my Dutch, but it's starting to come back reasonably well."

"More than reasonably," said Oscar. "You only have a slight accent."

"How cool, America," said Didi. "Oscar and I were in New York last year. It was so impressive."

Hennequin said nothing. She took some baby clothes out of the basket.

"Where exactly did you live in the States?" asked Oscar.

"In Vermont," she lied. Vermont was a beautiful state, but it was also relatively small and unfamiliar to most Dutch people.

"When did you come back?"

"Two months ago," she lied. "After my divorce I didn't have much reason to stay."

"Oh, what a shame." Didi looked at her with pity from the bed.

It was almost laughable.

"Were you married for long?"

"No." She smiled. "It's fine. We just weren't right for each other. At any rate, I'm glad I was able to get back to work as soon as I returned to the Netherlands."

"There are always jobs in healthcare," said Oscar.

"Yes, lucky for me."

She reached for a towel and started folding it. It really had been child's play. The healthcare industry was desperate for workers, and she had an impressive CV. It hadn't even occurred to Dora to verify any of her credentials with the training college or hospital. Otherwise Hennequin wouldn't be standing here now, folding laundry.

She gazed once more at the young family. At Didi, who lay wearily in the raised bed with a pale, unmade-up face. Oscar beside her, virile, sharp, full of energy, with his daughter safe in his muscular arms. Somebody had to capture this scene.

"You three look lovely like that," she said.

Didi smiled gratefully. "Thank you. I don't feel very lovely at the moment."

"You will eventually. It'll be at least six months before you start feeling like your old self again." She pointed to the digital camera that had been lying around in the living room, barely used, since her arrival. "You know what? Let me take a picture of the three of you. You probably don't have one yet."

"I'm not sure if—"

Hennequin brushed the protest aside. "You look beautiful, Didi. Honestly. Doesn't she, Oscar?"

He looked up in surprise and turned to his wife. "Yes. As always, darling." He was about to lean toward her and give her a kiss, but then remembered that there was a sleeping baby in his arms and remained stiffly upright.

Hennequin grabbed the camera, took a few steps back, and bent down to eye level with her subjects. She framed their faces through the viewfinder. The lapel of her white uniform clung around her breasts. Through the lens she could see that Oscar had noticed it.

"Everybody smile. Yes, like that. Oh, it's a great shot!"

She walked toward them and passed just in front of Oscar to show the screen to Didi. Subtly, she rubbed her body along his. "Look. Nice, isn't it?"

Didi took the camera and gazed at the picture. She nodded, but didn't look particularly happy.

❧

As expected, the Alfa Romeo was registered in the name of Hennequin Smith. There was nothing out of the ordinary about the car. And Baljuwstraat 66 was home to a young family. The father was Oscar Stevens, thirty-four years old. According to his LinkedIn profile, he was a sales manager at a large recruitment agency. His wife, Dineke Stevens-Vos, had just given birth to a daughter. This information was not in the system, but had been announced by Didi, as she was known, on her Facebook page. Nearly a hundred friends had replied to her status update. "We'll pop in soon." "That's great news, so happy for you." "Are you feeling any better?" "Indy, what a beautiful name." Miriam gathered, from some of the responses, that there was something wrong with the mother or had been during the pregnancy. She suspected that Didi had mentioned it on her Facebook page, but most of it was private. Probably overcome with emotion, Didi had forgotten to restrict her most recent post about the birth. Miriam looked at both Didi's and Oscar's lists of friends and connections. There was no link with Hennequin Smith. It was looking increasingly likely that Hennequin was working for them after all.

Miriam enjoyed nosing around on social media. People tossed all sorts of information online that could be of interest to the police and would be very time-consuming to find out by other means.

On the other hand, logging in to the police database, as she'd just done via her work BlackBerry, was a last resort. At least when it concerned a private investigation that had to remain a secret from her chief and colleagues. These kinds of searches were recorded automatically.

It was possible to check at any time which officer had accessed what information. That sort of thing would only be examined in the event of an investigation, but still. With her impulsive Belgian adventure, she'd squandered Van der Steen's goodwill and she didn't expect him to give her a second chance.

※

Didi had dozed off. So had Indy. The shrimp was lying on Oscar's arm with her mouth open. Her bodysuit read "I love Daddy." Daddy himself was playing on his iPhone with his free hand.

Hennequin bent forward to put the folded laundry into the basket. She arched her back slightly.

It had the desired effect. Oscar glanced at her cleavage and looked away again sheepishly. Like a schoolboy who'd been caught in the act.

She smiled to herself. The husband was going through a dry spell, and had been for months, no doubt. All that time, Didi had probably rejected him, pushed him away, because a baby was growing inside her and her body no longer felt like something sexual, but like an incubator. Or perhaps *she* had still desired him, had craved his closeness and comfort, but he just hadn't been able to face it. Incontinence, weight gain, mood swings, pain, and a steadily growing, constantly moving baby: incubators weren't sexy.

But tanned, toned maternity nurses in tight-fitting uniforms were.

Hennequin placed the laundry basket on her hip and walked slowly out of the room. She knew that he was looking at her, and in what way.

She would let him dream about it for one more night.

※

She should have just gone to sleep. It had been stupid to get out of bed. A rookie mistake she hadn't made in a long time. Now she was too sleepy for the night shift, and she could only hope nothing would happen that required a quick reaction time. It was never a good idea to draw a weapon with a trembling hand. In four hours, she was due at the station for the briefing. If she took a sleeping pill now, it wouldn't wear off in time. Caught between a rock and a hard place.

Miriam had a few packs of Red Bull in the cupboard for emergencies. She took two cans from the box and put them in the fridge. She poured a glass of apple juice and opened the curtains.

Boris was in his studio now. He was wearing a checked flannel over a T-shirt. His thick black hair was tucked under a beanie, a gray chunky-knit cap he often wore. She'd always found young men in such caps a bit pretentious, but had changed her mind when she'd met Boris. The cap suited him, as did the shirts printed with his own crazy slogans or designs. Even the half-grown black beard looked good on him, despite her usual dislike—even loathing—of facial hair. Boris had been going out with a pretty girl who dyed her short hair black and had full-sleeve tattoos. But Miriam hadn't seen the girl for a few months. They'd probably broken up.

Sipping her juice, she watched Boris. She liked the way he focused on his work. The palette, which looked like a whole box of paints had exploded on it, was resting on his forearm. He mixed the colors and applied layer upon layer to the canvas. Boris's paintings often seemed like moving photographs. Cityscapes, sidewalk cafés, passing cars, restaurant interiors.

He looked up. It was too late to hide. His mouth crinkled into a smile, and he raised his chin in greeting. He had a nice smile, Boris. White teeth. Sweet, dark eyes with laugh lines.

Miriam went weak inside. Raising her hand, she wiggled her fingers. She smiled sheepishly. Then she turned away from the window. It was a bit weird to peep at your downstairs neighbor. At least he didn't seem to mind.

❦

Hennequin walked barefoot through her apartment in her silk kimono. The resin floor was as hard as glass, but felt pleasantly warm. She'd just taken a shower. Her dark hair glistened in the lamplight. The music was blasting. She spread her arms and danced through the living room in slow motion. Pet Shop Boys, "It's a Sin." She hummed along and whispered the lyrics.

After the notes had died down, she sat on the sofa and grabbed her iPad. Six o'clock, time to order some food. There was plenty to choose from: Italian, Surinamese, Thai, Japanese, Dutch, Chinese, you name it. She could also book a chef to prepare a meal in her home. It was all available, almost all at the click of a button. One of the advantages of city life. Here, everything was close at hand, quite unlike in the mansion in Belgium or before that in the house with its own jetty on the west coast of Florida. Hennequin chose a Thai salad with seafood and lime, coconut prawn soup, and fried squid and entered her address on the restaurant's website.

She hadn't so much as touched a pan since the death of Bart de Moor. He smiled at her from a corner of the home screen. She tapped on the photo. Her hazel eyes ran over the not-unattractive, slightly rugged face of her deceased husband. Despite his relatively young age, his hair was already pretty thin and gray. Hennequin could've had better-looking men than Bart. Younger men. Nevertheless, he'd been her best catch ever. The man who'd made it all possible. The generous benefactor of all this. All the nice things she could now do, the freedom his money afforded her.

She stood up and walked to the bedroom. In front of the full-length mirror, she pulled the cord of the kimono and let the garment slip off her shoulders. With her chin raised, she looked at herself in the large mirror, turned around, and ran her hands over her curves. That body, it was gorgeous. Taut and bronzed, rounded in all the right places. Money well spent.

Tomorrow she would put it to use to pry open the hairline cracks in the budding happiness of the Stevens-Vos family.

❦

Miriam had just put on her uniform when the phone rang. She looked at the screen. A long number. It took her a full second to realize what that meant. Evidently, Chucky Lee hadn't used her retainer to take his wife and children to Disney World after all.

She answered it. "Hello?"

"Chucky Lee, Investi-Gators. Good afternoon. Is this Ms. De Moor?" said a voice in English.

Afternoon—it was nine p.m. here. But that clearly hadn't occurred to Lee.

"Correct. That's me."

Chucky got straight down to business. Miriam struggled to understand the man. He had a terrible accent and spoke far too fast. Less than two minutes later, the phone call was over, and Miriam stood staring into space.

Smith wasn't Hennequin's original surname. It had come from an ex-husband, a real estate agent called Keanu Smith. She'd been married to him for five years and they'd lived in Fort Myers on the west coast of Florida, among other places. The real estate agent was now dead, but when Chucky tried looking further back, he'd stumbled across something remarkable. Hennequin wasn't her original first name either. "The woman has erased her past," Chucky had said. "Neither the first nor the last name she was given at birth in the Netherlands is registered anywhere here."

42

Chucky said that he would keep trying to get to the bottom of it. He would have to send her another invoice, since there were extra costs involved with obtaining information from the relevant authorities.

Miriam bit her lower lip. Hennequin Smith wasn't really called Hennequin Smith. That explained a lot. More than once, Miriam had entered her name into the system, to no avail. It was only due to her obsession with Hennequin that she'd kept trying from time to time, against her better judgment. Her heart had nearly stopped when, at the start of the week, the system had suddenly come up with an address and a social security number. By moving to Rotterdam, Hennequin had appeared on her radar.

Day Three

THURSDAY

"Did that ointment I sent you do any good?" Oscar's mother was sitting on one of the leather chairs by the bed. She dropped her rusk back on the plate on her lap.

Didi looked at her mother-in-law. She was quite tall, and had short gray hair and a strong face. Henriette always reminded her of the big Italian woman from *The Golden Girls*. "Yes, thanks," she said. "It's been a huge help."

"Good." She took another bite of the rusk and nodded toward the kitchen. "You've got a great maternity nurse. She's a beautiful girl too."

"Isn't she? We're lucky to have Hennequin. She's amazing."

While Oscar's mother made conversation, his father sat silently with Didi's iPad on his lap. He was looking intently at the photos from after the birth. Oscar's parents had been the first to be informed of Indy's arrival, and they'd also been the first to come and congratulate them; less than an hour after the birth, they'd turned up at the bedside with an enormous Miffy doll in their arms.

Physically, Oscar took after his father. He had the same slim build as the bank manager and the same slightly wide-set gray eyes, but his personality was a mix of both his parents. Oscar could be as gregarious and outgoing as his mother, and could turn on the charm when necessary, but he also had a reserved, rather distant side, which had been on full display since Indy's birth.

Didi felt less, rather than more, connected with him than before. That worried her, although she realized that the birth and their new situation were life-changing for him too.

Indy, who'd been sleeping contentedly on Didi's chest, jerked her arms up as if something had frightened her. She moved her head searchingly from side to side, her mouth open, and made soft protesting noises.

Oscar stood up. "I'll go and warm up a bottle."

Hennequin came out of the kitchen with a tray. She put the visitors' empty breakfast plates on it. "Would anyone like more tea?"

The group nodded in agreement.

"And you, Didi? Green tea with honey?"

"That'd be lovely."

Hennequin went into the kitchen, humming to herself. Didi watched her. Oscar's mother was right: Hennequin was a great maternity nurse. Didi didn't know what she would have done without her support.

❦

Miriam took off her uniform and put it on a hanger. Her closet was so full she hadn't been able to close the doors in months. As she gathered together a sports bra and tracksuit, she realized that she needed a bigger closet. Or fewer clothes, perhaps. *Or a day off to declutter.*

She got dressed and went into the bathroom. After brushing her hair, she tied it up with an elastic band.

Last night she'd paid the inevitable price for her failure to presleep. The first half of the shift had been hectic. Lots of arrests, including a mugging and a break-in. The latter had turned out to be unexpectedly spectacular. When she'd arrived at the scene after the burglar alarm had gone off, the control room had received a call from a neighbor. He'd seen a man climbing over his fence and thought he might still be hiding in the garden. Miriam had gone in with several colleagues, not knowing whether the burglar was armed and if so, with what, and whether he was prepared to use it. Some thieves were desperate, and people sometimes flipped out at the sight of a uniform. But this burglar had made a run for it. They'd caught him after a wild chase.

For the first few hours, the adrenaline had kept her alert, but after that, the night had become bogged down in routine, and she'd started to feel her fatigue. Ringing in her ears, nausea. For a while, she'd even struggled to string a sentence together. Two Red Bulls had gotten her through.

And now it was half past eight in the morning, and she felt completely beyond sleep. Nevertheless, she would have to try to get some after her jog, because she was scheduled for another night shift later.

Miriam made some coffee, buttered a slice of bread, and ate it standing up at the counter until she realized she had no reason to hurry. Munching on her bread, she unplugged her cell phone from the charger and sat down at the breakfast bar. No email from Chucky Lee.

She'd transferred another five hundred dollars to Florida—one thousand in total. She knew she could get hold of the same information as Investi-Gators through official channels, but using the police's facilities was out of the question. At least, if she wanted to keep her job. The money she'd inherited from Bart had been well spent.

Miriam loaded the dishwasher and turned to the window. Boris was there again, in the studio behind his gallery. Her downstairs neighbor was wearing jeans and green sneakers, his crossed long legs resting on his desk. He was on the phone. She ran her eyes over his physique and couldn't help smiling at the way he emphasized his words with his hands. Boris was very expressive.

In the middle of the call, he suddenly looked up. He immediately broke into a wide grin and then winked.

Miriam smiled back at him and held her hands up, palms facing forward, as if to say, *OK, OK, you caught me. I surrender.*

Was she really flirting with her neighbor—and he with her? It certainly looked like it.

She waved at him again, turned away from the window, and plugged her earbuds into her phone. Then she grabbed her house keys from the hook beside the tea towels. She shut the apartment door behind her and ran at a leisurely pace toward the river.

The muffled voices of Oscar's parents were coming from the living room. They were talking about Oscar's sister, who'd given birth to a son two years ago. Sophie hadn't come to see Indy yet because her little boy was in bed with flu.

"It's been hard for you, hasn't it?" Hennequin whispered. She ran her fingertips delicately over Oscar's forearm. For just a moment. She gave him her most sympathetic gaze.

Pleasantly surprised, Oscar looked at Hennequin. He reacted exactly as Hennequin had expected. This was presumably the first time in a long while that anybody had paid attention to him, acknowledged him. It would have been no different for Oscar than for any other man in his position. For the past six months, everybody was bound to have been asking him how his wife was doing and if everything was all right with the unborn baby. Perhaps he'd been dragged dutifully to childbirth classes, where he'd done his very best to act like a loving, understanding husband among all those sweaty, asexual pregnant women, even though he'd have infinitely preferred to be home on the sofa watching soccer or out playing tennis. Relaxing. But Oscar hadn't been allowed to relax. No doubt Didi had also cajoled him into accompanying her to the midwife checkups, where he would've had to listen to the baby's heartbeat and sit on a hard chair in a corner of a darkened room that smelled of disinfectant, feeling totally out of place and excluded in this shadowy women's world. In the evening, when he came home from work, but also early in the morning, and perhaps even in the dead of night when she couldn't sleep, Didi had probably grabbed his hand and placed it on her round, elongated belly so that he could also feel the soft kicks that Didi felt so clearly and that meant so much to her, but which he could barely distinguish from her breathing, muscle twitches, or bowel movements. And then, on top of that, Didi had become an invalid.

He obviously felt as though, for six whole months, nobody had cared about *him*. Nobody had given him any thought. He hadn't even existed. And now here was this woman, this slim, tanned woman, who stood close to him, looked deep into his eyes, and actually saw him and understood everything.

"It'll be OK." His voice was hoarse, his pupils dilated.

"You're strong," she said softly. "A very strong man." She flashed him a subtle smile, then lowered her eyes, and tugged, as if nervous, at a loose wisp of hair on her neck. Turning around, she took the bottle out of the microwave.

The milk was warm.

❦

Miriam relished being outdoors and enjoyed the monotonous movement that helped her to clear her head. Three, sometimes four times a week she ran her regular route along the quayside of the river before tracing a wide arc around the new housing estates and tower blocks and arriving back where she started. German bombs had ripped the historic heart out of the old port city, but this had created a new blank space that, even seventy years later, still attracted young architects, artists, and other creative people from all over the globe. Miriam loved the contrasts that could coexist here. Old and new, the mix of nationalities and cultures. The city was always buzzing. And nowhere else in the world could you run through so many areas with a different look and feel in the space of an hour.

Running had always been one of her favorite sports. She'd practiced judo for years and had even risen to become champion of South Holland. Her trainer had been devastated when she stopped. He'd hoped to coach her to become Dutch champion, and beyond, but that sort of career hadn't appealed to Miriam. She'd seen it happen to friends: sports stars had no life outside sports. Though now that she'd worked her way up to chief duty officer in the police, she had to admit that she had no life outside work either.

Her phone vibrated in the inside pocket of her tracksuit. She unzipped it and dug out the device.

It was an email. From Chucky Lee.

❦

She'd done it; she'd made it through the first round of visitors since Indy's birth. Didi loved her in-laws, but she didn't feel comfortable talking to them about intimate matters concerning her body. And she was well aware that it could easily come across as attention seeking. Nobody wanted to be around a whiny new mother who'd just brought a perfectly healthy child into the world.

This morning she'd had yet another reason to be thankful that she and Oscar had decided to give Indy expressed milk from a bottle: she hadn't had to breastfeed in front of her in-laws. She could never have managed that—not without a face contorted with pain.

Her breasts were even larger and heavier than yesterday. Added to that, her nipples felt overworked and sore, and looked it too. She was worried that it would never get better.

Didi closed her eyes. She was exhausted from all the talking. She'd spent the whole morning putting on a front and pretending that everything was fine. Now, all she wanted to do was sleep. For hours.

"Your in-laws are really nice," said Hennequin, clearing away the remaining cups and saucers beside the bed. She stood there with the dishes in her hands.

Didi opened her eyes. "They are, aren't they? Thank you. They're lovely people."

"Can I ask you a personal question?"

"Of course," she said.

"Are your parents still alive?"

"Yes. At least . . . my mother is, but not my father."

Hennequin looked around the living room as if Didi's mother might jump out from somewhere. "I haven't met her yet."

"She hasn't visited yet. She lives in Norway with her new husband."

"Does she know she's a grandmother?"

Didi explained that she'd called her mother not long after the delivery. Nelly had been overjoyed at the news and promised to come to the Netherlands as soon as possible.

That was the last she'd heard from her. No phone calls, nothing. Perhaps it was difficult to book a flight on short notice, or perhaps she would turn up on the doorstep tomorrow. As a surprise.

It was anyone's guess.

Hennequin paused and then asked, "What happened to your father?"

"He was in a motorcycle accident. I can barely remember him. I was only three at the time. My mother remarried, but . . ." She paused and looked ahead. That year had been the darkest of her entire life. She still dreamed about it sometimes. Bad dreams. She would probably never get over it. Should she mention it to the maternity nurse?

No, better not. It was so long ago.

She cleared her throat and said, "Anyway, the marriage didn't last, and after that my mother and I lived on our own for several years."

"You don't have any brothers or sisters?"

Another shadow passed over Didi's pale face. "Not anymore."

"Oh?"

"I had a sister. She was a few years younger than me. She died in an accident when she was four."

Hennequin looked at her sympathetically. "Gosh, Didi. You've had a lot of hardship and bad luck in your life. To lose both your father and your sister . . ." To her delight, she saw Didi's eyes fill with tears. She kept a straight face.

Didi whispered, "Indy is named after her. After my sister."

Hennequin raised her eyebrows. "Oh, how lovely."

Didi picked up a notebook that was lying on the bed. She leafed through it and, after some searching, took out a pink card. "Look. Indy's middle name is my late sister's first name."

Hennequin took the card. Modern, square, with a photo of a baby's foot on the front. On the back it read in italics:

Here in our arms,
safe from all harm,
remember, little star,
how dear to us you are.

We are delighted to welcome our beautiful girl

Indy Claartje Stevens

Hennequin gave the card back to Didi. "What a beautiful tribute."

Didi put the birth announcement carefully back into the notebook and snapped it shut. "Are you spiritual?"

"Spiritual? In what sense?"

"Do you believe in life after death, in spirits?"

"Spirits?" Hennequin raised an eyebrow. The dead people she'd seen had been stone dead, and none of them had come to visit her from the afterlife. "I've never really thought about it."

Didi stared into space. Her voice was quiet. "You know, sometimes I think . . . I think she's still here. That Claartje can see us, down here. That she knows that she now has a niece and is watching over her. Maybe, just maybe, she's been *reincarnated* in Indy." Warily, she looked at Hennequin. "Do you find it weird, that I think that?"

"No, not at all." Hennequin's eyes lit up. "It's actually a very inspiring thought."

❦

Miriam sat down on a bench near the river. She curved her hand around the screen of her iPhone to block out the autumn sun. It was still the middle of the night in Florida, which meant that either Chucky Lee's working hours were as irregular as her own or the email had been delayed in transit.

Chucky's rambling note told her that it hadn't been easy to track down Hennequin's original name. Once again, he mentioned that Hennequin's current surname came from her last known American husband, Keanu Smith, a real estate agent. Before marrying him, she was registered as Hennequin Wilson. That surname was the remnant of a brief marriage to a certain Jonathan Wilson, a dentist she'd lived with in Las Vegas for a few years. *How many ex-husbands can one woman have?* Thanks to her relationship with this dentist, Hennequin had been able to obtain a green card for the United States. Miriam scrolled through the text and shifted on the bench.

Hennequin's birth name sounded a lot less exotic: Catharina Kramer. She'd been born thirty-five years ago, on April 2, in a Dutch village Miriam had never heard of.

She had to hand it to Chucky Lee—he'd been very thorough. All his findings came with dates. Hennequin/Catharina had lived in the United States for almost nine years and, in that time, as far as Chucky knew, she'd been married twice. She'd divorced the dentist; the real estate agent had died of alcohol poisoning.

In his email, Chucky wrote that there was more he could do for Miriam. For example, he could try to make contact with husband number one and with any relatives of husband number two to discover more about Hennequin and piece together her life in America. Another option was to request the deceased husband's autopsy report and find out how his estate had been divided. These things would obviously come at a price.

Miriam closed the email and put her phone in her pocket. Hennequin had had three husbands in relatively quick succession. Two had died. Coincidence? She looked out across the glistening water, a wide gray stream that flowed out into the North Sea somewhere in the distance. The sun had disappeared behind the clouds.

Miriam shivered, zipped her tracksuit all the way to the top, and stood up. Chucky Lee had done enough for the time being. She had a name, plus a date and place of birth.

From now on, she could rely on her own experience and networks.

❦

Hennequin was tidying up the kitchen when she heard Didi crying. This was no soft, subdued sobbing, but a fit that sounded unstoppable.

In the material she'd downloaded from the internet, this was called the baby blues. It was most likely to start on the third or fourth day after childbirth. Didi was right on schedule. Hennequin had read that emotional outbursts were normal even for mothers who'd brought a healthy baby into the world after an easy labor and a trouble-free pregnancy.

Didi's pregnancy could hardly be described as trouble-free, and she hadn't been blessed with an easy delivery either.

Didi's family situation was also a factor. She'd lost both her father and her only sister at an early age, and her mother was clearly in no hurry to come and see her grandchild.

This afternoon, shortly after the visitors had left, Oscar had also been called away by work. "You can manage for a few hours, can't you?" he'd said, with one foot already in the hallway, his coat in his hand. "Hennequin is here for you and Indy, so I don't need to be by your side the whole time, do I?" He'd then jumped into his leased Audi and sped off.

That had been a bit insensitive of him. But, Hennequin thought, understandable. A man like Oscar needed air. Space. He was bound to be going crazy in this house, stuck all day between these four walls with a sickly, unstable wife and a maternity nurse who sent his hormones into overdrive. The man was struggling with his emotions. He didn't burst into tears like Didi; he ran away.

But he would come back. And Hennequin would still be here, seductive and willing, gently whispering sweet nothings in his ear. There was no escape.

Didi was sobbing her heart out. She no longer even tried to keep it together. She cried with long howls.

Hennequin stood listening, leaning against the counter with her arms crossed. Her eyes closed, and the corners of her mouth curled upward.

She was loving it.

❦

Miriam took a sip of her chamomile tea. Normally this helped her to feel sleepy, as did the hot shower she'd taken after her run and the silent darkness that filled the room after she'd closed the curtains. But now, none of it had any effect. Her laptop hummed. The screen lit up her face and part of the small living room.

Hennequin's birthplace turned out to be a hamlet in the far southwest of Gelderland, near Zaltbommel. It had a little over six hundred inhabitants, a Reformed church dating from the eleventh century, and one primary school, which was called De Rank and had about a hundred students.

Miriam used Street View to walk through the village. The images had been captured in the summer. Blue skies, fleecy clouds, fruit trees, and flowering shrubs. Almost all the houses were detached, and they appeared to be at least a hundred years old. Beautiful renovated farmhouses, some of which were built on knolls; large homes with gabled roofs and white eaves with woodcarvings—a wonderful place to grow up.

Pensive, Miriam crept virtually through the village. *What kind of child were you, Catharina Kramer? What made you move to America from such an idyllic place and become Hennequin Smith?*

Miriam took another sip of her tea. What could you really learn from a birthplace? Perhaps Hennequin had been born in one of these fairy-tale houses, but had grown up somewhere else entirely?

The sound of her phone brought her back to the here and now. The device vibrated on the breakfast bar like an angry buzzing insect. She looked at the screen. A number she didn't recognize. "Hello, Miriam speaking."

"Hi, it's Boris."

She grabbed the iPhone with both hands, immediately annoyed at her adolescent eagerness. "Hey, Boris."

"Are you busy?"

"No. Why?"

"I was wondering . . . Have you eaten?"

"No. Not yet."

"Great. I was going to order a pizza from next door. Shall I get some for you too?"

She smiled. "Sounds good, but—"

"But what?"

"I really should be in bed by now. I've got another night shift later."

A deep laugh on the other end of the line. "Shit. I keep forgetting that you're a police officer. Except when you're in uniform . . ." He paused and coughed. "Isn't it funny? We practically live together, but we barely know each other."

"That's what happens in cities. Some people like it."

"Including you?"

"Sometimes." When he didn't respond, she quickly added, "But not right now."

"So you wouldn't mind sharing a pizza?"

"No. Actually, it sounds good."

"OK. Um, are you free on Saturday?"

"Yes, I am."

"Any requests?"

"A Hawaiian or else a Roma. Shall I bring some beer?"

"Perfect. I'll see you on Saturday around six." With a brief goodbye, Boris hung up.

Miriam sat there in a daze. Was this a date? Or had it spontaneously occurred to him that they needed to get to know each other better— simply as neighbors?

Now it was really going to be difficult to get to sleep.

"Oh, oh, finally I've got you! I keep getting your damn voice mail, and you never call me back." Dora's voice sounded crystal clear, as if she were in the same room.

"Sorry," Hennequin replied. "My phone's been acting weird for the past few days. It's driving me crazy. But I was planning to call you." The warmth in her voice didn't match the hard look in her eyes. Hennequin ran her fingers through her hair in annoyance. It was still damp from the laps she'd swum in the communal pool in the basement of the apartment building. Her gaze lingered on the plastic bag on the dining table. The Thai food yesterday had been so delicious that she'd ordered from the same place today. The aromas of lemongrass, ginger, and coconut filled the room. She had to keep this phone call brief.

"How's the Stevens family doing?" she heard Dora ask.

"Great. Really good. They're nice, kind people, and Indy, the baby, is no trouble at all. Didi still hasn't quite gotten the hang of the breast pump, but I have no doubt she'll master it eventually."

"How is her pelvis?"

"Not so good. She still can't do much. She told me she's going to start physiotherapy again next week. I really hope it'll help her, because it's so sad. She can't even bathe her own baby."

"Yes, that's terrible. But pelvic problems are very rarely permanent, so you can reassure her about that. By the way, regarding the breast pump, we've had good experiences with a lactation consultant here at the agency. If there's no improvement, please let me know, and I'll ask her to help out. Often it only requires a few minor adjustments."

"No need," said Hennequin firmly. "It's getting a bit easier every day. I'm sure we'll manage on our own."

Dora paused, then said, "That's the same thing the family told me."

The family? Are they in contact?

"Oh?"

"After three days, I call the family and ask how everything's going, if they've hit it off with the maternity nurse, and if they have any questions. I talked to the father, Oscar Stevens, earlier today, and he spoke very highly of your services."

Hennequin grinned at her own reflection in the large window of the penthouse. She saw the white kitchen behind her, and the low white sofa next to the rug. On the other side of the glass, gray clouds were racing over the city. It would be dark in an hour.

"It's good to hear that we're on the same page," she said. "How is Jantine, the nurse I replaced?"

Dora suddenly sounded glum. "Still not great. We still don't know if her tailbone will ever fully heal. At the moment she's in a lot of pain, and there's no way she can work."

"Most accidents happen in the home," said Hennequin.

"Yes, so they say. But Jantine insists that she was pushed down the stairs."

"By a boyfriend? Husband?"

"Jantine lives alone. The police took her suspicions seriously, but they didn't find any sign of forced entry."

No, of course they didn't. Jantine is a silly cow who leaves the window above the kitchen door open for the cat and also leaves the back door key in the lock.

"Was anything stolen?"

"No, nothing."

Hennequin picked at her cuticle. Jantine obviously hadn't noticed that she was missing a uniform. Then again, she had six of them in her closet, and in various sizes no less. "Yikes, what a scary story, Dora. I don't know her, but I don't suppose anyone would make up something like that. It's enough to make you believe in ghosts."

"Well, let's not get carried away. In any case, I'm glad you showed up when you did so that you could take over. It was probably meant to be. I don't know what I'd have done without you."

"I'm sorry it had to come at somebody else's expense, but I'm really pleased that you gave me this opportunity. And they're such a nice family; I love working with them. I hope you'll send me to a new family after next week."

"If you keep doing such a great job, I certainly will. But do me a favor and get your phone fixed. It's such a hassle to get ahold of you."

"Will do," said Hennequin. She said goodbye to Dora and hung up.

She went over to the dining table, grabbed the plastic bag, and without even looking inside, threw it into the trash. Picking her tablet up off the sofa, she ordered a new meal.

She hated lukewarm food.

❦

Indy was crying. Her voice was very soft and shaky and sounded muffled through the wall, but for Didi it was heartrending. She lay in the guest bed, wide awake, looking at her phone. Half past three. She'd tried. She'd done as Oscar had asked earlier this evening and not immediately called him to pick up Indy every time she made a peep. But now she'd been crying nonstop for twenty minutes, and Didi couldn't stand it anymore. It was as if she had an invisible link to her daughter. She felt her every sound, physically, like a cramp, deep in her empty stomach. Her breasts reacted to it as well.

She cursed her pelvis. Why couldn't she just stand up and go get her child and hold her in her arms? It was true what Hennequin had said this afternoon: *You've had a lot of hardship and bad luck in your life*. What had she done to deserve all this? At the same time, she felt guilty for her own self-pity. Indy was just hungry. That was all it was. Didi's milk production had increased slightly, but it still wasn't enough for Indy.

Hennequin had assured her that this was temporary. Despite the pain and stress, Didi was producing more and more milk. It would be a matter of days before supply caught up with demand. A week, at most.

Indy was still crying. She really was calling for her.

Didi grabbed her phone and called Oscar again. Why had she ever agreed to sleeping in separate rooms? Of course, this bed was on risers, which made it easier for her to get in and out. But it had also driven her out of the marital bedroom and banished her to a corner of the house.

Didi gently pressed her breasts. They felt heavy, and every now and then a twinge of pain shot through them. She was supposed to start pumping again now, but the breast pump was downstairs in the kitchen. Once again, she called Oscar. She heard his ringtone straight through the doors. He didn't answer.

"Os? Oscar? Os?" She raised her voice. *"Oscar!"*

Indy cried and cried.

Should she get up? Then what? She couldn't even lift her baby. She was too scared that her legs would give way.

"Oscar!"

Suddenly, he appeared in the guest room. His eyes were bloodshot, and his hair was sticking up. He was still wearing the same shirt as this afternoon.

"Why did you make me scream for you like that?" she asked.

His jaw tightened. "Why can't you let me sleep, for God's sake?"

She was shocked by the look on his face. "Indy's crying."

"Yes, Indy's crying. She cries all the damn time! Go to sleep, woman. I'll see to the baby at seven o'clock. I do have a life, you know."

Slowly, she felt herself growing cold. "How can you . . . How . . . Jesus, Oscar, Indy needs us. Can't you hear that? She's hungry. I can't do it. OK? I can't get her out of bed. The most I can do is hobble over there and look at her. Do you have any idea how frustrating it is?"

He looked at her in silence, his eyes dark. Then he said coolly, "This wasn't my choice, Didi."

"What wasn't your choice? Me not being able to walk? No, it wasn't mine either. I—"

"That's not what I mean. I mean the child."

His words hit her like bullets. "But you said—"

"I remember exactly what I said! That I wasn't ready to start a family. And you knew that. You knew that when you decided not to get rid of it."

Didi shook her head in disbelief. "You said that you'd support me. That you'd get used to the idea. You even said you were looking forward to it." Her vision had become blurry, and tears were running down her cheeks.

"Maybe that was true at one time; maybe I got carried away by the idea." He put his hand on his neck and stood like that for a moment. Just when Didi thought he was going to apologize, his expression changed, and he pointed at her. "But you, Didi Vos, you're driving me crazy with this breast milk business. I need my sleep! Next week I'll be back at work, and I really can't afford to be woken up in the middle of the night by your constant phone calls. If there really is a problem, fine, I'm willing to do what's necessary, but that baby is just hungry. And that, Didi"—his face transformed into a grimace as he pointed at her again—"is your fault. Your choice. Don't make it my problem."

"But what should—"

"Just give the kid formula, you stupid woman. Millions of children have grown up on it. And ours can too."

Didi thought about the forums she'd read on the internet. About all those men who supported their partners if they wanted to breast-feed. Who were kind. Gave massages, hugs. Tea. She was so shocked she'd stopped crying. She felt herself growing colder and colder inside. Emptier. Quieter.

"You're just not cut out for it," he snapped.

"Hennequin says—"

"I don't care what Hennequin says. Have you seen your boobs? They'll never be the same again. I think you should decide what's more important to you. 'Cause I can't take this anymore." He stalked out, then came back with the baby and dropped her clumsily on Didi's lap. "I'll go get a bottle," he grumbled.

She was about to call after him to bring the breast pump as well, but thought better of it.

Day Four

FRIDAY

Miriam parked her car on the side of the road and got out. She zipped up her leather jacket against the wind. The village didn't seem to have a center and was situated in a landscape of meadows and orchards. It consisted of a collection of winding lanes with knotty old trees, farmhouses, and ancient-looking manor houses and mansions. In the distance, the traffic was racing along the A2 highway, the main road between Maastricht and Amsterdam. This roar detracted slightly from the idyllic, almost mystical quality of the place.

But the real disappointment was the primary school. Miriam looked at it, her hands tucked deep into her pockets. White and orange bricks. A gabled roof, glass, Trespa cladding. If Hennequin had been born and raised in this village, she would have gone to school here twenty-five years ago. And this building clearly hadn't been built back then.

She went into the playground and walked up to the entrance. One of the double doors opened under her hand. The interior smelled like all primary schools in the country. A mixture of wood, linoleum, finger paint, and damp children's jackets, which were hanging from hooks under shelves of books.

Through the glass of one of the doors, Miriam could see children sitting in a classroom. The desks were arranged in groups of four.

"Are you looking for someone?" A man with side-parted hair approached her, stopping a few steps away. He peered at her suspiciously from behind his rimless glasses. The man had to be in his thirties, but the way he moved made him appear older. He had the sort of demeanor and expression you'd expect in a priest or monk. Miriam suddenly felt a long way from Rotterdam.

"I'm sorry to walk in unannounced," she said, without a trace of regret. "The door was open. My name is Miriam de Moor, Rotterdam police. You are?"

The man seemed taken aback for a moment. "Addo van Zuilen, head teacher."

"Good, just the person I was looking for." She held out her hand, which he shook half-heartedly. "We're conducting an investigation, and I would like to ask you some questions. I hope you can spare a few moments. Normally I would've warned you I was coming." She didn't explain why she hadn't on this occasion, but continued, looking around inquisitively. "Is there somewhere quiet we can talk?"

The direct approach always worked with reserved types. The head teacher led her to an office at the back of the building. A large window overlooked deserted, muddy pastureland and the highway. Miriam took in the interior. A slightly shiny wooden desk, bookcases. The furniture was older than the school itself. There was a tea and coffee machine in the corner, but the man didn't offer her anything.

He pointed to a chair opposite the desk. "Take a seat, Ms. . . . er, what was your name again?"

"De Moor, assistant prosecutor." She saw the man's expression change. She had to chuckle to herself. "Assistant prosecutor" was simply a more impressive-sounding term for chief duty officer.

She sat down. "This building doesn't look very old."

"Right. It was only built six years ago."

"Did this village have its own primary school twenty-five years ago?"

"It did indeed." He pointed at the wall behind Miriam. "Back then it was still housed in the old building, down the street, closer to the church."

Miriam only half listened to his explanation about the poor condition the original school building had apparently been in for many years before it was abandoned. As soon as the head teacher paused for breath, she asked, "Are you from this area?"

He shook his head. "I grew up in Barneveld and moved here four years ago for this job."

"Are there any teachers still working at this school who taught here in the late eighties?"

"No. Our team is young. We're proud of that. A new generation with new methods and ideas while preserving the values and . . ."

The head teacher rattled on, in great detail and even a little defensively, as if she were a school inspector. It was fairly common for people to get nervous once they found out you were from the police. And she'd heightened the effect by introducing herself as assistant prosecutor.

Eventually she interrupted him. "What about your records?"

"What do you mean?"

"If I want to find out which children attended this school twenty-five years ago, can I look that up in your records?"

The man shifted in his seat. "Normally, that would be possible, but . . ." He looked out the window, as if he might find a solution to his problem out there. "Unfortunately, something went wrong during the move."

"And that means?"

He looked really nervous now. "It means that we no longer have the names and addresses of former students from before 2003."

Miriam took a moment to think. She didn't even know if Hennequin had attended this school, and this man was clearly unable to tell her. Eventually, she asked, "Could you put me in touch with a former teacher?"

His face brightened. "There's one who lives here in the village. Corné Dillen. Nowadays he's on the parish council."

Miriam took a notebook out of her pocket and wrote down the name and address. She then asked the head teacher for more names and addresses, or perhaps a janitor she could contact, but he couldn't help her.

"Dillen might remember people from back then," he said.

Normally, Miriam would have given the man her card at this stage and asked him to call her if anything else sprang to mind. But there was little point in that now. After thanking the head teacher for his time, she quickly said goodbye, and went outside.

She could only hope that Corné Dillen would be at home.

Didi's colleagues were sitting in a semicircle around the bed in the living room.

Hennequin could see that this was a courtesy visit. It was obvious. The women showed no genuine interest in Didi or the baby. They couldn't wait to leave.

"Well, Didi, I see you're in good hands."

Hennequin gave Didi a bib and smiled at the woman with short blonde hair. "It's my job to help."

From her bed, Didi looked at her admiringly. Hennequin noticed that her skin seemed to be becoming more transparent every day. A soft white layer covering her ravaged muscles and bones, with purple veins at her temples like delicately branched coral.

"Hennequin is too modest," said Didi, folding up the bib and putting it down beside her. "She's amazing, a godsend. I don't know what we would do without her."

It was almost touching how grateful Didi was. And how blind.

"I'm happy to help," said Hennequin with a smile, putting the plates and teacups on the tray. "Would you like another cup of tea, ladies?"

The women stood up almost simultaneously, as if on cue. "No, thank you. We'd better get going." They grabbed their handbags off the floor and the backs of their chairs.

"It's no trouble," Hennequin persisted. "Stay a bit longer. We haven't had that many visitors."

The women looked at one another knowingly. A dark-skinned girl, the youngest, began to sit down again, but was silently rebuked by the others.

After a brief, awkward silence, the woman with short blonde hair said, "Sorry, I have to be somewhere at twelve thirty."

"Me too," said another.

"How about I come again next week?" suggested the youngest colleague hesitantly.

"Great! The door is always open," crowed Hennequin. "It's not every day you have a baby. I'll show you out." Hennequin led the women to the hall, gave them their coats, and opened the front door. "Thank you for the lovely gifts. It's really kind of you," she called after them, shutting the door.

It was quiet in the living room.

Didi was lying in the raised sickbed, still as pale as before, her eyes closed and her arms rigid at her sides. Lying there, she looked like a corpse. A dead Didi—what a nice thought. But for now, a suffering Didi was even more appealing.

Humming to herself, Hennequin wheeled the chairs back into place. She heard footsteps upstairs. Oscar had finally gotten out of bed. Like Didi, he'd slept badly last night because the shrimp kept waking up. Hungry. The creature screamed the lungs out of her newborn body to alert her parents. But Didi couldn't help her child.

Through the ceiling, Hennequin could hear the muffled sound of running water. Oscar was taking a shower.

"Why on earth did you say that?" asked Didi.

Hennequin carried on humming and stacked the plates on top of one another.

Didi repeated her question, a little louder this time. "You said we haven't had many visitors. Do you really think so?"

Hennequin came and stood beside the bed, rubbing her hands. "To be honest, yes. It's usually busier."

"Lots of people came to the baby shower Oscar and I held in the garden last summer."

Hennequin put her hand up. "You know, Didi, you're right. I shouldn't have said that in front of your colleagues. It's none of their business. Sorry."

Didi laughed nervously. "No, no, it doesn't matter. You can say whatever you want, of course. I'm just a bit upset after last night. I . . ." She lowered her eyes. "I had an argument with Oscar."

Hennequin's eyes lit up. "Oh really? What about?"

"He thinks I shouldn't keep wasting my time with the breast pump."

"And he thinks that's worth arguing about?"

Didi nodded. Nervously, she locked her fingers together on top of the blanket. "He's not usually so irritable. It's because he isn't getting enough sleep; he can't cope with that."

"All babies cry. It's their only way of letting us know that they're hungry, or cold, or too hot."

"I know, but . . ." Didi looked at Hennequin. "Indy cries a lot at night. Much more than during the day. Oscar thinks I should let her cry, but I can't. She's calling for me; she's lying there all alone in that bed in the dark. I really wish I could have her in my room with me at night."

"I understand that, but it really is better this way, for you and for Indy. You know that, don't you?" Hennequin looked at her thoughtfully. "You know what, let's put you in the guest room today. It's quieter

67

in there, and you can try to get some sleep. That'll lift your mood and boost your milk production. If any more visitors turn up, I'll ask them to come back tomorrow or the day after. Deal?"

Didi nodded wearily.

"Good. I'll take the breast pump upstairs for later. You don't need my help with it anymore, do you? I'll bring you a cup of tea in a minute."

❧

Compared with most houses in this village, Corné Dillen's home looked like a dwarf's cottage. It was plastered in white and had a gently sloping and rather low tiled roof. At the front of the property there was a green metal ornamental gate.

The gravel crunched beneath Miriam's shoes as she walked to the side of the house. She rang the cast-iron bell beside the door. It made so much noise, the whole village probably knew whenever Dillen had visitors.

Miriam looked around. In real life, the village felt different than she'd expected. It was bound to be beautiful here in summer, as she'd seen on Google Maps, when everything was in bloom and animals were grazing in the meadows. But now, more than anything, it was silent. The mist that rose up from the surrounding pastureland gave the area a sinister feeling. It was an eerie place, far too quiet.

Fortunately, the man who opened the door looked a lot less unworldly than the young head teacher. He was stocky, with bushy dark eyebrows, crew-cut gray hair, and friendly eyes. He was wearing a blue fleece sweater and corduroy trousers. At the same time, a keeshond appeared in the doorway and started running around her in circles, yapping hoarsely.

"Miriam de Moor, Rotterdam police. Are you Corné Dillen, who used to teach at De Rank Primary School?"

"That's me."

The dog kept yapping.

"May I come in?"

Dillen made no move to let her in. He rubbed one of his thick black eyebrows with an extended forefinger. "What is it about?"

"It's about one of your former students. I'm trying to find out more about her childhood as part of an investigation."

He looked over his shoulder into the house. "I have to leave for a meeting in a minute. Could you come back another time?"

"It won't take long," she persisted.

"Who is this about?"

"Catharina Kramer."

The man's expression changed. He said nothing.

"We believe she may have attended the school here in the village in the late eighties and early nineties. Am I right in thinking the name rings a bell?"

"Catharina?" He moved his lips as if he were biting off a piece of skin and, to her surprise, opened the door wider. "OK. I have a few minutes."

❦

"You look a bit tired, Oscar." Hennequin took a glass out of the cupboard and put a tea bag in it. She turned on the hot water dispenser. Hissing and bubbling, a jet of boiling water spurted into the glass. She put it down and looked at Oscar, who was leaning his lower back against the kitchen counter, drinking an espresso. He was wearing jeans and a red polo shirt. His dark hair was still damp from the shower. He looked a little glum.

"This is a very exciting time," she continued. "You should get more rest."

He set his espresso down on the counter. "No chance. Indy was awake all night. I didn't get a wink of sleep. This is the second night she's kept us up."

"Given her birth weight, she should have no trouble sleeping for several hours between feedings. But sometimes babies cry themselves to sleep. They do it to tire themselves out. Often the only thing you can do is just let them cry."

He looked at her with bloodshot eyes. "That's what I want to do, but Didi keeps calling me 'cause she thinks I should get Indy out of bed. Obviously she can't do that herself." He ran his fingers through his hair. Hennequin noticed that the corners of his mouth had drooped a little in the past few days.

But he still looked good.

"I'll talk to her about it later," said Hennequin.

Oscar smiled wearily. "Thank you. That's sweet of you. You have—"

Hennequin came closer to him. She could smell Oscar's shower gel, which she knew was the Rituals brand; over the past few days, she'd become as intimately acquainted with the Stevens-Vos family's bathroom as her own. She'd gone through all the cabinets and drawers.

Oscar had stopped talking.

Hennequin's breasts were almost touching him. She had to tilt her head back to look into his eyes. "I understand what you're going through. Didi isn't herself." She put her hand on his forearm.

He glanced at it, but didn't pull his arm away.

"Listen, Oscar. I'm not just here for Didi and the baby. I'm here for you too," she said, in a soft, sickly sweet voice. Her thumb made circular movements on his arm. "Make the most of it. If you need any help, if there's *anything* I can do for you . . ."

❧

It had been a long time since Miriam had drunk filtered coffee—she wondered if they even sold such machines anymore. And it had been even longer since she'd eaten a Bastogne biscuit. The house was very small, but cozy thanks to the dark carpet and blazing gas fire. The furniture looked extremely solid. All in all, it felt a bit like she was visiting her grandpa and grandma. Except Grandpa and Grandma Dillen lived in a kind of public fairy-tale theme park rather than a bustling neighborhood of Rotterdam.

On the other side of the living room, Mrs. Dillen was sitting at the dining table, playing Wordfeud on an iPad. Her dog was curled up on her lap like an orange ball of fluff so that you couldn't tell its head from its tail.

Dillen logged on to his computer. "A while ago I scanned all my class portraits by hand. Every now and then, former students contact the school to request these old photos, and whenever that happens, they get referred to me." He leaned forward and typed in a few more details. "Here it is. Year 6, 1990." He clicked on the picture, enlarged it, and zoomed in on a chubby girl with thick glasses and long, wavy, but clearly rather straggly and unkempt hair. "And this is Catharina Kramer."

Miriam stared at the photo. It was impossible to imagine a starker contrast with Hennequin Smith, who didn't wear glasses and was slim, tanned, and beautifully groomed. People could change over the years, but still. "I can hardly believe it's her," she said.

"Sometimes I get mixed up, but not when it comes to Catharina. She was the sort of student you never forget. School must have been hard for her." He zoomed in even closer, until the unhappy-looking girl took up almost the entire screen.

Miriam peered at the photo. Those eyes. If she ignored the glasses and pictured an older, slimmed-down version of that face and body . . . It was possible.

Perhaps.

"Why was it hard for her?"

"She was bullied terribly. Not in the early years. I think she got along pretty well at first. Later, that changed."

"Why?"

He looked at her sideways. "Do you know this area?"

"Not really."

"People here are conservative. Traditional. The church is very important in this community, and everything revolves around the family. That was even more the case when Catharina grew up here than it is today. There was a lot of social control. Catharina was an only child in a village where families with eight, ten, even fifteen children were the norm. With so many siblings for company, those children didn't need much contact with others. In Catharina's case . . . well, she was all alone."

"Let's be honest, Corné; she was a strange girl. She had a few screws loose," Miriam heard Dillen's wife say.

Miriam turned to the woman, but she just stared at her tablet, as if she were talking to herself.

"Catharina, in herself, wasn't that strange," said Dillen defensively. "She just didn't fit in here. Her parents were from out of town, from the city, like you. Perhaps they moved here for the beauty of the surroundings and the fact that nice houses were more affordable in this area than where they came from."

"They were hardly short of money," Mrs. Dillen chimed in.

"Where were they from?"

"Arnhem, I believe. And what my wife says is true. The father was often away from home for long periods of time; he worked on oil rigs, if I remember correctly. It was something to do with oil, in any case."

"That chap was never at home," said Mrs. Dillen. "And his poor wife just rattled around in that big house with that strange child. It must have been too much for her. Perhaps she couldn't stand the isolation anymore."

Dillen coughed, clenched his jaw, and looked straight at Miriam. "They were outsiders in the village because they weren't religious. The fact that Mrs. Kramer—her name was Heidi—only had one child was regarded as a punishment from above." He raised his hand and circled his index finger. "Some people here still think like that." He leaned toward her, as if he were about to reveal a big secret. "Some people don't even have TV or internet."

"What happened to Mrs. Kramer?"

"She hanged herself."

Miriam jerked her head toward the man. "Who found her?"

"A housekeeper. As far as I know, Catharina didn't see it, though I can't say for sure. There are all sorts of wild stories making the rounds. You've probably heard them already. Oh well. In the last term of Year 5, the girl lost her mother. And suicide . . ." Deep in thought, he bit a flake of skin off his lip. "In these parts, that's regarded as a very serious sin; it also reflects badly on the rest of the family. But Catharina came back to school. That was brave. She went on to a middle-tier secondary school, but she could have done better. The girl was smart. Gifted, as we say nowadays."

"Does the father still live here?"

"No. They moved away when Catharina started secondary school."

"To where?"

He shrugged his shoulders. "Some said they went abroad; others said they moved to Nijmegen. Nobody really knows. Perhaps you could check the population register?"

Miriam looked out the window, at the fields. The mist had grown thicker. She then looked back at the computer screen. "Could you email me that photo? And do you have any more pictures of Catharina, by any chance?"

"What kind of investigation is this exactly? Did something happen to her?"

"Sorry. I'm afraid I can't go into that."

The man scratched one of his thick eyebrows. It made a scraping sound. "OK. I'm sorry to have to cut this short, but I have a meeting in a minute, and I need to get changed." They stood up together.

"May I call you if I have any additional questions?" asked Miriam.

"Of course." The man plucked a business card from a holder next to the computer and handed it to her.

"Did she do something to somebody?" Miriam heard Mrs. Dillen ask suddenly.

She turned to the woman. "What makes you think that?"

"I always had such a strange feeling about that girl. She wasn't quite right in the head, if you know what I mean." Mrs. Dillen twirled her forefinger next to her temple.

Dillen raised his voice. "You expect everyone to behave just like you. We can't all be the same."

She shook her head firmly. "This is something you can sense as a woman, Corné. Men are simply less attuned to it." The woman turned to Miriam. "She could give you such a piercing look sometimes. As if she felt superior to us."

"Did you ever visit the Kramers' home?" Miriam asked.

"No. I didn't have any contact with those people. Nobody did. We barely even said hello to each other."

Miriam followed the man to the door.

She turned around. "Where exactly did Catharina live?"

Corné Dillen straightened up. "If you drive to the end of the street and then turn right at the church, it's the third house on the right. A tall white building. You can't miss it."

❦

Didi sat motionless on the bed in the guest room. Her shoulders were bent, and she was leaning forward slightly. The breast pump was attached to both her breasts, and she was holding the transparent shields in place with her hands. She stared at a spot on the wall. It was extremely painful. She hated this device, which made a continual monotonous chirping sound and did even more damage to her nipples.

It was getting more and more difficult. The Vaseline that Hennequin had recommended this morning helped a little, but not enough. Her breasts just couldn't take it anymore. And her milk production was still pitifully low.

Yesterday, Hennequin had given her a bottle with an extra-small teat so that Indy would have to put in much more effort to get at the little bit of milk. After all that work, she would fall asleep from exhaustion. At least, that was the plan, but Indy couldn't be fooled.

Didi felt like a failure. She wasn't producing enough milk due to all the stress and pain—or perhaps, she feared, because she just wasn't cut out for motherhood. Her breasts were too delicate for this device. Pregnancy and childbirth had been hard enough. Without medical intervention, she wouldn't even have survived, and Indy wouldn't have been born. *Perish the thought!*

Last night she'd seriously considered giving up and switching to formula. Perhaps Oscar was right. So many people had been raised on it, it was the most normal thing in the world, so why wouldn't it be fine for Indy? At the same time, she'd hated herself for that thought. She just had to persevere and keep pumping. It would be a matter of days, at most a week, before she got the hang of it and started producing enough milk for her daughter. Hopefully by then it would also be less painful.

She looked at the clock. Only five minutes had passed of the twenty she was supposed to spend using the device. It felt like hours.

Where was Hennequin with her tea?

❦

The soft skin slipped past Hennequin's incisors and into her mouth. She closed her lips around it and tasted the preseminal fluid on her tongue. *I could bite him now,* she thought. *Very hard. I could bite the whole thing off and put an end to his rotten, cushy life, and Didi Vos's too.*

Oscar became excited. He thrust his member deeper inside her.

Trust.

It never ceased to amaze Hennequin how men could so casually expose their most important, oh-so-precious body part to danger, how they could surrender that delicate flesh so carelessly to a total stranger.

She let him get on with it, relaxed her throat muscles, let him go deeper. With the corners of her mouth curled up slightly, she lifted her eyes and looked up.

Oscar was holding on to the counter, clasping it with both hands, out of breath as if in pain, his eyes firmly shut. This would not last long. Oscar didn't need much.

The swollen flesh slid back and forth over her tongue, pressed against her uvula, slipped past her molars. It would be so easy. One hard bite, merciless, totally unexpected. One moment, euphoria. The next, dickless Oscar, father of a daughter he could never see again, hospitalized, maimed for life, *and* divorced before the year was out.

But that wouldn't give her much pleasure. If she yielded to this impulse, it would be game over. Hennequin liked to think of herself as a cat: a tabby cat, slender and lithe, with golden eyes like her neighbors' cat in her childhood village. The cat had spent hours playing with her prey. As a child, Hennequin had often sat and watched. First, the prey would be wounded to the point that it couldn't run away. Next, the cat would tap the creature, which then staggered away from her in a daze. When it was almost out of reach, she lashed out and dug her claws into its back in order to pull the little creature toward her. Purring with pleasure, she then watched it thrash around. Cats could keep this up for hours. Hennequin was going to take much longer than that.

Oscar started panting. He tried his very best to be as quiet as possible, but if Didi was alert, she might be able to hear him from the guest room. Perhaps she could bite him *gently*. Just tease Oscar a little, pin the skin between her canines and pierce it, hard enough to tear it open slightly, to make it bleed—accidentally, of course. *Oh no, I got carried away. I'm so sorry.* Kiss it—lick off the blood with the focus and intensity of a cat grooming her fur. *Sorry, sorry, how can I make it up to you . . .*

Above her, Oscar stood moaning faintly as if he were being tortured, unaware of what she was thinking. His breath stopped short; his body tensed up and made a brief, jolting movement.

He spewed inside her. Without even bothering to warn her.

With eyes full of hatred, she looked up at the contorted face above her, the mouth wide open in a silent scream.

Next time she would hurt him. Really hurt him. He deserved it.

She spat into the sink, took a sip from the tap, rinsed, and let the water run out of her mouth. Dabbing her lips with one of Indy's bibs, she turned around.

Oscar buttoned up his trousers. He looked around wildly, with red cheeks. Sweat beaded on his temples. He was already racked with guilt, or perhaps it was shame. He fixed his gaze on the tiles.

"Oh God," he whispered to himself, as if she weren't even there.

🦋

The childhood home of Hennequin Smith a.k.a. Catharina Kramer was slightly set back from the narrow asphalt road that meandered through the village and had a gravel driveway leading up to it. An enormous weeping willow stood in the middle of a poorly maintained lawn. The tree was at least as tall as the house itself and blocked out so much sunlight that nothing grew beneath it. To the right of the house, at the end of the driveway, was a detached off-white stone garage with a high tiled roof.

A strange atmosphere surrounded the house. Eerie, somewhere between magical and creepy, just like in the rest of the village.

Miriam parked on the side of the road and got out. The house wasn't very big, but it looked like it had once been grand, with a small set of tiled steps that led up to the front door. There were red shutters at the windows, and the walls were covered in a coat of white paint with a dusting of mold.

So this was where Hennequin had been born. This had been her home until the age of twelve. And in this house, Hennequin's mother had taken her own life.

As chief duty officer, Miriam had seen lots of dead people. She'd lost count of how many—twenty, twenty-five? When a body was found, she was often the first to be called to the scene. Usually it was a case of death by natural causes, sometimes suicide, and only occasionally murder. But even though she'd gradually gotten used to the sight of dead bodies, she still struggled with hangings. These were among the most horrific for witnesses. Dillen didn't know if Catharina had found her mother's body. But it was possible, and if she had, it would've had a devastating impact on her emotional development.

Miriam saw movement behind one of the windows on the first floor. She walked toward the front door, went up the steps, and rang the bell.

The woman who opened the door looked a lot younger and more modern than Miriam had expected judging by the house's appearance and surroundings. She couldn't be much older than thirty and was wearing jeans and a black hoodie. She introduced herself as Anita van Wijk.

"I don't live here. This is my parents' house." She said that she, her boyfriend, and her two brothers had all taken the day off to help her parents redecorate.

Packs of laminate were piled up in the narrow hallway, and Miriam could smell paint and wood. She could hear loud male voices and shuffling upstairs.

"My parents are getting older," explained Anita. "They want to downsize, but the house won't sell in its current state."

"It's a big job. Your parents must be grateful for your help."

She looked at her conspiratorially. "You'd think so, wouldn't you? But no, not a chance. They love their moss-green carpet and paneled ceilings."

"When did your parents buy this house?"

Anita tugged at the strings of her hood and narrowed her eyes. "I celebrated my tenth birthday in this house. So . . . well, that would be twenty years ago." She paused and then said, "What brings you all the way from Rotterdam to this backwater?"

"An investigation into the previous occupants of this house."

"Oh, then I don't think I can help you. The house was vacant when we moved here, and I don't think my parents ever had any contact with those people. Or rather, with that man. Because the woman . . . well, you probably know about that." Her eyes lit up. She suddenly became excited. "Is that what this is about? Are you from one of those cold case units?"

Miriam shook her head. "Sorry, it's still too early to go into that. But I'd like to speak to your parents."

"They're out shopping. I think they'll be back in an hour."

The women stood facing each other awkwardly.

"Um . . . would you like to come in?"

"Yes, please." Miriam stepped forward. The hall had an old-fashioned terrazzo floor, and the walls were covered with yellowed pine paneling. "Did your parents do much work on the house when they moved in here?"

Anita shook her head. "None at all. Apart from the children's rooms, it's barely changed. My parents were happy with it the way it was. It's like a museum." She rolled her eyes. "That's why it was desperate for a makeover. It's not easy to sell a house these days."

"Is it OK if I take a look around?"

"Um . . ." Anita tucked a loose wisp of hair behind her ear and smiled apologetically. "Sure. Why not. You're a police officer, aren't you? So it's not as if you're going to steal anything."

Oscar had gone out. That was the only answer Didi's husband seemed to have to pretty much any of the difficult problems and situations that arose within the smoothly plastered walls of Baljuwstraat 66: jump into his company car and run away.

Perhaps Didi hadn't been so lucky in love after all—Oscar had succumbed remarkably easily just now.

Hennequin was cleaning out the breast pump. She sterilized the flanges and tubes with boiling water and laid out all the separate parts to dry on paper towels. Then she took a tub of table salt, sprinkled some onto her damp forefinger, and smeared it on the inside of the flanges.

Humming to herself, she washed her hands and looked out into the garden. The day before yesterday, Oscar had cleaned out the hutch and given the rabbits fresh water and food. Since then, he'd probably forgotten all about them. On her arrival this morning, Hennequin had seen the water bottle lying in the grass in front of the hutch, and it was still there now. That was careless of Oscar. And it gave her an idea.

Quietly, she went over to the hall, stood motionless at the bottom of the stairs, and listened. Deathly silence up there. The baby was asleep, and Didi probably was too.

She went back into the kitchen and opened the connecting door to the garage. The space was almost completely taken up by Didi's car, a red Opel Corsa. A washing machine and dryer had been installed against the short wall. Long white shelves were mounted above them. There were also two bicycles. An upright bicycle with a low step-through frame, which allowed enough room for a baby seat on the handlebars, and a sleek road bike. The priorities in this family were clear.

Hennequin scanned the shelves. She quickly found what she was looking for: a jerrican containing a blue liquid. She read the label, unscrewed the cap, and sniffed at it cautiously. The ethylene glycol in antifreeze was strong stuff. You only needed a tiny amount. Hennequin took a bottle out of her pocket and poured some of the liquid into it. She then slipped back into the kitchen.

Outside, the water bottle was still lying in the grass. The lop-eared rabbits were bound to be thirsty.

She opened the sliding patio doors and walked toward the hutch.

❧

This wasn't how Didi had imagined motherhood. She'd expected it to be more romantic. Mellower. Of course, she was having trouble with her pelvis, and she'd been realistic enough to accept that the problem wouldn't go away right after she gave birth. And she *had* expected having a baby to put a strain on her relationship with Oscar, especially in the beginning. But still. Instinctively, she'd formed a rosier mental picture of this time. She'd envisioned herself standing beside the crib with Oscar, marveling at the living creature they'd made together. Bathing the baby together, taking turns feeding her, and going for walks on sunny days. Just being a loving family together: Oscar, the baby, and herself. An inseparable trinity. For that was what she'd always been convinced they would be. Even Oscar had started to believe it, after his initial misgivings.

And now this.

Early this morning, Oscar had apologized half-heartedly, telling her that he hadn't meant what he'd said and that he needed time to adjust to their new situation. But that couldn't hide the fact that something was seriously wrong. Oscar had been acting distant ever since Indy's birth, and it only seemed to be getting worse. Even when he was present in body, he was clearly absent in mind. And now he was gone—gone again, even though after last night she needed to talk to him and feel his arms around her more than ever. That closeness seemed to be precisely what he seized every opportunity to avoid.

He hadn't even told her where he was going. She'd already called him three times, but he wasn't answering his phone.

On her digital camera, Didi looked at the photo that the maternity nurse had taken of the three of them. The young family who stared out from the screen appeared anything but happy and radiant. Oscar actually looked a bit strange, his eyes fixed on something below the lens. Indy was barely visible, buried under the baby blanket. And her own face was pale and puffy, with red-rimmed, almost expressionless eyes and a forced smile.

No wonder Oscar didn't want to be here.

She picked up her phone and called him again.

Voice mail.

🌿

The front door of the house worked like a time machine. Inside, the clock seemed to have turned back at least thirty years. The staircase was lined with yellowed paneling, all the way to the top, and the closed-tread steps were covered with moss-green carpet. Miriam looked up. The stairs to the attic were concealed behind a sloping wall. Mrs. Kramer couldn't have hanged herself in the stairwell.

"So you're aware of what happened here?"

Anita followed close behind. "You know what villages are like. We've heard the stories."

They came out onto the first floor. In one of the rooms, a man was steaming off the wallpaper while two others were pulling up the carpet. When they saw her, they stopped working. It was obvious at a glance that two were twins. The brothers appeared to be quite a lot younger than their sister, in which case they would remember even less than she did. Anita introduced Miriam.

"What do you know about the family who lived here?"

"Not very much. They had one child, a girl. The father worked on an oil rig or something."

"Mrs. Kramer hanged herself here," one of the men remarked.

Miriam looked around. "Here?"

"No, in the garage."

Her eyes rested briefly on Anita. "Did you know that when you moved in? It must have been a scary thought for children."

"Our parents didn't tell us; we only heard about it later at school. I was worried that the mother would come and haunt us, but nothing ever happened. Although I never liked going into the garage."

"Me neither," said one of the brothers.

The other brother had stuck a cigarette in the corner of his mouth and was searching his pockets for a lighter. "I don't know how seriously you should take those stories." He pointed with his chin toward the front of the house. "Some people said that the woman hanged herself from that tree out there."

Miriam looked out through the sheer curtains at the weeping willow.

"They all contradict one another," said Anita's boyfriend, a slim, olive-skinned man in a garish Diesel T-shirt. "But you can check the police reports, can't you?"

"That's certainly a possibility," said Miriam.

Unfortunately, that wasn't true. The system only went back five years. To delve any deeper into the past would be difficult. Difficult, but not impossible—at least if this were an official case.

"So it might not have been suicide?" asked Anita.

"We're keeping all options open, but the investigation is still very broad at this stage. I also urge you not to discuss this with anybody else, as that could jeopardize the investigation."

"Of course."

"I'd like to take a look around on my own, including in the attic and the garage. Is that OK?"

"No problem. Could you let us know when you leave?"

❦

Humming to herself, Hennequin poured the boiling water out of the pan. She fished the baby bottles and nipples out of the sink and laid them out on the counter. The whole kitchen smelled of vinegar. It made the plastic of the bottles nice and clear. According to the protocol, she was now supposed to rinse the bottles thoroughly with cold water, but she didn't bother. Indy probably wouldn't appreciate the taste of vinegar, but that wasn't Hennequin's problem. She would be out of here in half an hour.

Didi was pumping upstairs in the guest room for the fourth time today. She was doing pretty well. Much better than she realized. That woman kept on producing milk, and lots of it, despite the fact that the breast shields were far too small, which caused more and more damage to her nipples.

Hennequin took two bottles of milk out of the fridge and opened them. The sickly smell wafted up, straight into her nostrils. She turned her face away. Vomit, that was what it smelled like. Disgusting. She filled two clean bottles halfway with milk, added an equal amount of tap water, shook them, and held the bottles up to the light. The milk had become slightly more transparent, but the difference wasn't that obvious. Oscar and Didi hadn't noticed it yesterday or the day before. And why would they? They had no reason to believe there was anything wrong with the milk.

Hennequin dumped the rest of the breast milk into the sink. Mesmerized, she watched the precious liquid disappear down the drain.

❦

The garage was a lot bigger than it had looked from the road. There was space for four cars. It was dim and dusty, filled with boxes of old paper and strewn with tools. The daylight filtered in through a few grimy square windows. High above Miriam's head, raw wooden beams supported the tiled gabled roof.

She'd walked around the entire house, which was still largely in its original state. This had made her feel as though the young Catharina could appear at any moment, drinking her milk at the kitchen table before school or running through the adjoining rooms. It was a fascinating stroll through Hennequin's childhood, but ultimately Miriam hadn't learned much from it.

So far, what had struck her the most was the change in Catharina's appearance. Miriam found it incredible that the elegant, groomed woman of today had once been a chubby, awkward child, grinning into the camera. An outsider at school and in the village. A lonely child too. Corné Dillen's wife claimed that Catharina hadn't been "quite right in the head." That she could give people piercing looks and had an air of superiority about her. This description was consistent with Miriam's impression of her sister-in-law. Hennequin's manner toward her family had seemed very friendly at first, but if you observed her long enough, you saw that she approached everybody in almost exactly the same way: with a smile that appeared to be made of plastic. Fake. For that reason alone, Hennequin had given Miriam the creeps. Now, she was suddenly reminded of that humming of hers. She didn't know anyone who hummed as much as Hennequin did; it was as if she were constantly chuckling to herself or hatching a plan. Miriam felt another shiver run down her spine. She'd never understood why her brother had fallen for a woman like that or how he could have been so blind. Every day, she still regretted never having the guts to broach it with him.

Miriam was about to go outside when she noticed a number of posters on the wall, half-hidden behind an open shelf unit. They were yellowed and covered with cobwebs and a thick layer of dust, with creases down the middle and tears in the thin paper where staples had once been. She blew off the dust. Talking Heads, Duran Duran, the Pet Shop Boys—bands from the eighties. She looked at them pensively. Catharina had lived in this house from her birth in 1978 until 1990. Miriam had been told that the current occupants had left it largely intact, but did that include not even taking down the posters from the walls? Could they be Hennequin's? Had she put them up in here herself as a child? She decided to go and ask Anita.

❦

Oscar came home just in time. Hennequin was due to get off work in five minutes.

She heard the car turn into the driveway, and moments later the front door opened. Oscar didn't go upstairs. His footsteps clacked on the tiles in the living room.

"You're still here," he said when he saw her in the kitchen. He looked a little drawn. "Where's Didi?"

"Upstairs," she said calmly.

"Listen, Hennequin, what happened this morning, it's—"

She put her hand on his forearm. "Shh. Nothing happened, nothing important."

"But—"

"You enjoyed it, didn't you?"

He looked at her with a mixture of astonishment and confusion.

"It's my pleasure," she said. "I like to help. You needed it; I could sense that." She gestured with her chin to the first floor. "Your wife can't do that for you right now, can she?" She chuckled to make her words sound more lighthearted. "It's on the house," she joked, with a twinkle in her eye.

Oscar looked timidly in the direction of the living room, as if his wife might appear at any moment. "Do you do this often?"

She frowned. "Don't think about it. Just enjoy it. You've been having a hard enough time, and you still are. Next Monday is my last day here. After that, you'll never see me again."

"I can't believe—"

She stood on tiptoe to kiss him gently on the cheek. "While I'm working here, I'm not just here for your wife and child, but for you too—at least, if that's what you want." She grabbed his hands and looked at him earnestly. "It's no trouble, Oscar. And you deserve it. You thoroughly deserve it." She gave him a beaming smile. "Shall I make you a cup of tea?"

Hennequin pattered into the living room. The door to the hall was still open. She stood at the bottom of the stairs and raised her voice, "Would you like tea as well, Didi?"

"Yes, please" came a voice from the guest room. "With two sweeteners."

Goodness. The corpse couldn't even walk, and she was worried about her figure.

Humming to herself, Hennequin went back to the kitchen. Oscar was still there. She reached into a cupboard for tea and two mugs.

"Could we maybe . . . see each other sometime, somewhere else?" she heard him whisper behind her. "I just find this . . . It doesn't feel right." There was a hint of doubt in his voice, but the guilt was gone.

"We'll talk about it tomorrow, OK?"

As she held the second mug under the hissing water jet, she heard Oscar leave the kitchen and go upstairs.

Smiling, she tossed the tea bags into the mugs. She was feeling increasingly at home with the Stevens-Vos family. She would miss these people when they were gone.

Picking up the mugs, she turned around. Through the glass patio doors, she had a clear view of Jip and Janneke. The lop-eared rabbits looked perfectly fine. Snug in the straw. Dozing peacefully side by side, their noses twitching up and down.

The water bottle was already a quarter empty.

❧

It turned out that the posters *had* been on the wall when the family moved into the house in 1991. "It was just a garage," Anita had said to Miriam. "My father went in there sometimes, but we never did, because of those stories." Anita had also told Miriam that she'd recently found out that her parents had bought the house at a bargain price and had therefore turned a blind eye to its troubled history.

All the way home, Miriam was lost in thought. She kept thinking of that chubby, unhappy-looking child in the class photo, that child who was excluded and whose mother had committed suicide. The contrast between Catharina Kramer and the confident, even slightly intimidating, adult Hennequin Smith was startling. Miriam suspected that Hennequin had gone under the knife. That was common among people who'd had a tough childhood or had bad memories of their parents or family. They turned to plastic surgeons to transform their faces because they couldn't bear the constant reminder of their hated or dreaded family traits. Hennequin had lived in the United States for many years. She'd changed her name there, so why not her body and face as well? No doubt she'd also taught herself all kinds of social skills, behaviors that didn't match what she felt inside. And for the most part, she got away with it. Not many people had a sufficient level of social sensitivity to notice the discrepancy between Hennequin's behavior and personality. After all, Bart hadn't spotted it. And perhaps the previous two husbands hadn't either. Even Miriam's parents had regarded Hennequin as a lovely, sweet girl.

Anita and her brothers hadn't been able to tell Miriam where Mr. Kramer and his daughter had moved after Mrs. Kramer's death. They'd promised to consult the title deeds, which listed the house's previous owners, and call her with Kramer's details. With a name and a date and place of birth, Miriam could quickly find out if the man was still alive and where he lived. If he was still in the Netherlands, at least. Oddly enough, she couldn't remember whether Hennequin's father had attended the wedding. She didn't think so. Most of the guests had been Bart's friends and business associates, a bunch of people who liked the sound of their own voices. Miriam could kick herself for not asking Hennequin many questions at the wedding and then hardly speaking to her in the eighteen months that she'd been part of Bart's life. In fact, she'd barely even talked to Bart himself. She, Bart, and her parents had all gotten wrapped up in their own jobs and lives in recent years. Under normal circumstances, that wouldn't have mattered. Miriam had always had a good relationship with her brother, and she was sure that they'd have become close again at some point. The fact that that moment would never come made the sense of regret and loss even stronger.

Perhaps her colleague Rens was right: perhaps she was still grieving and was finding it so hard to get over her brother's sudden death that she needed a scapegoat. If so, that would have a significant effect on her professional judgment. After all, it was perfectly possible that Hennequin had changed her name and appearance purely to erase any reminder of the unhappy, lonely child she'd once been. Miriam couldn't rule that out. But the fact that she'd gone through three husbands in such a short space of time, and that two of them had died, was pretty extraordinary. And then there was Mrs. Dillen's remark: *I always had such a strange feeling about that girl. She wasn't quite right in the head, if you know what I mean.*

It wasn't looking good for Hennequin Smith a.k.a. Catharina Kramer.

❧

It was dim in the guest room; all the lights were off except for a reading lamp. Oscar was standing beside the bed in his boxer shorts, his hair disheveled.

"What's wrong with her?" Didi wondered aloud. Indy had clearly been hungry, searching with a half-open mouth for the bottle, but once she'd found it, she'd turned her head away and started howling.

"She's not hungry," said Oscar.

"Of course she is. You can see for yourself that she wants to drink." Didi looked despairingly at her child, who was turning redder and redder from crying, and pushed the bottle against her mouth again. She moved it from side to side, squeezing a drop of milk into the baby's mouth. Once more, Indy turned her head away. No, she really didn't want it. Earlier this evening it had been a similar ordeal.

"I've heard that the taste of the milk is affected by the mother's diet," said Oscar. "What did you eat today?"

"Nothing unusual. The same as always."

Oscar nodded to the baby. "Really? She doesn't seem to like it." He stretched. "Or she's just had enough. Hennequin says that babies sometimes cry to tire themselves out, and that it's fine to leave them to it."

Didi looked despondently at her child. She was certain that Indy was hungry. Not just tonight. She had been for days. *You can't give her what she needs, and your milk doesn't taste good enough.* Didi felt tears pricking behind her eyes.

"Come on, I'll put her back in the crib." Oscar held out his hands.

Reluctantly, Didi let go of her child. She couldn't even lift Indy up to pass her to Oscar, as that would send a sharp stab of pain through her lower body. She watched Oscar carry Indy into the nursery. Moments later a soft instrumental lullaby started playing from the mobile above the crib. Didi heard Oscar close the door behind him. Indy was silent for a moment, overwhelmed by the new sights and sounds, but soon realized that she was being left alone and began to cry again.

Oscar appeared in the doorway and ran his fingers through his hair. He glanced at Didi and then looked away from her again, as if he were about to tell her something but changed his mind.

"Is something wrong?" asked Didi.

He shook his head. "No, nothing. Good night."

❦

Miriam sat cross-legged on the sofa with her computer open on her lap. There was an empty beer bottle on the coffee table, and a repeat of

Absolutely Fabulous was playing on TV. She wasn't paying any attention to the sitcom. She'd spent the past few hours furiously entering all sorts of names into the search engine. It felt like she was firing shots in the dark, hoping to hit something: Catharina Kramer, Hennequin Smith, Hennequin Wilson, Keanu Smith, Jonathan Wilson . . . She'd even immersed herself in the phenomenon of oil rigs—offshore industry—in the hope of coming across a Kramer, but that was like looking for a needle in a haystack. She hadn't learned much about any of them. In one photo, a graying Jonathan Wilson smiled at her with a mouth full of unnaturally white teeth. Below it was the address of his practice and an offer for a free X-ray with the first paid consultation. She couldn't find any mention of the dentist's private life.

In any case, Chucky Lee's information clearly hadn't come from the internet.

She sighed and stretched. It was half past eleven. Tomorrow was a normal working day, which meant that she would have to be at the station at seven o'clock and work until three. That gave her enough time to shower and freshen up for her date with Boris—if it even was a date. Perhaps she was reading too much into it. At any rate, she had to go to bed.

She was about to close her laptop when she had an idea. Now that the trail seemed to have gone cold in Hennequin's childhood, it might be better to approach it from the opposite angle. She had information about Catharina Kramer the primary school student and the adult Hennequin Smith, who'd settled in the United States at the age of twenty-six. There was a gap of fourteen years that she needed to piece together.

She opened her email and drafted a message to Chucky. Perhaps he could consult the emigration documents and find out Hennequin's last known address in the Netherlands.

Day Five

SATURDAY

Hennequin knew the statistics: one in a hundred full-term or near-term babies died during labor or within four weeks of birth. That was a pretty large number. Worryingly large. The Netherlands had one of the highest rates in Europe. Various organizations and professional bodies all scrambled to blame one another or dispute the figures. But the fact remained, being born in this country was a risky business.

Hennequin looked into the crib. Indy didn't give the impression that she was going to give up without a fight. The shrimp had clearly chosen to join the 99 percent of infants who pulled through. She howled and she cried. She clenched her fists. She stamped her little feet inside the swaddle. How had anyone ever gotten the idea that babies were cute? It was pure mass hysteria. Right now, there was nothing cute about Indy, who was making a racket and turning redder and redder. Hennequin watched, her arms crossed. Indy had worked out how the game was played. She didn't care about her mother next door, ravaged by a traumatic pregnancy and a grueling delivery. Indy was hungry, so she screamed. Indy had a dirty diaper, so she screamed. Indy wanted attention, so she screamed. Indy thought about Indy. The baby in that crib embodied the survival of the fittest in its most ruthless form.

Hennequin felt a deep hatred rising in her when she took the child out of the bed. She removed Indy's soft sweater and undid the three fasteners at the bottom of her bodysuit. With her nose in the air, and quick, careless movements, she changed the diaper.

Indy had stopped crying, startled by the heavy-handed treatment. She looked in her direction with those little blue eyes. Hennequin knew that she was staring into space. Newborn babies couldn't focus. They couldn't see you; they could only make out light and dark and rough outlines. And the half smiles that delighted Didi were nothing but uncontrolled twitching. Indy was a horrible, self-centered creature.

Hennequin lifted the baby under the armpits and held her with outstretched arms. The child dangled between Hennequin's slender hands like a tattered rag doll, her head slumped forward and to the side since her neck still wasn't strong enough to support it. She made sobbing noises.

Once again, Hennequin was engulfed with hatred. She toyed with the idea of laying the shrimp down on her front rather than her back or putting a little antifreeze in her bottle. Such a tiny baby wouldn't need much.

In fact, she'd be doing Didi a favor.

🍂

It was funny how a few night shifts in a row could wreak havoc on your system for days afterward. Miriam was sure that the suspects she'd dealt with this morning hadn't noticed anything unusual, but she'd felt dizzy and slightly nauseous the whole time. She was thankful that Rens was shadowing her. He drove while she sat beside him, half dozing, half listening to the chatter in her ear.

It was Saturday morning and fairly quiet. She knew that this was the calm before the storm. Later tonight, her colleagues would have their hands full with people attacking each other in a variety of ways while under the influence of alcohol or drugs, or both. At home, on the street, or in the pub, during the weekend there was always some incident that required intervention. It was one of the most satisfying but also most dangerous aspects of this job and the reason that she and her colleagues wore bulletproof and stabproof vests under their uniforms.

"Get a move on," she heard Rens say beside her. He was talking to the car in front, a black Ford driven by a woman who, with a police car in her rearview mirror, was sticking too closely to the speed limit.

"You can thank the wannabes on the speed patrol for that," remarked Miriam.

"It's not my fault," said Rens testily.

Miriam nodded toward the car. "She can't tell the difference."

As Rens passed the woman, Miriam's iPhone began to vibrate. She took it out of her pocket. An email from Chucky. It was probably an invoice. Even in America there was no such thing as a free lunch.

To her surprise, the email contained information. Her fatigue vanished in an instant. She tilted the phone slightly so that Rens couldn't see the screen.

Chucky Lee had an address for her: Hennequin Smith a.k.a. Catharina Kramer's last known residence was in The Hague.

❦

Shakily, Didi took off her oversized sleep T-shirt and draped it over the side of the bath. The shirt was doable. The underpants—a strange, white mesh garment she'd been given at the hospital—were trickier, even though they were very thin and stretchy. She couldn't just step out of them. Rolling the pants slowly down her thighs, she hissed and squeezed her eyes shut when it was time to lift her leg.

She changed the maternity pad, straightened up, and removed her nursing bra. That horrible thing was ugly enough, but it was nothing compared with what she saw in the mirror. It was exactly as she'd feared when she woke up this morning: her breasts had swollen up. The white skin was stretched tight; the flesh underneath was bumpy and crisscrossed with enlarged blue veins. She could only just recognize the pair of breasts that Oscar had once worshipped. The strain on her skin was painful without the support of the bra; it felt like she was carrying boulders inside her chest. She turned her head away from the mirror and was about to step under the shower when she heard Indy crying.

Her little voice was very soft. It sounded just like the bleating of a lamb. So small, so fragile. The crying suddenly stopped. Didi took a step toward the bathroom door. Hesitating, listening. She couldn't just run out and check on her baby; first, she would have to put the mesh underpants back on, and that would take five minutes.

Indy was crying again. It sounded different this time, as if it were more than just hunger or a dirty diaper. *It's as if she's calling me.*

Didi felt a strange cramp in her abdomen: a physical reaction to her child's voice. Oscar had gone shopping, but Hennequin was somewhere in the house. Was she still downstairs? Could Didi hear footsteps, or was she just imagining it?

Suddenly, the noise stopped again. Didi stood listening for several minutes, but nothing happened. Indy had probably gone back to sleep, and there was nothing to worry about. She was being paranoid.

Just as she reached for the shower tap, the bathroom door burst open. Hennequin appeared in the doorway, holding Indy in a blanket. The maternity nurse looked flawless and radiant. The contrast with Didi was stark.

Hennequin met Didi's eyes, but not before taking a good look at her body. It made Didi uncomfortable, but she suppressed the feeling. After all, Hennequin helped her to use the breast pump and examined her stitches every day.

"Do they hurt?" said Hennequin, nodding to Didi's breasts.

"Yes. They feel very heavy."

"You've got fluid retention. That's common after childbirth."

"Do all women have it?"

"Not all. Every woman is different. But it'll get better."

"Pumping is so painful."

Indy stirred. Didi heard her child making soft protesting noises. She didn't seem to like the way Hennequin was holding her. Didi resisted the urge to grab Indy out of Hennequin's arms. A maternity nurse was bound to know better than she did how to hold a baby.

"I know. It's very unpleasant for you. Some women produce lots of milk without any trouble, but for others it's a bit more difficult." Hennequin's eyes lingered on her breasts once again. "And more painful. I'm afraid you'll actually have to start pumping even more to reduce the fluid retention."

"I was reading about that on the iPad last night and—"

"Never do that." Hennequin looked at her sternly. Reproachfully, almost.

"W–what?"

"Stay away from the internet."

Didi was startled by the sudden hardness in Hennequin's voice and the fierce look in her eyes. The bundle in Hennequin's arms started moving again.

Hennequin looked straight at Didi. "There are so many different opinions; everyone contradicts each other, even within our profession. And what's more, a lot of the information is out of date, and the forums are full of the most awful scare stories."

Didi couldn't help it. She began to cry. Hennequin's outburst—she didn't understand it. Had she said something wrong?

Hennequin suddenly appeared beside her and put a hand on her arm. "Oh gosh, Didi. You're very emotional today. Sorry, I should have noticed that. The last thing I want is for you to get upset. That's why you should stay off the internet." She looked at her, up close. Hennequin's eyes were strikingly green. Deep green. Didi had never met anyone with such an intense eye color.

"Just trust me," said Hennequin. "It'll get better."

"Really?"

"Really."

Didi put her forehead on Hennequin's shoulder and began to sob softly. At times like these, she missed her mother so terribly that it hurt more than all her physical ailments put together. Nelly hadn't even called. Wasn't she going to come visit?

Hennequin pulled away and took Didi's hand. She looked her in the eye. "Is that better? Sweetheart, what you're going through right now is temporary. As a redhead, you have very thin, delicate skin, which makes you more fragile and sensitive than other women. It's just one of those things. But it'll pass. Your skin just needs to get used to this new situation, and whatever you do, you have to keep pumping. In your case, a little pain and discomfort are simply part of the process." She shifted her gaze to Indy, whose face was barely visible, buried in the swaddle. "This is why you're doing it, remember? For your child. She won't get a second chance. This is your sacrifice to her."

Didi sniveled. She grabbed a tissue from the shelf and blew her nose.

"I'll take this little lady downstairs. Why don't you have a nice relaxing shower, and then I'll make you a cup of tea?" Hennequin disappeared and closed the door behind her.

Didi blew her nose again. Hennequin was right, of course. She had to pull herself together. Surely she couldn't give up now, just because she was having a bit of a tough time? Breast milk was the best form of nutrition, and she wanted to give Indy the best possible start in life. She owed it to her child.

❧

It was nearly two o'clock. Miriam was drinking a cup of coffee in the control room, a large, high square space that, with a little imagination, looked a bit like a modern church. Desks with monitors were arranged in a large U-shape in the center of the room. Her colleagues were sitting behind the computers, wearing headsets. It was always hectic in the control room, but sociable too. She often came here to catch up with her desk-duty colleagues over a cup of coffee. Today, they were laughing and swapping anecdotes as usual, but Miriam was barely listening.

In the car she'd already used her iPhone to check the route to the address Chucky Lee had emailed her. It would probably take no more than twenty minutes, half an hour at most. At least, if there were no holdups on the A13. That was less likely on a Saturday, but a collision or even just a broken-down car on the shoulder could quickly cause a major traffic jam on the road between Rotterdam and The Hague. She'd done the math. Her shift would be over in an hour, and she'd arranged to meet Boris at six. In between, she was going to try to speak to one or more of Hennequin's old neighbors and then shower and change when she got back. It was going to be tight. But first of all, she would have to go home. She could hardly drive to The Hague and knock on people's doors in her uniform. She'd already abused her position enough in Hennequin's childhood village.

"What are you thinking about?" Emma, a colleague, put a hand on her shoulder.

"Nothing. I didn't sleep very well."

"Those night shifts are taking their toll, aren't they?"

She rubbed her face. "It's a mug's game. My internal clock is always messed up."

For a moment she toyed with the idea of feigning the flu so that she could go home early. Her sense of duty stopped her. Today she was the only chief duty officer in the area. Rens wasn't authorized to make decisions yet. If she went home, a direct colleague in a neighboring district would be saddled with her work.

Miriam's personal phone vibrated in her pocket. She looked at the screen but didn't recognize the number. "Hello."

"Is this Miriam de Moor?"

"That's me."

"Oh great. I promised to pass on the details of the previous owner of my parents' house, remember? We found it on the title deeds, as expected. The man's na—"

"Hang on a minute." Miriam stood up and walked toward the bathroom. She took her notebook out of her pocket. "Go ahead."

"Arnoldus Hendrikus Kramer. He was born on May 7, 1953, in Druten."

"Fantastic. Thank you." That was all the information Miriam needed. She hung up and immediately entered the details into her work BlackBerry.

"Bingo," she said softly.

Hennequin/Catharina's father was still alive and lived in Arnhem. Miriam's enthusiasm quickly waned. She couldn't just drop in on the man for a chat. After all, she didn't know whether father and daughter were close. Perhaps they spoke to each other every day.

If she did contact him, she would have to tread carefully. She couldn't afford to get in trouble at work. And that was exactly what would happen if anyone found out about this.

❧

Two women were at the door. One was a skinny, nervous-looking blonde in her late twenties. The other, a plump woman wearing glasses, was a lot older. Her short dark hair was shot with gray.

Distinguished visitors.

"Come in." Hennequin stepped aside to let the women in.

The blonde shook her hand and introduced herself as Ella, a nurse from the Municipal Health Service. "I'm here for the NBS test."

NBS test? Hennequin nodded as if she knew exactly what that meant and turned her attention to the other woman. "You must be the midwife." She shook the older woman's hand. It felt hard and rough. Strong too. More like a man's hand. In that one brief moment when their hands touched, Hennequin realized that this businesslike woman was her polar opposite in life. She helped bring new life into the world, whereas Hennequin saw herself as an active and very passionate death doula.

"Have we met?" asked the midwife. She glared at Hennequin from behind her thick glasses.

"No, we haven't." Hennequin took their coats. "I'm new."

"How is Mrs. Vos?"

Hennequin turned to the midwife. "Didi spends most of the day in bed. She still can't walk properly."

"It would be surprising if she could. Mrs. Vos only gave birth four days ago."

Hennequin swallowed the jibe without flinching. "Didi is in the living room; the baby is sleeping upstairs. Would you like some coffee or tea?"

"No, thank you," muttered the midwife, walking past her into the living room. "I have a punishing schedule today."

Suddenly, the nurse seemed to be in a hurry as well. "Could you go and get the baby?" she squawked. "I always do the screening with the mother present." She also disappeared into the living room.

As Hennequin climbed the stairs, she decided to offer the two of them coffee or tea again in a minute. With a few drops of ethylene glycol in it, so that in no time at all, they would feel so sick their stomachs would turn inside out.

❦

It wasn't the most affluent area of The Hague. Massive blocks of deck-access apartments, separated by large green spaces. Built in the sixties or seventies, Miriam guessed, when a lot of people had to be housed in a short space of time. The area looked rather desolate under the cloudy sky. That impression was reinforced by the large balding trees and playgrounds where teens loitering on scooters appeared to have scared off any children.

She drove slowly past the apartment where Hennequin had apparently lived around eleven years ago. Miriam had little hope of finding anyone today who could give her more information. Buildings of this sort had a high turnover. Young families with children preferred houses with gardens, and apartments like these weren't popular with older people either. Besides, there was rarely much community spirit in these kinds of neighborhoods.

Since access to the lot was blocked by a barrier, Miriam parked on the street. She grabbed her leather jacket from the back seat and got out. Locking her car, she walked toward the entrance. Halfway there, she slowed down and looked up along the walls. It had been exactly four days since she'd stood looking at Hennequin's Rotterdam apartment block in the same way. That building was located in the trendy heart of Rotterdam and attracted a different, much wealthier kind of resident. Hennequin Smith was clearly in a more enviable position than her younger self, Catharina Kramer.

❧

Indy lay nestled up against Didi. The nurse had just made a pinprick above her heel and collected the bright-red blood. Indy had burst into tears. "Don't worry; it's just the shock," the nurse had said, but Didi wondered how the woman could be so certain. It would obviously hurt if someone stuck a needle in you, whether you were an adult or as tiny and innocent as Indy. The hearing screening had been much easier. Indy had lain happily on the bed with her while the nurse performed a series of tests.

The midwife had then examined Didi's stitches and remarked that they needed bathing in baking soda. Next, she had double-checked the size and position of her uterus. The results had differed slightly from Hennequin's earlier measurement. That too was a cause for concern, she said. Out of sight of the midwife, Hennequin had rolled her eyes. Didi had struggled to contain her laughter—for the first time since the birth, she felt the urge to burst out laughing. Perhaps she was becoming hysterical.

"Well, I'd better be going," she heard the midwife say. "Or do you have any questions, Didi?"

She did; she had lots of questions. She wondered, for example, whether it was normal for pumping to be so painful and for the flanges to irritate her nipples.

She looked at the midwife. Hennequin was standing diagonally behind her. Could she . . . could she really ask the midwife the same questions she'd asked Hennequin earlier today? Wouldn't Hennequin take offense? It might sound as if she didn't trust Hennequin's expertise.

The midwife already had her car keys in her hand; she would be gone soon, whereas Hennequin would still be here for the next few days to care for her and Indy. She didn't want to spoil the bond she'd forged with the maternity nurse.

"No questions?"

Didi shook her head.

"OK, then. I'll be back in a few days. Maybe two, maybe three. We're terribly busy at the moment, and almost all of them are boys, so when Indy grows up, she'll have her pick." She smiled and shook Didi's hand. "See you then."

❦

Number 276, Hennequin's old address, was home to a Moroccan family with young children. The mother didn't speak Dutch. Miriam had quickly abandoned her attempt to communicate. After all, it was unlikely that this woman knew Hennequin. In the apartment to the left—there was no name on the bell, nor downstairs on the mailbox—no one was home. On the other side, according to the nameplate, lived "Klaas & Wendy." In the kitchen window, there was a plastic plaque with a motto about cats having staff rather than owners and a "Beware of the Dog" sign featuring a French bulldog. Here too there was no answer. She had better luck farther down the walkway.

The door was opened by an Indonesian lady who introduced herself as Susi Tanardo. She was very small and slight, with a tight gray bun on the back of her head. Susi said she'd lived here since 1976, when the area was still developing rapidly.

She remembered Catharina Kramer.

A few minutes later, Miriam was sitting in the darkly furnished living room, which overlooked the neighborhood and parts of the city. In the corner by the window, there was an aviary containing several birds. On the wall hung black-and-white portraits taken in a junglelike setting, wooden masks, and shadow puppets. There was a strong smell of incense in the air. Susi Tanardo said that she lived alone. Her husband was dead, and she had no children.

Miriam took a sip of her coffee. "Did you have any contact with Catharina?"

The woman bowed her head slightly and said in a soft voice, "Not much. Not much at all. She kept to herself. And Catharina didn't live here for very long, around two years. She'd just graduated from college."

"Do you know what she studied?"

"I'm not sure. I think it must have had something to do with computers. What do you call it, computer science? She had four in her living room. Back then they weren't flat like they are today, were they? They were these cream-colored boxes with curved screens." She indicated the size of the monitors with her slender, wrinkled hands.

"Did you visit her place?"

"Not very often. I saw her working sometimes when I was passing by on the walkway. Catharina was always sitting behind those computer screens. She once told me that she wrote programs for companies."

"Do you know where she moved to?"

"No. She didn't tell anybody. More coffee?"

"Yes, please."

Susi poured more coffee from an old-fashioned percolator on a tray on the coffee table. Before Miriam could say that she drank her coffee unsweetened, the woman had already sprinkled it liberally with cane sugar.

"You said she kept to herself?"

"Yes. She didn't have much to do with her neighbors."

"Did she ever have visitors?"

"Few, very few. But she did go out. She was sometimes gone for whole weeks or weekends." The woman looked at her birds and said, "I got the impression that she spoke to us a bit more than the other residents because her guardian and my husband knew each other through work."

Guardian?

Miriam leaned forward in her chair.

🦋

Hennequin filled the shallow tub with boiling water and added a whole container of baking soda. Many times more than what was needed to treat Didi's wound, "the cut," as the midwife called it euphemistically. Softly humming a song by The Police, she kept stirring until most of the baking soda had dissolved.

She glanced sidelong at the garden. The rabbits had barely moved today. They were sleepier than usual. This morning Hennequin had put more drops of poison in the drinking water and also sprinkled some on their food.

As she hummed, she heard "King of Pain" playing in her head. Sting sounded so pure and clear, it was like he was standing next to her. A black spot on the sun, how wonderful.

She took a tub of table salt from the spice cabinet and scattered the contents in figure eights over the steaming water. Humming, she made another figure eight. And another.

The midwife had said it herself: Didi's stitches required extra attention. That had been an excellent observation. Strange that she hadn't thought of it herself.

Didi was in the bed in the living room. Hennequin didn't know if she was fast asleep or just dozing. But what she did know was that in the next half an hour, Didi would be wide awake.

Hennequin sang along softly under her breath. Yes, it was her destiny.

❦

Miriam grabbed her notebook. "Guardian, you said? Do you know his name?"

"Of course. It's Walter Engelen. He was an engineer at Stork."

Miriam jotted down the name. "Did you know him?"

"My husband knew him better than I did. He worked for Walter. It was my husband who told Catharina about the apartment here."

"Do you happen to know where Walter Engelen lives?"

"I do." She stood up and shuffled over to a dark wood desk against the wall. Pulling open a drawer, she took out a well-thumbed notebook. Then she put on a pair of chained reading glasses and began to leaf through the notebook. She read out an address in Bennebroek, which Miriam immediately wrote down.

"I hope, for your sake, that Walter and Liesbeth aren't in Curaçao yet. They go there every winter."

"Are you friends with them?"

"Not really. We drifted apart after my husband died three years ago. But we still send each other a Christmas card. It's just one of those customs, isn't it?" Susi took off her glasses and put them carefully back into the drawer. "I've heard that people send cards over the internet nowadays, but I prefer the old-fashioned way. I think it's classier, don't you?"

Miriam looked at the aviary in the corner of the room, a tall, square cage containing a haphazard arrangement of jagged branches on which six zebra finches hopped nervously back and forth. Amid concrete and steel, Susi Tanardo had created her own exotic paradise.

When the woman had sat down again, Miriam asked, "What did Catharina look like?"

"Very pretty. Very Dutch, tall, with long legs. And well groomed, better than many girls her age. She was also quite slim, but she worked hard for her figure. She exercised a lot."

"What kind of exercise did she do?"

The woman thought for a moment and then said, "Tennis and fencing. She often went running too, and she once told me that she swam every day. Come rain or shine. Every morning she went to the swimming pool."

Miriam took another sip of coffee. "What color was her hair at that time?"

"Reddish brown." Susi held her slender hands at shoulder height. "Down to here. Thick and slightly wavy."

"Do you have any idea how Catharina first met the Engelen family?"

"The Engelens were a couple, not a family," Susi corrected Miriam. "They didn't have any children. Catharina was older by the time she came to live with them. She must have been about sixteen, seventeen. She had another year or two of secondary school and then went to study in Delft, where she lived in a dorm. And Walter paid for it all. After she graduated, she rented the place here." She lowered her voice. "You'd expect more gratitude from a girl in her position."

"What happened?"

"One day she just moved out. I saw them, the moving men, although it only took them a couple of hours because she didn't have a lot of stuff. No pictures on the walls, no plants. How can you live like that? It never occurred to me that she hadn't told Walter and Liesbeth she was leaving. I only found out about that later."

Her eyes lingered on her birds, which made soft meep-meep sounds and hopped tirelessly from one branch to another and back again. "Catharina had sent them a letter to say that she was fine and that she didn't want anything more to do with them." Susi now looked Miriam straight in the eye. "You often hear that about adopted children. So ungrateful. It's not your own flesh and blood, and that matters."

Miriam knew countless examples of families who proved Susi wrong, but she nodded amiably. She was here to gather information, not have a debate.

She glanced at her cell phone. It was half past four. She felt the urge to thank the woman for her time and drive straight to Bennebroek. Walter and Liesbeth Engelen had looked after Hennequin for at least nine, maybe ten years. They were sure to know what had happened to her between the ages of twelve and sixteen, after she'd left the hamlet in Gelderland with her father.

"So, Walter and Liesbeth Engelen became Catharina's legal guardians," she said. "Do you know why?"

"Nobody ever told us. My husband and I always had the feeling that there was something wrong with that girl, that something had happened to her. But no one ever mentioned what it was."

Miriam nodded and made a note. She was becoming more excited and curious by the second, but if she drove to Bennebroek now, she would have to miss her date with Boris.

In the two years she'd been living above him, she'd watched him with unusually keen interest while he worked down in his studio. Even last year, when she'd had a brief relationship with a young detective from another force, she'd never gotten Boris completely out of her system. She was dying to get to know him better.

But she also wanted to find out who Hennequin was.

She owed it to her brother.

"More coffee?" said Susi. She bent her narrow back, preparing to stand up.

"Thanks. That's very kind of you, but unfortunately, I have to be going."

❦

Hennequin poured a glass of wine. Her second in half an hour. Absently, she took a wafer-thin slice of Iberian ham from a plate and put it in her mouth. After work she'd driven straight home and hadn't left the building since. There was little point in hunting for a new Mr. Money on the weekend, as the four- and five-star hotels would be full of families and couples. To meet lonely, receptive businessmen, you had to be there on weekdays.

She swirled the wine in her glass. A Saint-Émilion Grand Cru. She'd paid more than fifty euros for it, but it didn't taste good. She still felt agitated. The restlessness wouldn't go away. Not even after she'd spent an hour working up a sweat on the cross-trainer in the building's gym and then half an hour swimming laps in the pool. And now, this stupidly expensive wine wasn't helping either.

Annoyed, she searched for Mali's number in her phone and dialed it.

It went straight to voice mail, with a greeting Mali had recorded in broken English: *Sorry, I am not to reach for the weekend. From Monday you can contact me. Leave message or send email malithaimassage-at-hotmail-dot-com.*

Hennequin hung up. She could call another masseuse—there were plenty in the city—but Mali knew exactly what she wanted and how she wanted it. Anybody else would only irritate her.

She went up to one of the windows with her glass of wine and watched the neighborhoods and streets down below, which were nothing more than dark, intersecting lines in a mixture of modern and prewar terraces. Viewed from this height, crowds of people were often likened to swarming anthills. That comparison was flawed. People were not like ants in any way whatsoever. Ants were quiet, efficient creatures with a military disposition. They worked perfectly as a team: each group had its own area of expertise, and their diligence was unmatched. The group came before the individual. No. The world down there was more like a big, stuffy, overcrowded chicken coop, where everyone was trying to come out on top. Cocks fought each other incessantly; everybody got pecked and wounded. Eggs were laid, trampled, and hatched, and sometimes new chicks grew up and had to find their way in that chaos, where arbitrariness was equally decisive as the law of the jungle. The deafening chatter never stopped.

Up here it was quiet, except for the soft whispering of the wind.

Too quiet.

Far too quiet.

Once again, she noticed the strange, empty feeling in her chest. It had been there for so long. There was no point in fighting it. It would never go away. She could only drown it out.

She turned away from the city and switched on the sound system. Heavy bass lines and synth notes filled the apartment, booming against the high white walls. Killing Joke, "Love Like Blood."

Hennequin put her empty glass on the kitchen island and went to her bedroom, where she undressed and put on her kimono. Then she went back to the living room and turned up the volume even higher. Barefoot, and with half-closed eyes, she danced across the white floor, her arms outstretched, her head rolling along her shoulders from left to right. Right to left.

🍃

Boris's ground-floor apartment was sandwiched between the gallery and the studio. As a result, the space was narrow and rather illogically laid out, but thanks to the wooden floors and colorful paintings, it had a warm and pleasant atmosphere. The living room had an open kitchen, and behind it, tucked away in a dim corner, was a spiral iron staircase.

It led down to the basement—Boris's bedroom—where daylight came in through a small window located at the front of the terrace just above street level.

After a brief and slightly awkward tour, Miriam had sat down on a red sofa in the living room. Boris was sitting on a canvas pouf with one leg tucked under his big body, chewing a bite of pizza, a bottle of beer in his hand. The beer was slightly lukewarm, since Miriam had bought it at the last minute in the local supermarket after returning from The Hague. She'd decided not to drive to Bennebroek after all. Now that she was sitting opposite Boris, she had no regrets. He'd taken off his beanie, which was on the floor beside him. His long dark hair was tied up with an elastic band.

"Do you have any other siblings?" he asked.

"No, sadly. How about you?"

"I have three brothers."

"Three?"

He chuckled. "My mother kept hoping for a girl, but she gave up after the fourth boy."

"Are you close?"

He nodded. "Funnily enough, we all ended up in the cultural sector. My two elder brothers live in Berlin, and my younger brother, Benjamin, works at the Stedelijk Museum in Amsterdam."

"So, you come from an artistic family."

"Yes, kind of." Boris told her that his mother had worked as a ballet teacher for many years and that his father was a freelance journalist who wrote reviews and articles for the culture sections of a couple of magazines. "What do your parents do?" he asked.

"Nowadays they run a bed-and-breakfast in Zeeland, but my father used to work in the finance department of an insurance company, and my mother was a beautician. I take after my granddad. He was a policeman, and he always told such exciting stories about his job that I caught the bug. As a matter of fact, he was born and brought up in this area and never left."

"Is your granddad still alive?"

"Unfortunately not. But he did live to see me join the police. He was over the moon." Miriam reached for a slice of pizza.

They ate out of the boxes, which Boris had placed on a tree stump with a sawn-off red-varnished surface. She tore off a triangle, supported it with her other hand, and took a bite.

"If I met you on the street, I wouldn't think you worked for the police. You don't look like the type at all."

She chuckled. "What are police officers supposed to look like, then?"

"Different. Less . . ." Boris turned his head away slightly and raised his hand apologetically. "Hey, never mind. Forget I said that."

She looked at him fixedly. "Don't backpedal. Spit it out."

"Less petite. You know? I thought police officers had to be able to fight and shoot people."

"I can. Make no mistake."

"With all due respect, Miriam, you weigh barely a hundred pounds."

"One hundred fifteen, actually," she said calmly. She took the time to finish a bite. Their neighbor Daoud was an Egyptian who tried, not very successfully, to pose as an Italian, but he could make pizza with the best of them. When her mouth was empty, she said, "And if necessary, with those one hundred fifteen pounds I can take down a full-grown man, purely through technique and experience."

Boris looked at her from under his dark eyelashes. His voice was deeper than before. "I like the sound of that."

Laughing away the sudden tension, she sought refuge in her bottle of beer. She was extremely annoyed with herself. She didn't hesitate to take on the most hardened criminals and broke up pub brawls without a second thought, but she struggled with these kinds of personal situations. That uniform and the bulletproof vest underneath it not only gave her authority but also acted as a buffer. In civilian clothes and without backup, she felt vulnerable. She even missed the comforting murmur of voices and emergency calls in her earpiece. Eventually she said, "I think you need to reconsider your idea of police officers. It's not accurate."

"So you say."

"And I should know."

He smiled disarmingly. "That's true."

She thought for a moment. "Would you like to accompany me on a shift? An evening shift, maybe?"

"Is it that simple?"

"Not exactly." She looked at him probingly. "But it can be arranged if you like."

"It actually sounds really cool."

"I'll take care of it, then."

He took a sip of his beer, revealing his wide, muscular neck. Boris was tall, with long legs and big feet and hands, but he was also slim and sinewy. A nice combination. "Shall I make a confession? I always flinch at the sight of someone in uniform."

"Guilty conscience?"

He pointed at her. "You see? See what you're doing? I consider myself pretty law-abiding, apart from the occasional joint, which is legal anyway, but as soon as I see a police officer, I feel like I'm doing something wrong. Like I've forgotten my ID, or had too much to drink, or my bike light has stopped working all of a sudden . . . I usually make myself scarce."

"You're not the only one. I'm surprised you dared to ask me over for dinner," she teased.

"It only took me two years, didn't it?" Boris chuckled at his own joke. He stood up and gathered up the pizza boxes. While he took them to the kitchen, his cat came into the room. The animal was white, with orange ears and a bushy orange tail. It was the biggest cat Miriam had ever seen.

The cat walked over and rubbed his chin and the side of his head against her knee. He was so big he didn't even have to jump up. His bushy tail quivered and curled over her thigh. Miriam had often seen the animal wandering around in Boris's studio, and very occasionally he went for a walk along the walls of the inner gardens. She held out her hand to feel the thick white fur.

"Don't stroke him; he's vicious."

She yanked back her hand and stared at the cat. Boris was right; on closer inspection, he didn't have a very good-natured look in his eyes.

"You have a vicious cat as a pet?"

"Nouc is a pedigree. It's gone to his head. Even when my mother bought him as a kitten, he was a real handful, but when he got bigger, she couldn't cope with him anymore. The breeder didn't want him back, so I took him."

"You're a saint."

"He's not that bad. If I leave him alone, he leaves me alone. And he doesn't pee in the house. As long as he keeps that up, he can stay."

Nouc cast her another inscrutable glance before turning around and disappearing into the studio.

"I thought you had a girlfriend?" Miriam heard herself ask, trying to sound nonchalant.

"I did. Bregje and I split up. She's traveling. Nepal, India. I can't leave this place. Or rather, I don't want to leave. I couldn't just start again from scratch somewhere else. I'm finally beginning to build a good clientele."

"Do you miss her?"

Boris plopped down beside her and put his arm on the back of the sofa.

She was almost afraid to move. Around Boris, she felt a little insecure. Perhaps it was because she really liked him—and because, if this didn't work out for whatever reason, he would still be her neighbor, and his mere presence would be a daily reminder of the breakup.

He tucked his legs sideways under his body and turned to Miriam, bringing his face closer to hers.

For a moment she thought he was going to kiss her and held her breath, but the movement stopped a handbreadth away from her face.

"Miss her, now that you're here?" he said, grinning, with a raised eyebrow. "Like a hole in the head."

🦋

Music was soothing. It had made Hennequin feel much better. Or perhaps the third glass of wine had helped silence the restless energy she'd carried inside for so long. Still dressed in her kimono, she logged on to the internet via an anonymizing network. This had once been her life. Her work as a programmer and website developer had not only provided her with a good income but also afforded her the privacy she cherished. She'd always been self-employed and worked from home. Only after marrying Keanu Smith and moving into his beautiful waterfront villa in Fort Myers, Florida, had she shut down her business. Keanu had been filthy rich, so she hadn't needed to work.

Hennequin smiled at the memory of how Keanu had looked at her in the few minutes before his heart gave out for good. That was when he'd finally realized what was happening, right at the very end. Beautiful and sad at the same time. Beautiful because that had been the first moment she'd felt a real connection with her husband, and sad because it had been so brief. The official cause of death was alcohol poisoning. Keanu was a heavy drinker. Everybody knew that. He had been even when Hennequin had first met him in a big hotel in Las Vegas. She'd spotted him right away. A man on his own. Socially awkward with women. Trying to impress by throwing money around. He'd worn expensive suits, but they hadn't flattered his stocky frame.

A typical American. And she, Hennequin Wilson, would be his savior. Even Keanu's mother had believed it. All hope was riding on her.

Since her marriage to Keanu, Hennequin had used the internet solely for recreational purposes, joining various chat groups whose members met only in cyberspace and mostly preferred to keep it that way. She had no idea how old they really were, where they lived, or what job they did. They could be male or female, married with four children, or eternal bachelors living in their mother's basement. It didn't matter. Their experiences and fantasies, which they shared without restraint, were what united them in that virtual world. In these private communities, each individual seemed crazier than the last. Yet Hennequin felt a deeper connection with them than with anyone she encountered in daily life.

Her fingertips drummed over her keyboard. She was talking to Delicieux, who used a male avatar and had strange, disturbing fantasies—they went a bit too far even for her, but she loved chatting with him. He was as intelligent as he was unhinged.

The bell rang. Hennequin's fingers froze. This wasn't the chime of the buzzer from the lobby downstairs, a sound she invariably ignored. It was the shrill bell of her own penthouse. Someone was at her door.

Turning off the monitor, she walked barefoot to the video screen in the hall. She switched the camera on.

He was standing right by the door, his lips pressed together, looking around. His face was slightly distorted by the fish-eye lens.

Oscar.

❧

Didi tried to shift in the bed. She hissed softly in pain. It hurt when she moved, and it hurt when she lay still. Everything hurt. Forced by the pelvic pain to lie in the same position all the time, over the past few weeks she'd developed a bedsore on her lower back. Last week Oscar had given her a calendula ointment from his mother that he rubbed on it whenever she asked him to. The effect never lasted very long. She would love to sleep on her side. Or on her stomach. That felt like a life-time ago. To be able to *walk* normally again, that would be absolutely fantastic.

Before she got pregnant, she'd played tennis a couple of times a week. She was worried that she'd never be able to do that again. Hadn't Hennequin already hinted at that? When she'd told the maternity nurse that the doctor had assured her the SPD was hormonal and would clear up on its own, Hennequin hadn't seemed convinced. Far from it. She'd paused and then said something like, "I'm glad they put it to patients that way. As a new mother, if you start stressing about things like that, it'll affect your milk production."

Hennequin wouldn't say such a thing without reason. In her job she came into contact with lots of women and probably had plenty of experience with these kinds of health issues.

What if she could never walk again?

Didi tried to shift once more. A stab of pain shot through her entire body and made her stiffen up. It was worse than yesterday. Even during her pregnancy, it had varied from day to day, but she'd hoped it would gradually get better after the birth. And that had seemed to be the case. Until this afternoon. Ever since she'd lowered herself into the bath of baking soda and almost instantly sprung back up in pain and shock, it had felt like a nerve was trapped, which made everything much worse. Hennequin had convinced her that the bath really was neces-sary, that her wound needed to be disinfected, and that the pain was normal. She'd helped her and supported her when she'd lowered herself once again into the vile, hateful liquid that made her wound sting. Hennequin had assured her that the burning sensation would go away.

But it hadn't.

Didi had mentioned it to Oscar, but he'd barely listened. As soon as he'd put Indy to bed, he'd gone to the tennis club. "I'll be back in a few hours," he'd said. "If there's a problem, call me and I'll come straight home."

"Your phone's always off."

He'd shown her his device. "Look. The sound is turned up. See? I'll put my bag next to the court, so I'll definitely be able to hear it. But you should get some sleep." He'd turned to her in the doorway. "Didi, we need to sort something out. I'm due back at work on Monday. And Hennequin isn't going to be here forever. Maybe you should find out if you qualify for home care?"

You.

He said "you."

Not "we."

As far as Oscar was concerned, it was all her problem. Caring for Indy. The SPD.

Indy was in her crib upstairs. Very occasionally, Didi heard her daughter's soft voice. It sounded like she was waking from her nap with a start and protesting when she realized she was alone.

Then she'd fall silent again.

❧

Oscar. Hennequin felt a deep hatred rising inside her. It almost made her nauseous.

What was he thinking? Where did he get the nerve to turn up at her home? Men. They were always so full of themselves, convinced that the whole world revolved around them. A little humility would do him good. *Would do them all good.*

She hurried to her bedroom, covered her hair with a net, and pulled the extremely expensive handmade blonde wig over her head. She checked the end result in the mirror. Fine. The bell rang again. Longer this time.

Cursing, she put in her emerald-green contact lenses and scanned the apartment. Had she forgotten anything? Left anything lying around? She closed the door to the computer room, as well as her bedroom door. Whatever happened, he could not go in there.

She rushed to the door and opened it.

Oscar looked both surprised and relieved. "Oh wow." He ran his eyes over her.

"How do you know where I live?" she asked icily. She wrapped the shiny kimono tighter around her waist and tied the sash.

Oscar struggled to tear his gaze away from her body. "I've been following you. Since yesterday."

"Following? That's a bit strange, Oscar. You could be arrested for less."

He looked dismayed. "Sorry."

"Only joking, Oscar. Come in."

He trailed after her through the white hallway. "I feel like an idiot. It's just hit me that you see it as work. And of course, this is your private life."

Without answering, she went into the living room and dimmed the lights with the remote control.

Oscar looked around approvingly. He noticed the high ceiling, looked at the reflective resin floor, and finally caught sight of the breathtaking view. "Jesus. How beautiful."

A smile played about her lips. "You weren't expecting this?"

"No." He crossed his arms and looked curiously out over the city through the enormous windows. Like a child on a school trip. The setting sun colored his face and shirt orange. He turned his head to her. "Do you live alone?"

She nodded.

"How—"

"How can I afford this, you wonder?"

"Er, yes. No offense, but it's pretty swanky for a home help."

"Maternity nurse," she corrected him. "I help people, but I'm not the help."

Oscar was still looking around. He noticed the designer kitchen, the Loewe TV. Hennequin thought she could detect a hint of envy in his eyes. He turned to her. "Not that it's any of my business, but . . . Where do you get the money for all this?"

"From an inheritance I'd rather not have had."

"Oh. Sorry. I shouldn't have asked. But you just wouldn't expect someone in your line of work to live in a penthouse like this, someone who—"

"Changes diapers and butters rusks for a living?"

"No, no, that's not what I mean."

"Don't lie, Oscar. That's exactly what you mean, but it doesn't matter. As I said before, I like to help people. This is my calling."

He chewed the inside of his cheek. When he finally spoke, his voice sounded deeper and softer than usual. "And what you did yesterday, do you often do that?"

A smile played about her lips. With a twinkle in her eyes, she looked up at him. "Only if I take a liking to the father in question."

His eyes darkened. "So you've taken a liking to me?"

"Evidently." Gosh. He'd gotten all shy. It had really made an impact.

He took a step closer. "I liked you from the moment I first saw you. I know this isn't appropriate, but what you said was completely true. Didi isn't herself. She hasn't been for a very long time. Before she got pregnant, we used to go out with friends, to the pub, to parties, everything. We were crazy about each other. And now I'm stuck at home, climbing the walls. It's all so . . ." He frowned and put his thumb and fingers between his eyebrows. "So confusing. I'm not sure I'm ready to be a father. I don't think I am. It feels like I'm suffocating."

"Shh. Calm down." Hennequin put the flat of her hand on his chest. "I know what you're going through. It's perfectly normal, trust me. But that feeling will go away. Life is unpredictable; nothing stays the same, ever. The things you worry about or take for granted today"—her hand slipped downward; her fingers played with the elastic waist-band of his tracksuit pants, and she noticed that he was holding his breath—"might not even be here tomorrow."

❧

"Well. I'll see you around."

Boris stood close to Miriam. His fingers were touching her upper arm. She could feel his breath brush past her face.

It felt nice.

More than nice.

"Thank you for a lovely evening," she managed to say. "I never knew I had such a great neighbor."

"No, thank *you*." Barely moving, he kept looking at her.

Miriam shifted her weight onto her toes and was about to kiss him lightly on the cheek when he turned his face to her and grabbed the back of her head. He pressed his lips against hers. Briefly, very briefly, before letting go.

"I hope to see you again soon."

"Yes," she said, so softly that it sounded like a sigh. "I hope so too."

❧

Withered leaves rustled on their branches, gently moving back and forth in the autumn wind. The bluish moonlight filtered through the trees, just enough for Hennequin to see what she was doing. She didn't use a flashlight. It might attract attention.

Hennequin was breathing jerkily, and her lungs were burning, as were the muscles in her arms, back, and shoulders. Clouds of conden-sation were coming out of her mouth. She'd heard it on the news this afternoon: today was the coldest October day in living memory. Now, long after the sun had gone down, the mercury had dropped even further. But Hennequin wasn't cold. Quite the opposite. She was sweating in her thick jacket.

Her feet sank into the loose soil. Just now, in the car, she'd wrapped plastic bags around her shoes to avoid leaving prints. One more thing to throw the police off the scent. To be on the safe side. It was unlikely anyone would ever search here. Let alone dig. But still.

Hennequin felt herself growing calmer, more peaceful, with every thrust into the soil, as if the monotonous movements were helping her to reach a different, deeper state of consciousness. She hadn't felt so good in a long time. So at one with herself. Softly, she hummed "I Scare Myself," and heard Thomas Dolby's teasing voice echoing in her head, and the piano attacks, the saxophone.

Earlier this evening, she'd almost succumbed to the temptation to deal with Oscar there and then. At the last moment she'd managed to control herself. These things couldn't be rushed. You had to plan them. Careless preparation or execution would catch up with you, every time.

Still, it hadn't taken her very long to come up with this plan. Less than half an hour after Oscar had left, she'd known what she was going to do and how she was going to do it. It was as simple as it was brilliant. Nothing could go wrong.

Because it all added up, fell perfectly into place. As if it were meant to be.

Day Six

SUNDAY

This morning, Miriam had a new look in her eyes. Gentler, less fanatical. A calmer version of herself stared back at her in the bathroom mirror.

Boris had kissed her. Very briefly and awkwardly, but it had felt good. Exciting and familiar at the same time. Still, she was glad that they'd stopped there. She had the impression that Boris was rather cautious too. They had to take it slow. If this didn't end well, they wouldn't be able to avoid each other.

She had no idea what had possessed her to ask him to join her on an evening shift. Now she would have to find out how to arrange that and then try to make it through the shift without setting tongues wagging by getting too cozy with him in the car. She and her colleagues never missed a thing. They knew one another too well and had shared too many experiences to be able to pull the wool over each other's eyes. In view of that, it was a miracle no one had noticed what she was up to by now.

Miriam put her toothbrush back in the cup, ran a brush through her hair, and tied it back with an elastic band. It was ten o'clock. She had the day off, and she was hoping to meet Walter Engelen, Hennequin's guardian.

❧

Jip and Janneke were in a bad way.

They were lying a short distance apart, flat in the straw. Hennequin suspected that they'd been dead since last night. No one had noticed. Neither Didi nor Oscar. Nor the visitors upstairs in the guest room with Didi.

She would mention it to Didi later, toward the end of her working day, when Didi was in the bed in the living room, and Oscar was home.

Dosage was important.

So was timing.

Humming to herself, Hennequin buttered four rusks and sprinkled them with pink sugar-coated aniseeds. Her movements were slightly less coordinated than usual. She could really feel the muscles in her arms and back, and there were blisters on the soft skin between the thumb and forefinger of both her hands. This morning she'd thrown her gloves in the trash. The hard work had proved too much for the soft, thin lambskin.

Hennequin arranged the rusks on a large plate and put it on a tray, together with a glass of tea. She picked it up and went out of the kitchen. When she reached the sliding patio doors, she paused and looked at the hutch.

As a young child, Hennequin had also had a rabbit. A bony black animal with a white nose and one white leg. Her father had brought it back from a petting zoo. During the rare moments when he was at home, he'd built a hutch in the garage and made a mesh run so that the animal could eat grass outside in nice weather. Polly had been intended to keep her company, but she hadn't brought Hennequin much comfort. The animal had been frightened of everything. Whenever Hennequin had tried to take her out of the hutch, she'd flattened herself in the straw, ears back and eyes bulging. Hennequin had also been given a book about rabbits and had read a lot about them, about their care, feeding, and behavior. Rabbits were probably the most unfortunate of all popular pets, because unlike dogs and cats, for example, they were prey rather than predators. They had every reason to look out into the world with a genuine fear of death. Birds of prey, dogs, foxes, wolves, tigers, cats, and snakes—they all had rabbits in their sights. Even in their own burrow, rabbits were never safe.

On a beautiful summer's day, Polly had been snatched from her run by an enormous buzzard. One minute, Hennequin had been watching her eating grass; the next minute, the run had been empty.

Only as a teenager had Hennequin come to realize that people weren't that different from caged animals. They behaved in exactly the same way. Even though some people ran away from difficult situations, in the end they always returned to their nest, their burrow underground. Into the cage they'd built for themselves. The fact was, people liked to be where they felt safe and nurtured. At home. With their family, their loved ones.

And that was where Hennequin sought them out.

She climbed the stairs with the tray of rusks in her hands. Grinning broadly, she entered the guest room. "I thought you might like these!"

❧

Walter and Liesbeth Engelen lived in a bungalow that looked like it had been very trendy and modern in the seventies, but above all extremely expensive. The L-shaped living room was full of Scandinavian designer furniture from that era, all chrome and cognac-colored leather.

Liesbeth Engelen had given Miriam a cup of coffee and was now sitting diagonally opposite her in an S-shaped armchair. "You're lucky to have caught us," she said. "Normally we'd be in Curaçao at this time of year."

"That's what Mrs. Tanardo said. It must be wonderful to be able to escape the Dutch winter." Miriam glanced outside. The large windows looked out onto a neat lawn bordered by flower beds, with a pond, birch trees, and ornamental grasses. The sky was overcast.

Liesbeth Engelen didn't look as if she spent much time in the Netherlands at all. Her almost white, short hair contrasted sharply with her tanned skin. Her eyes were rimmed with shimmering eyeliner. "It sounds more expensive than it is. My husband and I only pay for the airfare."

Miriam looked at her uncomprehendingly.

"We have a lot of family in Curaçao," she explained. "For decades I complained about how little we saw of one another, but now we can finally turn it to our advantage." She looked to her husband for confirmation. He hadn't said much so far. "Isn't that right?"

Despite his smooth, shiny scalp, Walter Engelen looked younger than his wife. "I don't think the police are interested in our winter holidays or how we can afford them. You asked about Catharina. What do you want to know?"

Miriam put her mug back down on the smoked glass coffee table. "When did you first meet her?"

"In 1994. She was still in Oosterhoek, in Grave, at the time."

Miriam sat up straighter.

Oosterhoek.

It was a big prison complex with a juvenile detention center. And a psychiatric institution.

That was for serious crimes.

What did she do?

Walter paused and rubbed his thin nose. "You must understand that we haven't seen Catharina for a very long time. Her disappearance hurt us deeply. It brings back painful memories to hear that the police are gathering information about her."

"What is she accused of?" asked Liesbeth.

"Unfortunately, I can't really go into that at this stage. It's a general investigation; we're currently looking into several people's backgrounds." She turned to Walter. "When did you last see her?"

"It must have been nine years ago. She was twenty-six. I believe she was working for a computer company."

"You don't know for sure?"

"She didn't have much to do with us by then." The man shook his head. His regret was plain to see. "We started seeing less of her when she went away to college. She only came home when she needed money or on special occasions. In later years, she stopped coming at all."

"Do you have any idea why she didn't want to see you anymore? Did something happen?"

"No," said Walter. "Nothing. We could never understand it."

Liesbeth looked past Miriam into the garden. The gray autumn light caused dark shadows to form on her face. "She's not a very trusting person," she said softly. "Catharina is extremely intelligent, but also extremely complex. You never really get to know her."

"How exactly did she end up with you?"

"When she was released from the detention center, she needed a fresh start, far away from where she'd lived before. She was only sixteen. Still a child," said Walter.

Liesbeth continued. "Walter and I have always believed that young people deserve a second chance. Even if they've done bad things. We couldn't have any children of our own, so we've taken in lots of troubled foster children over the years. Sometimes two at a time, sometimes just one, as in Catharina's case. We wanted to do our share. We had the space, time, and money, so why not?"

Walter shifted in his seat. "I heard about Catharina's situation through my brother-in-law. He works for the judiciary. That girl had no one. Nobody ever came to visit her. She didn't have any brothers or sisters, and her mother had taken her own life when Catharina was eleven. Yet she clearly came from a good home and had had an excellent start in life. Piano lessons, tennis, trips to museums. We were confident that here, in this environment, and with a stable upbringing, we could get her back on track."

"And what about her father?" asked Miriam.

"He disowned her."

❧

Didi was sitting half upright in the bed in the living room. The visitors were gone. Oscar's sister had finally come to see Indy, and a couple of old school friends she'd seen less of since marrying Oscar had dropped by. It was quiet now; she wasn't expecting anyone else for the rest of the day. Outside, the wind was chasing the autumn leaves through the streets. Across the road, a family came out of their house. They were in high spirits, laughing and talking. A brown dog was frolicking around them. The father folded up a stroller and put it in the trunk of the car while his wife strapped their child into a car seat. Didi felt a slight pang of jealousy. One day, would she, Oscar, and Indy be a happy family just like them and go for walks in the woods on Sundays? In the future, when Indy was a bit bigger, and she could walk normally again—and Oscar started acting normally again?

His behavior was still distant and slightly strange. Last night, after returning from the tennis club, he'd taken a shower and avoided her, hardly saying a word. He'd changed and fed Indy, but to Didi it had all looked mechanical. As if he'd been on autopilot. And now he sat reading the newspaper while the maternity nurse hummed and ironed his shirts. He said nothing. He did nothing. He was present only in body, and barely even that.

The whole situation was starting to get to her.

"Tea?" asked Hennequin.

Didi looked up. "No, thanks. I can't face any more tea." She was dying for a glass of wine. Or preferably something stronger, and in large quantities. Shots of Stroh Rum. One after the other, bottoms up! She would love nothing more than to get drunk. Perhaps it would make her feel better, more carefree and less glum, and she could briefly forget that even though walking had been a little easier since this morning, it was still extremely painful, and she still wasn't sure if she would ever fully recover.

She didn't do it. She didn't ask for a glass of wine.

She was due to pump again soon, and if any alcohol got into her milk, that wouldn't be good for Indy.

She stared out the window. On second thought, perhaps expressing milk wasn't such a good idea after all. She was the one who'd carried a baby for nine months and had to give up all sorts of treats—carpaccio, her favorite French raw milk cheeses, alcohol—and now, once again, it was she who had to deny herself everything. While Oscar could do as he pleased.

Tomorrow he would go back to work, every day, but only till three o'clock, so that he could take over from Hennequin in the afternoon. Didi would have preferred to apply for home care, but Hennequin had advised her to hold off for a while. She thought it was premature to submit the application right now, as she was sure that Didi would soon be able to manage on her own. Hennequin had been very convincing.

Maybe she was right, and Didi was worrying about nothing. After all, the pelvic pain had come on overnight. Perhaps it would suddenly clear up tomorrow or the day after.

Didi looked at Oscar, who was still quietly reading his newspaper and drinking a cappuccino that Hennequin had made and put in front of him.

"Have you taken care of Jip and Janneke yet, Os?"

"I'll go and check on them in a minute," he muttered.

"When was the last time you did that?"

"Yesterday." There was a wobble in his voice.

Didi felt herself becoming more agitated by the second. Had he been looking after her animals at all?

Hennequin rushed up to her. She leaned over Didi and plumped up her pillow. "Shall I go and take a look?" she asked softly.

"It's not your job, and it's no trouble for him," replied Didi, loud enough for Oscar to hear.

He didn't react.

"Shh. It's OK. I'll go and check on them."

Ignoring Didi's protests, Hennequin went into the kitchen. Humming to herself, she opened the sliding patio doors.

❧

Walter Engelen looked as if he still couldn't understand it, all these years later. "Catharina's father didn't want to see her again. He broke off contact with his daughter before she was even convicted."

"What exactly did she do?"

"Don't you know?"

Liesbeth shifted in her seat. The designer armchair creaked. "Surely, as a policewoman, you should know things like that?"

Miriam thought for a moment. Like any police officer, she could use her work BlackBerry to search up to five years back in the national database. She would have to enter her number to get into the system, and searches were logged, but that was rarely monitored. However, to access information on crimes committed more than five years ago, she would need authorization. And that wouldn't be granted without good reason. Furthermore, children were protected: juvenile trials were held behind closed doors, and sentences weren't made public.

"My colleagues are currently looking into it," she said, as calmly and reassuringly as possible. "They're due to report back to me in a few days. But perhaps you could tell me in your own words what you think happened?"

Walter looked at his wife. They seemed to be having an entire conversation without exchanging a word. Eventually, after a silence that felt to Miriam like several minutes, Walter said, "I think you should probably go to the boarding school Catharina attended before her conviction. I'd rather they told you."

Boarding school?

Miriam grabbed her notebook. "Could you tell me the address of this establishment?"

"De Horizon, it's in Boxmeer." Liesbeth gave Miriam an address, which she wrote down.

"When did she go to this boarding school?"

"From the age of twelve to fifteen."

Twelve—right after primary school. "What happened there?"

Once more, Liesbeth and Walter exchanged a knowing glance. Liesbeth shook her head almost imperceptibly. "We haven't seen her in a long time, but we still care about her, just like all the children we've taken in and brought up here."

Walter looked at Miriam. "I think you should go to Boxmeer. They'll be able to tell you more."

"How long was Catharina in prison?"

After a short silence, he said, "A year."

Miriam could barely contain herself.

A year.

That could only mean one thing.

❧

An unpleasant feeling came over Didi when she saw Hennequin walk back inside. The maternity nurse didn't look happy. She looked alarmed.

Hennequin stopped near the table where Oscar was still reading imperturbably.

Only then did Didi see the bottle Hennequin held in her hand. It was empty.

"Sorry," said Hennequin. "I should have kept an eye on them myself. I feel awful."

"What? What's wrong?" Didi gasped for breath.

Hennequin held up the bottle. "It was lying on the grass in front of the hutch." She pressed her lips together and shook her head. "I should have spotted it. Oh shit, why didn't I pay more attention?"

Oscar looked up from his newspaper.

"What happened?" asked Didi. "Are Jip and Janneke OK?"

Hennequin shook her head. "I hate to have to tell you this, but your rabbits . . ." She glanced at Oscar and then back at Didi with a strange look in her eyes. "They're dead. I'm so sorry. They're gone."

❧

The Engelens' living room faded into the background.

A year sounded short, but it was extremely long in Dutch juvenile law. The maximum sentence that could be imposed on children under sixteen.

Miriam's head was spinning. If this information was correct—and she had no reason to believe otherwise—it meant that Hennequin had murdered someone when she was fifteen. While she was at the boarding school.

❧

Didi's reaction was stronger than Hennequin had expected. The woman went deathly pale at the sight of the empty water bottle. Hennequin had briefly toyed with the idea of bringing in the rabbits themselves, but it would cast doubt on her excuse about being allergic. Considering how upset Didi was already, the effect would certainly have been interesting.

She looked at Didi with her most compassionate expression. "I feel terrible for you."

Didi threw off the blanket. Her pale face was contorted with pain, despair, and grief—a classic trinity. Slowly, but faster and much more roughly than was sensible, she struggled to the edge of the bed and slid off, landing on her feet. Without even bothering to put her slippers on, she walked stiffly toward the kitchen.

"What are you doing?" asked Oscar. He'd stood up and was walking toward her. "Go and lie down; you're overdoing it."

Didi said nothing. She didn't even react. Her face was blotchy; her eyes were sunken. She looked like a zombie and moved like one too. Her oversized sleep shirt hung like a shapeless rag around her body. She reached for the handle of the patio doors.

Hennequin rushed over to her. "You don't want to see it, Didi. You really don't. And it won't change anything. Leave this to me."

Didi shook her head. "They're my animals. I love them. I've had them for six years!" She jerked her head to Oscar and shouted, "I've known them longer than I've known him, for God's sake."

Oscar said nothing. He looked helplessly at Hennequin.

"Oscar's right, Didi," said Hennequin, as Didi started tugging impatiently at the patio doors. Overcome with emotion, she forgot to press the button on the handle, so the door rattled but wouldn't slide open.

"Open it!" Didi shouted at her husband. "Open this damn door, Oscar! It keeps getting stuck, and you were supposed to have fixed it ages ago, remember? Another thing you promised but didn't do!"

He stepped back and turned his head away, as if Didi's words were stones she was throwing at him.

"Shh . . ." Hennequin put her hand on Didi's upper arm. "Please calm down, or you'll end up in the hospital."

Didi tore herself away. Finally, she realized that she'd forgotten to press the button on the handle. She slid open the heavy door with such force that it bounced back at the end of the track and banged into her shoulder. Fighting off the pain, she pushed her shoulder forward and strode into the garden.

Hennequin stopped in the doorway.

So did Oscar.

Didi came to a halt near the hutch. She stood motionless in her bare feet. The wind pulled at her red tresses and the faded sleep shirt.

To Hennequin it was a wonderful sight, that woman standing there with drooping shoulders, looking at her beloved, dead animals. She'd have preferred to see Didi's facial expression. But this was beautiful too.

Didi's shoulders began to shake. "Oscar, the food bowl is empty as well," she said tearfully.

Oscar walked toward her. The expensive leather of his Van Bommel shoes got wet in the grass. "It can't be! I just filled it on Wednesday."

"Oh really?" Didi turned around. Tears were streaming down her face. "And the water too, right? Well? Can't you see?" She pointed to the empty bottle in Hennequin's hand. "Can't you see they had nothing to drink? Empty, completely. That's just not possible in four days."

"Calm down. I'm not an idiot. I'm sure I—"

"You son of a bitch, you killed them! You killed my animals! Just because you don't care about them. But I do!" She pointed to her chest with both hands. "I do, Oscar, you arrogant bastard. I hate you! I hate you! I hate you!"

Oscar looked at her in silence, his face a mask of anger and disbelief. "Fine. Suit yourself," he snapped. "You're not listening to me."

Hennequin felt the warm glow of triumph in her chest as she watched Oscar do what he excelled at in difficult situations: run away.

🍃

Miriam thanked Walter and Liesbeth for the information and for their hospitality, and got into her car. She immediately entered the address that Liesbeth had given her into her GPS and headed for Boxmeer. A drive of nearly two hours.

She felt sorry for the Engelens. The couple had looked shell-shocked when she'd left them in their bungalow filled with aging designer furniture. At the same time, she felt elated.

Her curiosity and excitement grew with every passing moment as she drove away from Bennebroek toward the boarding school.

"I'm onto you, Catharina Kramer," she whispered.

🍃

Hennequin rushed after Oscar and went into the house. She caught up with him in the doorway between the living room and the hall. "You can't just leave. Your wife isn't herself. She's only just had a baby; her emotions are all over the place."

"That may be, but I can't take this anymore." With a gloomy expression, he looked past her and out at his wife, who was leaning on the hutch with both hands, bent forward, as if out of breath. He looked back at Hennequin.

His expression changed and his pupils widened. "If I hadn't had you, this would have happened a lot sooner." He ran his eyes over her face appraisingly. "Can I come and see you later, when you've finished work?"

She shook her head gently.

"I need to," he insisted.

"Sorry, Oscar. Today is no good. I have plans."

His face fell.

"How about tomorrow?" she said, glancing at Didi, who'd overstrained herself and was now trembling violently. "Six thirty. But you can't come to my home. I have a friend visiting."

"Where, then?"

She gave him the name of a big, well-known hotel in Ridderkerk, right by the highway. "Don't go into the large parking lot at the front," she said softly. "There's a smaller one around the back for staff. It's less conspicuous."

"I've gotten to the point where I don't care if someone sees me with another—"

"I do." She gave him a piercing look.

"OK. Fine."

Hennequin put her hand on his forearm and stroked the thin skin on the inside of his wrist. Oscar's muscles were tense. Adrenaline was coursing through his body. He felt stressed and angry. And yet he reacted to her touch. A shiver ran through him. That was a good sign.

He would be there tomorrow.

❧

The boarding school was situated in the middle of a residential area. It turned out to be an old building with large windows and occupied half of the narrow, shady street. From the street side, you could look in through some of the windows. Desks and plastic chairs, white walls, maps. A strip of municipal bushes and a low wall separated the building from the street.

Miriam walked toward the main entrance, a low, wide step up to a double door with safety glass. There was a white sign screwed to the wall that read "De Horizon Boarding School" in plain blue letters.

It looked quiet. It was Sunday, so most of the children would be at home, with family or friends. But Miriam knew from experience that no boarding school was ever completely deserted. There were always some children who had nowhere else to go. And there would certainly be staff on the premises.

The door was opened surprisingly quickly by a wiry man in his fifties wearing jeans and a striped shirt. Glasses, blond and balding, severe acne scarring. He looked like he'd been a punk in his youth.

"Miriam de Moor, Rotterdam police," she said, shaking his hand. She tried to convince herself that there was nothing wrong in mentioning that. After all, she was on the police force. She just wasn't on this case.

It's not even a case.

The man introduced himself as Berend Luijten.

"I'm looking for someone who can tell me more about one of your former students."

"From long ago?"

"Between 1990 and 1993, we believe."

"That was before my time. Who is it?"

"Catharina Kramer. She attended this boarding school from the age of twelve to fifteen."

The man's expression changed at once. The corners of his mouth curled up slightly. "Kramer, you say?"

"Yes."

"I know that story, but only from hearsay. I wasn't there at the time."

"May I come in?"

The man turned his head to the corridor behind him. "I don't know if—"

"Five minutes," said Miriam.

"Hmm . . ." He smiled and shook his head. "I don't think the administration will be very happy if I discuss this with you."

"I'm not a lawyer; I'm from the police," said Miriam calmly.

Luijten tilted his head. He said nothing.

For a moment, Miriam was worried that he didn't believe her and would ask to see her badge. She had it with her, but what if he checked it with the station? "We've already requested the court documents," she said, as nonchalantly as possible. "But the wheels of justice turn slowly, and I'm not that patient."

He nodded as if he understood. "I think that story still haunts the admins. That incident—shall we say—had a pretty significant impact on the school's image. They did everything they could to keep it out of the papers. For the most part they succeeded, but people still talk."

"Can you tell me what happened?"

His voice took on a confidential tone, and he leaned toward her slightly. "Catharina Kramer killed her roommate. Her name was Hilde Vandenbroecke, a Flemish girl."

"Why?"

"Why did she do it?" Luijten put his hands up as if Miriam were holding him at gunpoint. "No idea. For no apparent reason, or so I'm told."

"For no apparent reason," repeated Miriam.

He shrugged.

"How?"

"She pushed her down the stairs, here in this building."

Miriam turned white. The words hit her like a punch in the stomach.

"Could I see where it happened?"

The man scratched the back of his head. He briefly looked away from her. Just when Miriam thought he was going to send her away, he suddenly said, "OK, fine. Come with me."

She followed him into the building. It was a lot lighter and more spacious than it appeared from the outside. The ceilings were high and painted cream. At the end of the corridor, there was a set of swing doors. Luijten held one open for her. "It's here on the right." He made a sweeping gesture, but looked downcast, as if he were unveiling a dubious work of art.

Miriam stopped at the foot of a stone staircase with wide steps that made a turn at the top and joined up with another staircase to the second floor. She threw her head back to look. It was very high. "Which floor did she push her from?" she asked.

Luijten coughed once into his fist. "From the top. Over the railing."

Miriam began to climb the stairs. Luijten followed close behind.

"Did she do it out of anger, or could it have been an accident?" she asked.

"I wasn't there." Luijten's voice echoed against the high walls. "But as far as I know, it was definitely not an accident. Although Catharina apparently maintained throughout the trial that she'd only been trying to scare her."

"Then how could she have been convicted of murder?"

"Two witnesses saw her do it."

Miriam came to a halt. She put her hand on the banister and looked down. It was extremely high. And hard. The stairs, the floors, everything was made of concrete and stone. "Who were they?"

"An English teacher, De Vries," said Luijten. He sounded slightly out of breath. "And a student from the lower school."

"Does De Vries still teach here?"

Luijten shook his head. "He retired years ago."

"I'd like to have their addresses."

Luijten looked at her rather doubtfully. "I'll have to check our records. But I really should get permission from the head teacher, Mrs. Scheltema. She's not here at the moment."

"Maybe tomorrow?" she persisted.

"No, sorry. She's on vacation all next week."

Miriam realized there was little point in insisting. She would have to come back after next week to ask for the names and addresses of the two witnesses and the victim's family. Of course, she could pull rank and demand that Luijten look up the details for her right now, but as an off-duty officer investigating a nonexistent case, she knew that wouldn't be a very good idea.

She went up to the top floor. There, she gripped the railing and looked into the depths once again. If you threw someone down from here, the fall would almost certainly be fatal. How frightened that girl had to have been in her final moments. She turned her face to Luijten. "Were Hilde and Catharina friends?"

"All I know is that they'd been roommates for several months and that Hilde was Belgian."

Miriam looked down again, at the black-and-white tiled floor so far below.

Beside her, Luijten coughed into his fist once again. "For more information, I think you should talk to Mrs. Scheltema."

"OK," she said softly, running her hands over the balustrade.

❦

A small rectangle had been dug out of the lawn. The loose dark soil was covered with a paving stone. "RIP Jip & Janneke" had been carved into it with a nail.

Didi's legs were shaking. She felt empty and broken. She glanced to the side, at the serene face of Hennequin, who stood looking at the grave, lost in thought, and felt deeply ashamed. As a maternity nurse, Hennequin was bound to have seen all kinds of situations; they probably weren't the first parents of a newborn baby to have terrible fights. But this was pretty extreme.

Yet Hennequin had acted as if it were the most normal thing in the world. Just now, she'd taken her inside and slipped her half a glass of wine—"Don't be silly. Your baby won't notice a little drop of alcohol"—and then gone into the garage to find a spade. Here, in a corner of the garden, she'd dug a grave and then—with rubber gloves on—she'd put Jip and Janneke into a cardboard box and buried them. Now, she was standing next to Didi, stroking her arm.

Didi looked at the empty hutch. There were still droppings in the straw. She could smell the scent of her rabbits, the scent of hay and their soft coats. But she would never be able to stroke them again. She'd always loved doing that. Very gently, with her forefinger between their ears, which made them close their eyes, confident that they were in good hands. And they had been. For years. Until now. She'd betrayed them. In truth, over the past few months, she'd barely thought about her rabbits' welfare.

And even less about Oscar's.

"I feel guilty."

Hennequin stroked her arm and held her closer. It felt good.

"Maybe I could have prevented it," Hennequin suddenly said. "I should have checked on them earlier. It's partly my fault."

"No, it's not your fault," replied Didi. Her voice croaked with emotion. "It's my own fault. It's all my fault."

❧

Once murderers had found a method that worked well, they usually stuck to it. Most contract and serial killers followed a pattern that became increasingly obvious over time.

Hennequin had pushed her roommate down stairs. Miriam's brother Bart had fallen down the stairs in his own house. Perhaps Keanu Smith really had died of an accidental alcohol overdose. But it was equally possible that he wasn't the only person in Hennequin's past to have died of alcohol poisoning.

Miriam wouldn't be surprised.

Hennequin had lived in several Dutch provinces, in Belgium, and in a number of US states. Miriam knew that police forces didn't always collaborate or share information with one another. Incompatible computer systems and different laws, cultures, and rules. As a result, some links between murders in other countries, states, or even provinces went unnoticed or were only discovered by chance. By moving around, shady characters could often continue their life of crime with impunity.

After today, Miriam was convinced that these three deaths in Hennequin's life were the tip of the iceberg. There was much more going on. The woman cast long, pitch-black shadows in her wake.

Miriam changed into fourth gear and passed a truck. It was Sunday, and there was hardly any traffic on the A73, a highway that ran parallel to the German border.

She was lost in thought. Based on all the information she'd gathered today, she tried to reconstruct Catharina Kramer's childhood.

After Catharina's mother had committed suicide, father and daughter had remained in the village for another year. The following year, Catharina had finished primary school, and her father had sent her to De Horizon. Miriam found that surprising. Sure, if Arnold Kramer really had worked on oil rigs, he would have been away from home for months on end, unable to care for his daughter. But then why had he stayed for the first year? Had he taken a year off? And after that, why hadn't he opted for a less drastic solution—a live-in nanny, for example? Miriam suspected that there wasn't much difference between the cost of a boarding school and a nanny. If he'd chosen the latter, Catharina would've had a permanent base, a home.

Miriam tried to get inside the mind of the young Catharina. First, she was deserted by her mother in the most horrifying way and then more or less disowned by her father. Banished. She had to have felt terrible. Abandoned. Combined with her unpopularity at school and in the village, it would undoubtedly have had a significant impact on her social and emotional development. You didn't need to be a psychologist to understand that Catharina had been traumatized at a very tender age and would therefore perhaps never be able to form close relationships or love and trust anyone.

But that was no reason, and certainly no license, to start doing bad things to others.

And that was exactly what Catharina had done.

Miriam reached a highway junction. She merged onto the A15 toward Arnhem. So far, she'd been reluctant to contact Arnold Kramer because she didn't know whether father and daughter were on good terms. Now that she knew they were estranged, she was more optimistic that he'd be willing to speak to her.

Hopefully he would be at home.

❧

Didi was lying in the bed by the window. It was already starting to get dark. Hennequin had been kind enough to stay an extra hour and had left her phone number so that Didi could call her if necessary. But that wasn't necessary. Shortly after Hennequin's departure, Oscar had come home. He hadn't wanted to talk. Silently, he'd warmed up the spaghetti Hennequin had cooked earlier in the afternoon. He'd brought some to Didi and then sat at the dinner table. When Indy had started crying, he'd gone upstairs without a word to change her and then handed Didi the baby and a bottle of warmed-up milk. After the feeding, he'd put Indy back to bed and left the breast pump on the table next to Didi. All in silence.

Then he'd left.

Not telling her where he was going, he'd mumbled on the doorstep that he'd be home in time for the next feeding. He'd sounded dejected. Sullen, even. Clearly, he was convinced he hadn't done anything wrong, and that hurt Didi the most.

After he'd closed the door behind him, Didi couldn't help thinking that she wouldn't mind if he never came back. She missed the old Oscar every second of the day, but the man he'd become since Indy's birth was a nasty piece of work.

In Arnhem, Miriam got out of her car. She looked at the large 1930s house, a grand-looking semidetached with white ridge beams, a leaded glass bay window, and a row of dark conifers lining the driveway that were starting to turn brown and bare at the bottom. This was Arnold Kramer's home.

The driveway was empty. That didn't necessarily mean that nobody was in. She walked up to the front door. On either side of it, a firethorn full of bright-orange berries was growing against the wall. A nameplate in the same brass as the doorbell was screwed to the doorframe. It was engraved with the names Arnold and Anne-Marie Kramer in a thin, italic typeface.

Catharina's father had remarried.

Miriam pressed the doorbell. It sounded like a carillonneur was ringing a series of heavy bells somewhere inside. She waited, looked around impatiently, and rang the doorbell again. She glanced at her watch. Half past six. She walked around to the front of the house, stepped onto the front lawn, and looked in through the window. A chesterfield sofa in dark-green leather. Root wood furniture. No lights were on; the surfaces were clean and clear. There was no one home.

Hennequin straightened up and stretched her back. She felt the damp chill rising from the soft woodland soil under her feet. Broken-off tree roots scraped along her legs and pulled at the fabric of her jumpsuit. She'd been working on it for two nights, but now it was ready. It was long and deep enough.

She used her shovel to help herself climb up. Patting off the soil, she sniffed the woodland air and wiped away the moisture from her nose with the back of her hand. Her hands hurt. The blisters had been torn open when she'd dug the rabbits' grave this afternoon. This grave was much larger. And more important, much deeper. It had to be. She had to do all she could to stop the smell coming up from the soil.

Once closed, this grave could never be reopened.

Day Seven

MONDAY

This morning, Didi had been able to take a few steps without the pain shooting down her spine and thighs like a lash. For the first time in months, she dared to believe she would make a full recovery. Her joy was soon overshadowed by the thought of Jip and Janneke. She became even more depressed when she thought about her marriage, or what was left of it. Just when they needed each other the most, it all seemed to be falling apart.

Oscar had decided that Indy was her concern, not his. But if she was honest with herself, his negative attitude hadn't come out of the blue. Didi had gotten pregnant by accident because they'd both been careless with contraception. When the doctor confirmed her pregnancy, Oscar had wanted her to terminate it. That had been out of the question for Didi. To her, the embryo was a living creature with a beating heart. A little person in the making who was completely dependent on her. *Her baby.*

Very gradually, Oscar had gotten used to the idea of becoming a father. At one point, he'd even said that he was looking forward to the birth. But then suddenly she couldn't walk, and everything changed.

Before she was confined to the wheelchair, they'd enjoyed their life together. During the week, they were both busy with work, and on Thursday or Friday afternoons, she and Oscar would hit the pub with their colleagues. On Saturdays they went shopping together and did chores in and around the house and then went into town or out dancing in the evening. On Sundays they slept late, before playing tennis or going for a run. The weekend invariably drew to a close with a burger or chicken satay in De Zaak, the pub where they'd met five years ago.

But now that all seemed like a very long time ago. Scenes from a different life featuring completely different people than who they'd become. Because she realized that it wasn't only Oscar who'd changed. So had she.

The creature that had grown inside her hadn't even existed nine months ago. Now Indy was the most important thing in her life. More important than her marriage to Oscar. Even more important than herself.

❧

Hennequin was poring over a form on the chest of drawers. The midwife was standing beside her. It wasn't the same woman she'd met a couple of days ago. This one was younger. She had a mass of curls and a much friendlier look in her eyes. And what was more, she turned out not to know Didi.

"I've promised the mother that I'll stay for ten days," said Hennequin. "She's counting on it. But I just found out I need you to sign off on that."

"Has this never come up before?" asked the midwife in astonishment.

"Never. Sorry. I haven't been doing this job very long."

"What did you use to do?"

"I've only just returned to work after a long break," Hennequin said quickly. "A lot has changed."

"And unfortunately, not for the better, with all the budget cuts."
The midwife now also turned her attention to the form. She went over
the boxes that Hennequin had ticked.

Hennequin watched intently. Seven days of maternity care was
standard, but too short for what she had planned. Hennequin had
hoped to be able to bend the rules and informally prolong her stay with
the family, but that wasn't going to work. It would arouse suspicion if
she didn't make things official.

"She really needs the extra help, Karin," she insisted. "Didi can
hardly walk. She can't even bathe Indy herself."

"I can see that. And what about the father?"

"He went back to work today."

"He can take paternity leave."

"Well . . . between you and me . . ." Hennequin looked toward the
stairs, then at Indy, who was sleeping in her crib, and finally straight
into the midwife's blue eyes. "I don't think we should expect too much
of the husband."

"Doesn't she have any family or friends who can help out?"

Hennequin shook her head.

"Gosh. How sad." Karin turned back to the form and grabbed
a pen. "You haven't filled this in properly," she said, changing a few
details.

"Thank you." Hennequin gave the woman her sweetest smile. "I'm
not really with it today."

The midwife signed at the bottom and put the pen down. "All
done. Ten days. Until this Thursday. If that's not enough, I hope the
family has some money in the bank, because they'll have to rely on
private caregivers."

"I know," said Hennequin.

"This will be our last visit, in any case."

"Oh really?"

"After a week, the health center takes over." The midwife's gaze lingered on Hennequin for a moment, and she raised an eyebrow. "You didn't know that either?"

"Yes, of course I do. Sorry. I'm still half-asleep."

"Be careful not to catch the flu. It's going around."

"I'll go to bed extra early tonight," joked Hennequin.

The midwife smiled back at her. She didn't seem to suspect anything. And why would she? At worst, she might think Hennequin was a bit scatterbrained.

"I'll just go and say goodbye to the mother. No doubt our paths will cross again somewhere in the district."

"Yes, definitely," said Hennequin, shaking the midwife's hand. She watched her go downstairs.

Humming to herself, she examined the form. Game time had been extended by three days. She was going to make the most of it.

❧

Miriam listened to the constant, reassuring babble of colleagues in her earpiece. Emergency calls, codes, and less important messages went back and forth. This morning was very quiet, as Monday mornings often were. The most serious incident was usually nothing more than a burglary that had gone unnoticed since the weekend and the odd traffic accident. Nothing remarkable had come up during the briefing she'd attended this morning either, except for a photo of a balding psychotic man in his forties who clearly had a grudge against uniformed officers and had attacked two colleagues with a hammer in the street last year. The man had recently been released from an institution, so she and her colleagues were warned to be extra vigilant. Next on the agenda had been a photo of a sixteen-year-old girl who was thought to have run away from home, then an arrest warrant for a guy who owed thousands in unpaid fines. The usual suspects.

Miriam ate a sandwich while steering her patrol car deftly through the traffic. She hadn't seen anyone who resembled the sixteen-year-old girl in the photo nor any balding psychotic men in their forties. However, she had seen other people on the road slowing down or automatically hitting the brakes as soon as they caught sight of her car.

Today it amused Miriam less than usual. She felt restless and frustrated. After her shift, she was hoping to drive straight to Hennequin's father's house in Arnhem again, even though there was no guarantee that Kramer would be in. Perhaps he was on vacation. Or spending the winter in sunnier climes, like the Engelens.

If she didn't get to speak to him this afternoon or this evening, she would have nothing to work with for the rest of the week. She'd have to wait until she could get the witnesses' addresses from the head teacher of the boarding school.

Miriam was jolted out of her thoughts when she heard her call number. She responded immediately. A dispatcher reported that there was a naked man waving a knife on the street not far from where she was. A smile played about Miriam's lips. This was why she loved her job so much. She felt a familiar surge of adrenaline rush through her body when she turned her car around and informed the control room that she was on her way.

❦

Hennequin hummed as she poured the breast milk down the sink and filled the bottles up with water. She screwed the caps on with the nipples turned inside out and put them in the fridge.

It was going to be a quiet day. Oscar was at work, there would be no more house calls from the midwife, and they weren't expecting any visitors. Today it would be just the three of them. Didi, Indy, and herself. Very cozy. Snug.

She hung a tea bag in a glass mug and filled it with hot water. Then she took the small bottle out of her pocket and dribbled some blue liquid into the tea. Not too much. Just enough to torment Didi a little, to make her feel sick. She screwed the cap back on and returned the bottle to her pocket. It was very tempting to use more. The effect would increase with the dose—it was usually lethal within twenty-four hours, but that wouldn't help matters. She couldn't get carried away. She added two lumps of sugar to the tea and stirred it well.

This morning, Didi had said that she was feeling better than yesterday. She'd even shuffled around a bit. The "cut" had almost healed up, and the stitches had come out. As a matter of fact, it was a miracle how well Didi was doing under the circumstances.

Hennequin was startled by the sudden yelling from the living room. "Hennequin, Hennequin! Come quick!"

❦

Didi saw a taxi pull up outside the door. A driver got out of the white Mercedes and took a suitcase and duffel bag out of the trunk. He then opened the back door and helped his passenger out of the car. A woman of about fifty. Not very tall, curvy, and red-haired like Didi, although the woman's neatly coiffed short hair was a darker shade.

The woman took her things from the driver and turned around. She looked at the house.

It took Didi a moment to realize who the woman was. Perhaps because she'd given up expecting her.

"Hennequin, Hennequin!" she cried. "Come quick; she's here!"

She tossed the duvet aside, grabbed her knees, and swung her legs over the edge of the bed. Sliding off the mattress, she put her slippers on. She threw on a dressing gown and staggered hurriedly toward the hall.

Hennequin was already there. She opened the front door for Didi and stepped aside to make room for her.

Tears were streaming down Didi's face. Jerkily, she hugged the small, sturdy woman at the door. "Mom!"

❦

Miriam was in the control room, drinking a cup of coffee and eating a sponge cake. She'd filled her colleagues in on the incident this morning: a marital spat had gotten out of hand, and the husband had ended up naked on the street, brandishing a kitchen knife. The couple was well known to the force; both the husband and the wife had a history of mental illness, self-neglect, and drug use. Many hours of police time were spent on people like these, addicts who often raised hell in the neighborhood. It was usually the same people who were arrested for theft, assault, or vandalism. Sometimes they fell off the radar for a while when serving a prison sentence or taking part in a drug treatment program. And then out of the blue, another call would come in, and the whole sorry business would begin all over again.

Miriam's iPhone started buzzing. She took it out of her pocket and stood up. Out of sight of her colleagues, she opened her inbox. Three emails from Corné Dillen, the retired teacher from Hennequin's primary school. Two photos of Catharina Kramer were attached to each. The first was a portrait of a very young girl with dark-brown hair, straight bangs, and missing front teeth. Miriam guessed her to be about six. She looked very normal, an ordinary bright-eyed girl staring into the lens. In the subsequent photographs, Miriam saw that little face change. With each passing year, the eyes seemed to grow duller, the cheeks chubbier. Eventually the cheeks even started to force her eyes closed slightly, making them appear smaller. In the final photographs, there was no trace of that bright-eyed girl—instead, she looked out into the world with suspicion, even reproach, in her eyes. No, Catharina

Kramer had not been a happy child. Miriam thought back to the large run-down house with yellowed posters and the stories she'd heard about Catharina and her parents. She took another look at the photograph of six-year-old Catharina. The face of an innocent child. But that innocence had disappeared a long time ago.

❧

"She looks like you, Didi." Nelly Vos was sitting on one of the chairs on castors by the bed in the living room. She looked adoringly at the little person she was holding in her left arm. Indy was drinking with greedy gulps from the bottle in her right hand. "Same nose, same cheeks . . . Isn't she beautiful?" She looked up, her cheeks flushed. "Gosh, I can hardly believe it. I'm a grandmother. Isn't that wonderful?"

Didi smiled. Her mother was right; it *was* wonderful. She just wished she were feeling a bit better. Since Oscar had left for work this morning, she'd had a knot in her stomach. And now she was starting to feel sick again. Nauseous, dizzy, as if she'd had too much to drink.

"I wanted to come much sooner, darling," said Nelly. "But Evert's car was acting up, and we had to wait for a part. Every day the guys at the garage kept telling me it would arrive at any moment." With the flat of her hand, Nelly Vos touched her dark-red, beautifully styled hair. Didi knew that the color came from a bottle. Her mother had already gone pretty gray by the age of forty. Now, at fifty-one, she looked possibly even better than she had back then. Norwegian nature and life on Evert's farm were doing her good.

Nelly continued, "I never quite realized how spread out things are in Norway. Everything's so far away; you drive for hours on end. And let me tell you, no one is in a hurry. That's what they say about people from the south, that they do things mañana, but the Norwegians could give them a run for their money. Eventually I thought, to hell with it, and rented a car to drive to the airport."

The bottle was empty. Indy was trying to get more out of it; Didi could hear her sucking the air through the nipple. She waved her little arms in protest, but Nelly put the bottle away and held Indy against her chest to burp her—all as naturally as if she did this every day.

Didi realized that her mother had always been more practical than she was. Nelly came from a farming family and had learned to help out with everything from a young age. The only thing she wasn't so good at was finding herself a decent man. Evert was husband number four, but he was the first farmer. "It's like coming home," she'd said—though Nelly also kept insisting how much she'd loved Didi's father. Didi's biological father was a skipper who'd been killed in a motorcycle accident when Didi was very young. She only had a few photos of him: a rugged, burly man with a beard, always in jeans and a grayish-blue T-shirt or a cable sweater. As a child, Didi had often fantasized that her father wasn't dead at all, but sailing the ocean somewhere as a pirate and would come home one day, full of stories.

Indy was still protesting.

"First, you do a burp," said Nelly softly. "And then we'll go and see if there's any more in the kitchen."

"I'm not producing much milk, Mom. We're trying to ration it."

Nelly nodded toward the bottle of milk Didi had just expressed with the breast pump. "You don't call that much? For goodness' sake, you could rear twins on that."

"The amount varies," she objected.

"That's normal."

The phone rang. Didi picked the handset up off the duvet and held it to her ear.

"Oh, Didi, it's you." Oscar sounded distracted. "I have to work late. Should I ask my mother to come help you?"

"No need. The reinforcements have arrived. You'll never guess who's here."

"Who?"

"My mother!"

"Well, that's good timing," he said wearily. "I'll eat here at work. Don't expect me home before nine."

"I—"

"Give my regards to your mother. See you later," he said, and hung up.

❧

Arnold Kramer appeared to be at home this time. The lights were on in the living room, and a large, slightly older but well-maintained Volvo was parked in the driveway.

Miriam didn't have to wait long for the door to be opened. A fit man in his sixties looked at her quizzically. He was immaculately dressed in beige pleated trousers and a blue shirt. His hair was remarkably dark for someone of his age. He reminded Miriam a little of a fifties film star. Hennequin had clearly inherited some of her father's features—including his strong, straight nose and wide cheekbones.

"Good afternoon. Are you Arnold Kramer?" She held out her hand, and he took it immediately. Kramer had a pleasant, warm handshake.

"That's right."

"My name is Miriam de Moor, Rotterdam police. I'd like to speak to you in connection with an investigation we're conducting."

"Rotterdam? You've come a long way."

"True." She paused and then said, "It's about your daughter. About Catharina."

The man's face clouded over. "I have no daughter."

"Yesterday I spoke to Walter and Liesbeth Engelen in Bennebroek." She looked around as if the garden were full of people and continued, lowering her voice slightly. "I think it'd be better if we continued this inside." Most people were sensitive about that. They didn't want conversations about private matters to be overheard by passersby or neighbors—especially conversations with police officers.

Arnold Kramer was of a different ilk. "There's nothing to talk about," he said. His face, which had initially appeared so open and friendly, had changed into an inscrutable mask. Even his body seemed to have become rigid. He didn't move.

"I understand that I've taken you by surprise," said Miriam. She paused to give the man some space. When there was no change in his demeanor, she continued. "Walter Engelen told us that you and your daughter are estranged and that this has been the case since her conviction in 1993."

Kramer still said nothing. Miriam tried to make eye contact with him, but he'd fixed his gaze on a point behind her. His stare was so intense that she glanced over her shoulder to find out what he was looking at. Nothing but a dark-green conifer hedge. *And a ghost from the past.*

"I urgently need your information," she said finally. "It concerns an important case, or rather cases. My colleagues and I would like to know why you're no longer in contact with your daughter. Is it because of her imprisonment and what she did back then?"

"I don't want to get involved. Is this genuine? Since when do detectives visit alone?"

Miriam raised her hands, her palms facing the man. "I apologize for any confusion. Let me show you my badge. By the way, I'm an assistant prosecutor, not a detective."

"Oh really? Interesting."

Miriam held up her badge and then quickly put it away again. "I'd really like to talk to you, Mr. Kramer. A few years ago, your daughter returned from the United States, where she was married twice. She's now living in the Netherlands. Her last husband died earlier this year under suspicious circumstances. The previous husband, an American, is also deceased." Miriam realized that she was seriously overstepping her authority. If this man contacted the station, the game would be up. She would probably be fired. For gross misconduct. Briefly, she considered simply telling the man the truth, but she didn't dare. She didn't know him; it was too risky.

It started to rain. Heavy drops fell from the low-hanging sheet of clouds and burst on the brick driveway and on Miriam's head and shoulders.

"May I come in?" she asked, with her face slanted toward the sky.

"I'd rather you didn't. Unless I'm obliged to let you."

"You aren't."

The man shook his head firmly. "Then I'm terribly sorry."

"But it would help me and my colleagues enormously if you could give us more information about your daughter."

Kramer's jaw tightened. "You've caught me completely off guard."

"May I call you later this week?"

"I'd rather you didn't," he said once again.

Miriam was about to take her card out of the pocket of her leather jacket, but before she could do it, she heard a thud. Kramer had slammed the door.

❦

The rain was beating against the large windowpanes of the house on Baljuwstraat. Nelly had lit the gas fire. She was sitting beside her daughter's bed with her slippers on, looking on the iPad at photos taken shortly after Indy's birth.

Hennequin observed the scene with a dark look. The shrimp had been sleeping sweetly for hours in a stroller next to the bed—this was an annoyance, but there was nothing she could do about it. It was Nelly Vos's fault. The ginger troll from Norway questioned everything. She was nearly always watching over Hennequin's shoulder; just now, she'd bathed Indy *herself* and said that it was "ridiculous" to make her grand-daughter sleep separately in her crib upstairs. So the child was now here. Hennequin's objections had been brushed aside. "It really won't do the baby any harm," Nelly had said to her daughter. "I can't believe they still preach that rest and routine nonsense in this day and age. These little ones just need to be close to their mother."

Didi accepted everything her mother dictated without question. A mother who'd abandoned her only daughter by moving abroad, for heaven's sake. But Didi never mentioned that. She clearly adored the woman.

Hennequin rushed over to the stroller, picked Indy up, and handed her to Nelly. "Would Grandma like to feed her? I'm done for the day."

"Yes, of course."

"I feel a bit sick," said Didi.

Hennequin ignored her and went into the kitchen. Didi's symptoms—double vision, dizziness, nausea—were a sign of mild ethylene glycol poisoning. The stuff was working well already. Perhaps she would give Didi another drop of antifreeze tomorrow or the day after, just for fun. Make her feel even sicker.

Hennequin took a bottle out of the fridge and warmed it up in the microwave. Didi's milk production had increased enormously in the past few days. Hennequin had immediately thrown some of the milk away, but now that Nelly had started to interfere with the pumping— "You can't use those breast shields; they're far too small. How on earth can they recommend those?"—it was more difficult. The woman had even stuck thin strips of paper on the bottles with the date and time.

Hennequin grabbed a few bottles, poured out some of the milk, and filled them up with tap water. She looked into the living room. Nelly sat cuddling her granddaughter, and Didi was staring ahead with a pained face. Hennequin had always planned for a visit from Nelly, but now that she'd actually come to stay with her daughter, it seemed almost too good to be true. Tonight, Hennequin would think carefully about what to do with her.

But first, there was something else to deal with, something she'd been looking forward to since her first day with the Stevens-Vos family.

One thing at a time.

Humming to herself, she removed the bottle from the microwave and took it into the living room.

❧

Miriam took one last bite of her burger. It was quiet in the Arnhem pub. There were two couples in their thirties and a man eating alone in the corner. He kept trying to make eye contact. Miriam ignored him and looked out the window. It was still raining.

Once more, she went over the brief conversation she'd had on the doorstep with Hennequin's father. Kramer's defensiveness was only natural. After all, Hennequin was his daughter. His own flesh and blood. What kind of father would turn in his own daughter? *That's how it must have felt to him,* thought Miriam. On the other hand, he hadn't seen his daughter for more than twenty years. Twenty years was an eternity. Was the bond completely broken? She realized that Arnold Kramer had been shocked more than anything. He'd slammed the door, both literally and figuratively, because he'd felt overwhelmed. He needed time. How much? A week? A day?

A few hours?

"Fuck it," she whispered to herself. She emptied her glass in a few gulps, stood up, and walked to the cash register.

❧

Didi waved to Hennequin as she drove down the street in her black Alfa.

Her mother got up from the chair and wheeled it back under the dining table. "I don't think you need that home help anymore," she said.

"Mom, it's called maternity nurse nowadays. It's nice having her here. She's been so helpful."

"That's her job."

"Of course. But she's often stayed late of her own accord to help me out."

"Well, she doesn't need to do that anymore. I've called Evert to say I'll be staying here for the time being, until you're back on your feet. At least, if that's what you want?"

Didi felt a wave of warmth sweep through her chest. "That'd be great, Mom," she said softly. "I'd love that." She hadn't seen her mother for more than eighteen months, and the prospect of having her here for another week—or perhaps even longer—was the best gift she could wish for.

"Well then, you can send that Hanneke home as far as I'm concerned."

"Hennequin. But that's not necessary, Mom. Thursday is her last day. To be honest, it's reassuring to have her here. She takes my temperature and the baby's, keeps track of how much Indy's drinking, whether she's having enough wet diapers, and things like that. She writes it all down. I need that guidance. I'm afraid of doing something wrong."

"I understand that. You know what? I'll photocopy those forms of hers, and we'll keep up that routine for a while. But not all of it."

"What do you mean?"

"Some of her advice is a bit strange. I think it's really heartless to make Indy sleep in her own room, for example."

"She said that rest and routine are the most important things for a baby, and that it's too noisy here in the living room."

"And what about those breast shields? They were far too small, weren't they? Anyone with an ounce of common sense would have realized they were going to hurt. And I'm sorry to say, but she's barely done anything about the inflammation around your nipples."

Didi shrugged. "I don't know, Mom. It's all new to me. I've read all sorts of horror stories on the internet about breastfeeding and pumping; not everyone finds it easy."

"But it *is* getting better now."

Didi couldn't argue with that. Since her mother had given her bigger flanges for the breast pump, pumping had been far less painful. Her nipples were already beginning to heal, much faster than she'd expected.

Nelly looked through the large window onto the street and rubbed her hands. "You know, Didi . . . I think she's a bit peculiar."

"Really? In what way?"

"I don't know. It's just a feeling."

"There must be a reason?"

She shook her head. "Oh, never mind." Her mother's face broke into a smile. "She can't do much more harm in the few days she has left."

He was still at home. The Volvo was still there; the lights were on inside. For the second time today, Miriam walked up the driveway and rang the bell. It was dark now, and the rain had left puddles on the street. She shivered. If Hennequin's father still refused to talk, she would leave him alone. But she hoped that in the intervening hours he'd been able to recover from the initial shock and had grown curious about his daughter.

Arnold Kramer opened the door. "Here you are again," he said, and to her great surprise, took a step back to let her in. "Follow me."

She walked behind him through a tasteful hallway to the living room. It was divided in two by a set of leaded glass doors. In the back half, there was a shiny wooden dining table surrounded by four elegant chairs.

"Take a seat."

Miriam sat down on one of the chairs. They had rounded seats covered with jacquard fabric. Kramer sat opposite her.

Miriam looked around inquisitively. There was a folded *NRC Handelsblad* newspaper on the smooth tabletop with a pair of reading glasses on it. Oil paintings hung on the walls, but no photos. On either side of the leaded glass doors were built-in bookcases, crammed with books. The space between the doors and the high ceiling was also filled with hundreds of books standing upright and lying flat.

"I see you like reading," said Miriam.

The man looked at his books with slight irritation, as if he'd only just realized he owned them. "I like to collect knowledge." He pushed the newspaper demonstratively aside and looked at Miriam. "What's going on with Catharina?"

He said his daughter's name with respect. Perhaps even love.

"We're trying to flesh out her background."

"That can't be very difficult with all the contacts and databases at your disposal."

"Catharina is a special case. Your daughter isn't the kind of person who wants to be found. It took us a while to discover that she was born as Catharina Kramer. She changed her name in America."

The man looked at her with interest. "To what?"

"Hennequin. Hennequin Smith."

He raised a thin, arched eyebrow. There was a flicker in his eyes. "Hennequin?"

"Yes, with a *q*. Does that mean anything to you?"

"Are you familiar with old folk tales and legends?"

Miriam shook her head. "Not really."

"I've been collecting them all my life." He made a sweeping gesture to the bookshelves. "I have hundreds of books about them. They can be gruesome stories, but they're of inestimable cultural and historical value. Catharina enjoyed reading them as a child."

"Is that connected to her new name?"

Kramer looked pensively at his books. "Stories about the character of Hellequin or Hennequin appear in various forms in medieval legends throughout Europe. In Normandy, the legend is known as *La Chasse Hennequin*. You may have heard of it."

Miriam shook her head again.

"As an emissary of the devil, Hennequin commanded a troop of demons who came out at night with horses and dogs to hunt for lost and evil souls and chase them to hell." The man paused. He lowered his voice and continued. "The name 'Hennequin' or 'Hannequin' is still used in that region of France to denote an *enfant désagréable*, a nasty, evil child."

Miriam felt a shiver run down her spine. She locked her fingers together on the tabletop.

Kramer continued. "Around 1300, the name also appears in Italy to designate a devilish theatrical figure. I believe it was Dante himself who, inspired by his visit to Paris, introduced the character of Alichino in his homeland." Kramer put his fingertips together. "In Italian theater, demonic characters had a more playful role than in France. More lighthearted, less serious. The *arlecchino* became a stock character in the popular *commedia dell'arte*. That term was then readopted in France as *arlequin* and is better known in these parts as 'harlequin.'"

"Like a clown?" Miriam rocked back and forth on her chair. She wasn't here for a history lesson, but she didn't want to interrupt him. If he felt at ease, he might open up about his daughter.

"No. Not a clown. A harlequin is more complex, and more intelligent too. A character with multiple faces, often with a tragic background. And usually masked." Arnold Kramer continued more quietly, as if he were no longer talking to Miriam but thinking out loud. "It's remarkable that she chose Hennequin as her name."

"Do you think Catharina sees herself as a theatrical figure or a devil?"

A nasty, evil child?

Someone who hunts for lost and evil souls?

"I don't know." He stared thoughtfully into space. "My daughter was fifteen when I last spoke to her. Still a child, an adolescent. But even then—" He stopped abruptly and shook his head almost imperceptibly.

"Even then what?"

The moment had passed. The man straightened up. "I've tried to put her out of my mind since then." He stood up. "I'm sorry I can't offer you anything to drink. I have to go out soon. But I've already told you everything I can."

Miriam was about to remind him that he'd barely mentioned his daughter, but stopped herself. He'd already been more open with her than just a few hours ago. Perhaps if she gave him a few days, or a week, he might be ready to tell her more.

She pulled her business card out of her pocket, crossed out the number of her work BlackBerry, and wrote her personal number beside it. This gave the impression that she had a new phone number, but hadn't gotten around to updating her cards. She handed it to Kramer. "If you decide you want to talk about Catharina, or if something comes to mind that might help our investigation, please call me. Day or night. People often say that, but in my case, you can take it literally. I regularly work the night shift, so there's never a bad time."

Kramer looked at the card and, to Miriam's relief, put it in his breast pocket.

He escorted her to the front door, where Miriam realized that she was still wearing her jacket. She stepped outside and turned around. "I really hope you'll call," she said. "But I can imagine this must be very difficult for you."

Countless emotions passed over Kramer's face. It was as if he were traveling through time in his mind, and all the events involving his daughter were flashing in front of his eyes. When he opened his mouth, his voice sounded different from before, softer. "You know, certain things happened after the death of my first wife that I didn't see coming. Perhaps I was away from home too much; I was often accused of that. Perhaps I was blind. Didn't want to see it." Shaking his head, he turned away from her. "Don't expect me to call, Ms. De Moor," he said, closing the door.

❦

Hennequin saw the Audi pulling up. The bluish beam from the head-lights swept searchingly across the parking lot and then moved in an almost straight line to the far corner, where she'd parked her Alfa. Oscar stopped his car next to hers and turned off his lights. It was fairly dark here. Hennequin could only see Oscar's outline. He didn't get out, assuming, of course, that she would get into his car.

Hennequin's fingers slid over the steering wheel. Together, apart, together . . . She looked to the right once again. It finally dawned on him.

He opened the door, briefly coming into the light. He was wearing dark chinos and a tight V-neck sweater under a thin dark jacket. She had to admit it looked good on him. Everything looked good on him. There was no way Didi could have kept this man to herself for the rest of her life.

He opened her door and looked questioningly inside. "Are you coming?"

"We're going to spice things up tonight," she said. Her voice sounded deep and a little husky. She slowly rubbed the passenger seat. "Get in, tiger."

At first, he looked at her with slight surprise, but he soon broke into a grin. It was almost touching, a childish sort of joy. He locked his car, briefly illuminating the parking lot, and slipped into the seat beside her.

She grabbed his face with one hand and kissed him passionately. Oscar responded eagerly, moaning softly. He'd been looking forward to this evening. And it was certainly going to be a special evening for him. Very special.

With her other hand, Hennequin quickly and discreetly searched his pockets. He didn't notice, too distracted by his own passion and her right hand, which was caressing his face and playfully pulling his hair.

She fished his phone out of the inside pocket of his jacket, and while gently sucking on his bottom lip, she threw it backward out of the open window. It landed in the dark between low bushes. That was perfect. She would return for it later.

"We're going for a ride," she whispered hoarsely. She cooed, rubbing her nose against his.

"Well, aren't you dominant all of a sudden?" he remarked, panting slightly with excitement.

"You like that, don't you?"

"I'm all yours."

With a satisfied smile, she started the car and drove out of the lot.

❧

Miriam turned off the highway and joined the city traffic. It was dark now, but at least it had stopped raining.

What an extraordinary story lay behind the name Hennequin. In light of that, and Arnold Kramer's erudition, Miriam began to suspect that her brother's widow was far better educated than her family had realized. Catharina Kramer a.k.a. Hennequin Smith turned out to be a highly intelligent, complex murderer who switched countries as easily as she switched spouses. And this woman was currently working as a maternity nurse in Rotterdam? It was possible, of course. But it was certainly a very strange twist in Hennequin's life story.

Miriam hesitated for a moment at a large intersection. If she turned right here, she would end up near Hennequin's apartment building. It was still early in the evening; she might be at home. If so, Miriam could drop in on her, for no particular reason, just to provoke her, get on her nerves. There was no need to pretend anymore. She'd never been close to her sister-in-law, and after Bart's funeral—throughout which Hennequin had worn dramatic jet-black sunglasses so that no one had been able to see whether she actually cried—Hennequin had ignored the family completely. But now, barely six months later, she had the nerve to turn up out of the blue. On Miriam's home turf. *My territory.* Why? Did it have anything to do with the family she was working for? Or was there a totally different reason for her reappearance? *Does it have anything to do with me?* No. She would have noticed it by now.

Miriam was frustrated that her investigation had reached a dead end. And she wouldn't have any new information until the head teacher of the boarding school returned. A surprise visit to her brother's widow might set things in motion. It would unsettle Hennequin and perhaps hinder her in whatever she was up to.

The traffic light turned green. At the last minute, Miriam steered her car back onto the main road. Somebody beeped at her; a man stuck up his middle finger. She had to laugh. How differently the same drivers would react if she were in uniform, at the wheel of a patrol car. People simply weren't intimidated by a young woman in plain clothes in an unmarked Peugeot.

She would leave Hennequin in blissful ignorance for one more night. Tomorrow, she would pay her a visit. Not in plain clothes, but in uniform.

❧

"Oscar's been gone a long time," said Nelly.

Didi looked at the clock again. It was five past ten. Oscar had never come home from work this late before. She'd called him several times, but kept getting his voice mail.

"Is everything OK between you two?" asked Nelly.

Didi pressed her lips together. She shook her head. "Not really."

Nelly shifted in her seat. "Why?"

"I think it's all too much for him. It frightened the life out of him when I ended up in that wheelchair; he was really worried about me. And he hasn't been himself since Indy was born."

"Having a baby is life-changing for many men too." Nelly tilted her head. "It's none of my business, of course, but I get the feeling there's more to it than that."

Didi bit her upper lip. "Indy cries a lot at night. Oscar says he's not getting enough sleep, and it's making him irritable. And he thinks I should give her formula instead of breast milk because pumping is too much trouble. Also—" She paused. No, she wasn't going to say it aloud. But inside, she cried out, *He doesn't want this child, Mom!*

She felt another wave of nausea sweep through her body, as if she were hungover. Occasionally she saw double. "I don't feel very well, Mom."

"Perhaps you should get some sleep. Shall I help you upstairs?"

"Oscar's not home yet."

"Oscar is a grown man. You don't need to wait up for him."

Indy cried out. Nelly took her out of the stroller and started walking around the room, gently rocking the baby back and forth in her arms. "It's understandable, but it's not right, Didi. It's not right for a man to run away." She turned to her daughter. "But lots of men are like that. They can't handle the pressure. And it's different for them. They haven't carried a baby in their body; they're less involved."

"What about me? Am *I* supposed to handle everything?"

Nelly looked at her gloomily. "If I'd known about this earlier, I'd have come here months ago. You should have told me what was going on and that you could hardly walk."

"I didn't want to worry you. What could you do? Evert needs you on the farm."

"Evert has farmhands, but you only have one mother. Come on, you should go to bed, get some rest. Then I'll change this lovely lady's diaper and give her a bottle."

"And what about Oscar?"

"I'll stay up till he comes home," said Nelly.

"And then?"

"I'll have a word with him. Because this can't go on, Didi."

❧

"I don't know if I—"

"Shh. Leave this to me." Hennequin closed her lips over Oscar's and whispered, "Just enjoy it."

Oscar was standing with his back against a birch tree. She'd already bound his legs. He'd protested, but not very much. His trousers were hanging around his knees, and his arousal was plain to see. The swollen white flesh stood erect in the patchy moonlight. Hennequin put her hand on it, fondled him.

She too was aroused—but not for the same reason. Her heart was beating rapidly; her breathing was raspy. This was new. New and exciting. But she knew it would work as long as she was quick and forceful enough.

She put the nylon rope over his chest and walked around the tree again, then tied his upper arms.

He tried to pull them loose. "I'm not really comfortable with this, Henneq—"

She pressed his arms against the trunk and kissed him again, first on his lips, then she drifted to his chest, his stomach—which trembled and contracted under her caresses—and farther down. A promise for later, if he stood still. When he was completely in her power. Only then would she do it. That was the game.

She stood up and uncoiled more of the rope. Three, four times around his arms. She pulled it. Tighter. Around his belly, his hips. He couldn't move at all now, but he tried to anyway. She saw him stretch his fingers and clench them into a fist, wriggle his shoulders.

Tighter. Even tighter.

He was still aroused. Humming, Hennequin put the rope on his neck.

Pressing it against his larynx, she pulled it tight. She looked deep into Oscar's eyes, which grew bigger and bigger, and smothered his panicky scream with an extra tug at the rope, which she wound once more around his neck and the tree trunk.

She leaned toward him, her cheek against his. "Now *I'm* enjoying this, Oscar," she whispered in his ear. "It's so kind of you to help me discover all these new things. I've never done this before. Did you know that?"

She heard him gasp for breath.

❦

Darkness had fallen. Miriam had switched the lights on and lit a few candles. She was standing at the stovetop in a tracksuit and slippers. Roughly once a month, she cooked several meals one after the other and froze them in individual portions. Stocking up the freezer stopped her from resorting to McDonald's too often or spending a fortune on takeout.

She fried sliced onions and garlic in a deep pan, pushing them back and forth across the sizzling surface with a wooden spatula. After adding the contents of two cans of peeled tomatoes, she took a large bowl of broccoli florets, dumped them into a pan of boiling stock, and put the lid on. Then she lowered the heat and set the kitchen timer for fifteen minutes.

She turned around and looked down through the curtains. The lights were on in Boris's studio. He was sitting on a raised stool, engrossed in his painting.

Miriam folded her arms and watched him mix paint intently on the palette resting on his forearm and then spread the color on the canvas. His eyes were focused, the sleeves of his hoodie rolled up to his elbows.

She kept looking at him furtively. It was comforting to know that there were still good things in the world and that she still had the ability to see them. And appreciate them.

On impulse, she grabbed her phone and dialed his number. After three rings, Boris answered.

"I have an evening shift tomorrow," she said. "If you have time, would you like to come along?"

❧

Dead weight. Hennequin had expected it to be heavy, but not this heavy. Oscar was slim, but he felt like a walrus now that all the muscles of his body had relaxed. She dragged the corpse behind her over the withered leaves. Strands of her blonde wig fell over her forehead. She felt elated and sad at the same time. Elated because she'd done it—she'd done it yet again, and what a wonderful experience it had been—but also disappointed because it was over. She wouldn't be able to entertain herself with Oscar anymore. His role was played out.

But there were still three people left. Three *generations*.

This was going to be something special.

Day Eight

TUESDAY

Didi sat with the phone pressed to her ear. Her heart was pounding in her chest. Oscar hadn't come home last night. That had never happened before. Ever. *This is Oscar Stevens's voice mail. I'm sorry I can't . . .*

She hung up. Had he run off? Walked out on her and Indy? But then why had he left all his clothes and things?

"Voice mail again?" asked Nelly. She looked at her daughter over the top of her reading glasses. Her hair was a little messy this morning, and her face looked pale without makeup.

"This isn't like him at all, Mom."

"Maybe he just needs some space."

Didi shook her head. "You should have woken me up. This is strange. Oscar has never stayed out all night before."

"He's never become a father before either." Her mother looked at her pensively. "You often used to hear about fathers going to the pub to celebrate the baby's birth and not reappearing till several days or a week later."

"That was in the past, Mom."

"It wasn't that long ago. At least, not for me. Number three was like that. In the end, he needed so much space to himself, there was no room left for me."

The home phone rang. Hennequin came in from the kitchen. "Shall I get it?"

"No. I will," snapped Nelly. She'd already stood up to grab the phone from the charging base. "Hello, Stevens-Vos residence."

She listened and shook her head. "No, he's not here . . . You're speaking to his mother-in-law. I'll mention it to his wife. No, she can't come to the phone right now." She turned away from Hennequin and Didi and picked up a pen off the table. "And what's your name? OK. We'll get back to you soon."

Didi was sitting up now. "Who was that, Mom?"

"Has Oscar ever skipped work before?"

Didi looked at her mother in astonishment. "No," she said softly. "Never."

"He has now."

❦

Miriam was woken by the sound of her phone. Thanks to the blackout curtains, she had no idea if it was morning. She looked at the clock. Quarter to nine.

She reached for her iPhone. The screen showed an unknown mobile number. She answered it with a drowsy voice. "Hello, Miriam de Moor speaking."

"Good morning. Is this a bad time?"

"No," she said, sitting up straight. "Who is this?"

"Reina Scheltema, head teacher of De Horizon in Boxmeer. I understand you spoke to Mr. Luijten last Sunday about one of our former students."

Miriam threw off the duvet and stood up. "That's right. I'm so glad you called! I wasn't expecting to hear from you till next week."

"Yes, that's when I'm due back at work. But I came across a message from Mr. Luijten in my email, and I thought I'd better call right away so that you can get on with your investigation. I was reminded of Catharina Kramer only a few months ago, when I attended the funeral of Klaas de Vries, her old English teacher."

De Vries? Miriam gripped the phone with both hands. De Vries was the name of the teacher who'd seen Catharina Kramer push her roommate over the balustrade. "One of the witnesses, you mean?"

"That's right. He'd been retired for a while and lived in Limburg, near Roermond."

"Alone?"

"Yes. Klaas had a partner, but they didn't live together."

"How did he die?"

"Alcohol poisoning. It's a very sad story, actually. I was shocked. After his death, they found bottles of booze all over his house. In the shed, in the attic, under his bed." She paused. "I don't understand what drove him to drink himself to death. But then I hadn't spoken to him for years. Maybe he couldn't bear the loneliness. I remember he wasn't really looking forward to retirement. He saw it as the beginning of the end. Perhaps he became depressed."

"There was another witness, wasn't there?"

"That's right. A grammar school student, Marie-Louise Diepman. She only boarded here for a short time, while her parents were working in Africa. I'm afraid we haven't been able to find a Dutch address in our records, although we did find the address of the company in South Africa her parents worked for at the time."

Miriam didn't think it would be much help, but she went into the kitchen and jotted down the long address on a notepad. She also wrote down Marie-Louise's date of birth; if the woman lived in the Netherlands, her name and date of birth would be enough to trace her current address.

"What kind of child was Catharina Kramer?" she asked.

"Unhappy and insecure. Extremely intelligent, secretive, unapproachable. Short-tempered at times. She wasn't very popular."

"I've spoken to one of her old teachers who knew her from before she came to your boarding school. Are you aware of her family history?"

"That her mother committed suicide, you mean? Yes. That must be devastating for a child."

So must social exclusion, thought Miriam. There had recently been a major study about violent individuals. The researchers wanted to find out why certain people were driven to commit terrible, destructive acts such as random shooting sprees in shopping malls or schools. The perpetrators turned out to have a distinctive feature in common: they'd been social outcasts as children, bullied and excluded by their peers. This led to measurable biological changes. For example, such people inexplicably developed a higher pain threshold; they were simply less prone to feel pain than others. At the same time, they lost some of their ability to empathize with other people's pain. It was as if the loneliness had caused a sort of callus, both physical and psychological, to form over their feelings. By the time Catharina was sent to De Horizon, the damage had probably already been done.

"I understand that Catharina was badly bullied in the village where she grew up," said Miriam.

"Really?" The head teacher sounded genuinely surprised.

"Wasn't she bullied at your boarding school?"

"No, quite the opposite; the other children were afraid of her."

🦋

"Did something happen?"

"That's what I'm trying to find out." Didi's voice sounded breathless and high, but she didn't care. "What time did he leave yesterday?"

"Five o'clock, as usual," replied Linda, one of Oscar's colleagues. "He said he didn't have to take over from the maternity nurse because his mother-in-law was there."

"Five o'clock. Are you sure?"

"Absolutely sure. We left the building together. Pim came to pick me up, and he chatted with Oscar by the car."

"So Oscar didn't have to work late?"

"Er, sorry, Didi. Not to my knowledge. Maybe he went out to eat and came back to the office later?"

Didi heard a voice in the background; someone had obviously been listening in beside Linda. It sounded like Koen, one of Oscar's colleagues.

"No, apparently not," Linda reported. "Koen says he was the only one here last night."

Didi's hands had started sweating. Her whole body was trembling. "How . . . how did he act yesterday?"

"As pleased as punch, of course. He showed us all the photos of his—hey, congratulations, by the way! Gosh. How silly of me to forget!"

"Thank you. It's OK." Didi's heart was thumping in her chest.

Where are you, Oscar?

What happened to you?

She paused and then said softly, "I have to go, Linda. Thank you. Give my regards to Koen." She hung up and looked at her mother. "Oscar left work at five o'clock yesterday."

"No overtime?"

"No."

All kinds of thoughts raced through her mind, each one crazier than the last. Another woman—or man—a gambling addiction, drugs, criminal activity? That wasn't Oscar's style. And he certainly wasn't the type of man to just up and leave. He preferred to talk things over. They'd always been open with each other.

But he didn't want this child, Didi.

"You don't think he had an accident, do you?" she wondered aloud. "He always drives way too fast in that car."

The maternity nurse came into the room. "If he had, I'm sure we'd have heard about it by now."

Didi looked at her. "Has this ever happened before, Hennequin?"

Hennequin shook her head.

"I have a really strange feeling about this. What do you think?"

Hennequin nodded to Nelly. "Maybe your mother is right, and he just needed space to think. He was very angry about the rabbits."

Nelly tried to make eye contact with her daughter. "Rabbits?"

In a flat tone, Didi told her what had happened. She tried not to cry, but she couldn't stop the tears from welling in her eyes or her voice from shaking. "He hadn't given them any food or water, Mom, but he kept insisting he had. It didn't make any sense. I was furious with him." Didi began to sob. "He was lying through his teeth."

Nelly sat down on her daughter's bed. She stroked her hair, made soothing noises.

"Nelly?" Didi heard the maternity nurse ask. "Shall I bathe Indy, or will you do it?"

"You do it, Hanneke," said Nelly distractedly, without looking at her. She hugged Didi, wiping away the tears with her thumb.

❦

Hennequin stopped in her tracks when she heard her unique name being mangled so carelessly by Didi's mother. With an icy gaze, she looked at the scene, the mother comforting her daughter, and felt a cold emptiness inside her. Just for a moment. It had already been replaced by a searing hatred by the time she walked away from them and went upstairs.

❦

Something strange was going on with Marie-Louise Diepman. The thirty-three-year-old woman who'd witnessed the murder of Hilde Vandenbroecke as a child had recently been reported missing by her parents. Miriam had found out more via Google, old news reports, and Facebook. Marie-Louise had a history of mental illness and probably suffered from schizophrenia. She worked as a drama teacher at a cultural center and still lived with her parents. Four months ago, she'd failed to come home after a night out. That wasn't cause for concern. Marie-Louise often stayed with a friend or someone she'd met the same evening, so her parents hadn't been worried at first. But eventually they'd called the police. And now, four months later, there was still no sign of Marie-Louise.

Miriam checked the national police website, where she found a passport photo and a brief description of the woman among those of almost four hundred other Dutch men, women, and children who were currently missing. As she stared at the photo of the brunette, Miriam slowly felt herself growing cold. Was Marie-Louise roaming around an unfamiliar city or another country in a state of psychosis triggered by drugs or alcohol? Or had she been murdered, her body yet to be found?

Two witnesses—one dead, the other missing—in the space of four months.

What a remarkable coincidence.

❧

Hennequin lowered Indy into the water. The baby felt slippery from the oil. She still couldn't see Indy as beautiful. To her, she looked like a plump shrimp with tiny eyes—shiny beads embedded in little cushions of fat. More a larva than a shrimp. She rocked her in the lukewarm water. Humming a song, she swayed her back and forth.

In the middle of a movement, Hennequin pulled her hands out of the water. The baby looked startled; she threw her little arms and legs automatically out to the side, like a frog. Tiny toes and fingers spread. She immediately sank to the bottom of the smooth plastic bath.

With a smile, Hennequin tucked a strand of blonde hair behind her ear and leaned over the bath. She looked down at the little girl. "What shall I do with you?" she whispered, just above the surface of the water. "Shall I pull you out? Like *this*?" She stuck her hands in, cupped the baby's back, supported her head, and lifted her out of the water, as if she were a priestess offering a sacrifice. "Or shall I leave you where you are?" She lowered the baby, let her go, and pushed down on her belly until she felt her back touch the bottom of the tub. She removed her hands.

It was thought that young babies could remember certain things from the womb, that they instinctively held their breath as soon as they went underwater. Hennequin wasn't sure exactly how long this reflex was supposed to last. A few hours, days, or weeks?

Underwater, Indy's eyes widened; the beads grew into buttons. Shiny blue buttons rimmed with white in a fat face. The body attached to it wriggled; as small and innocent as she was, she already realized she had to fight.

"What to do, what to do . . . ," cooed Hennequin.

Humming to herself, she watched the child struggle, the arms and legs thrashing in the water, and smelled the wonderful scent of baby oil. Hennequin loved that smell. She'd never forgotten it; it reminded her of better times, when the world still seemed beautiful and fair. She always found it calming.

"Eeny, meeny, miny, mo. Catch the baby by the toe. If she screams, let her go . . . ," she whispered, mesmerized by the struggling child, who now opened her mouth and blew out bubbles of oxygen. "Eeny, meeny, miny . . . mo."

Hennequin grabbed hold of the baby's slippery ankles as if she were pulling a big fish out of a pond by its tail. Gurgling, Indy came to the surface—the sound was weak, shaky.

Hennequin supported her body, held her against her chest, and tapped her on the back. Indy started crying softly.

"Ooo, wasn't that scary, Indy, darling? You got a fright."

Hennequin put the baby on the changing mat, patted her dry with a soft towel, and dressed her.

She noticed that Indy was coughing slightly. Water had gotten into the baby's lungs.

But not too much.

❧

Miriam had gotten dressed and opened the curtains. As she drank her third cup of coffee, she wondered what to do. Was it time to present her findings to her chief?

Better not.

When, shortly after Bart's death, she'd voiced her suspicions about Hennequin Smith's involvement in it, no one at the station had taken her allegations seriously. *You're grieving, Miriam, and in denial. Can't you see that?* Eventually her chief had suggested that she talk to the staff welfare officer and offered her compassionate leave.

Since then, she hadn't mentioned it to anyone. Except for Rens. But had he too only listened out of politeness? He'd never brought it up again, at any rate.

Miriam couldn't blame her colleagues for how things had turned out. She'd simply gotten carried away after Bart's death, culminating in the day she'd driven to Belgium in a patrol car without consulting anyone. There, she'd tried desperately to speak to the officers who'd been at the scene of the accident in Bart's house. That escapade had almost cost her her job. Her chief would hit the roof at the mere mention of Hennequin Smith. If she now confronted him with all sorts of cold case murders involving her brother's widow, she might as well head straight for the employment office.

She rubbed her hands over her face and breathed deeply in and out.

When she'd seen Hennequin go into that house on Baljuwstraat last Monday in a white uniform, she'd assumed Hennequin was a maternity nurse. But she could just as easily be working for the Municipal Health Service, or perhaps she was even a midwife. In either of those cases, Hennequin would have left again within half an hour for her next appointment. The problem was, Miriam hadn't waited to see.

One thing was certain: she wouldn't learn much here at home, behind her laptop. She put on her coat and grabbed her keys. Baljuwstraat was less than a ten-minute drive away, if she didn't hit too many red lights.

❧

Didi sat trembling on a dining chair. She was wrapped in her bathrobe. This was really happening. It wasn't a dream. Two police officers were sitting opposite her, looking very serious.

The woman, with short blonde hair and small, close-set eyes, did most of the talking, while her male colleague drank coffee and ate a rusk topped with sugar-coated aniseeds.

"It might be hard to believe right now, but there's a good chance your husband will simply come home during the course of the day or evening."

"You think so?"

"That's what normally happens. Especially when, as in your case, there are tensions and arguments. For us, alarm bells only start ringing when someone leaves the house in a stressed or depressed state of mind. Your husband went to work as usual."

"But he told me he had to work late, and that wasn't true."

The man leaned forward in his chair. "Has he ever done that before?"

"Not to my knowledge."

"I'm sorry to be so blunt, but if your husband doesn't use drugs, and there's no indication of any other addiction or involvement in criminal activity"—he looked demonstratively around him, at Hennequin, who was standing near the kitchen in her white uniform with Indy in her arms, and at Nelly, who was sitting next to Didi, holding her hand— "then that leaves us with only one obvious scenario." He looked Didi straight in the eye. "It probably all became too much for him, and he's taking some time out from his home life. He could be alone or with someone who makes him feel at ease and who may be completely unknown to you."

"My husband has never gone missing before."

"I'll take your word for it."

"And he's not having an affair either," Didi added. She was still shivering. The shivers seemed to come from inside, from her chest and stomach.

"How often did your husband have to work late?" asked the policeman calmly.

"Once, sometimes twice a week."

The policeman looked at his colleague and then back at Didi. Nobody said anything.

Nelly broke the silence. "Perhaps you could try to find his car? That can't be very difficult."

The man finished the last bite of his rusk. "In the Netherlands, an average of fifty people are reported missing every day. Eighty-five percent turn up within two days. And only about twenty people, or one in a thousand, are still missing after a year. Your son-in-law was last seen at work yesterday at quarter past five, so to be frank, there's little cause for concern at this stage."

"Maybe he had a serious accident, and he's in a hospital somewhere?"

The man straightened up. "We'd have been notified in that case; your husband is carrying his wallet, so he can be identified by his driver's license."

The woman looked up from her BlackBerry. "I've checked his license plate, but nothing's coming up." She sought Didi's gaze. "Your husband's Audi hasn't been involved in an accident, at any rate."

"Really?"

"We'd know about it," she said firmly.

The man prepared to stand up. "OK. If you still haven't heard from Oscar by five p.m. tomorrow, call me, and we'll set the wheels in motion."

"But now that we're here . . ." The policewoman looked at her colleague slightly reproachfully and then turned to Didi. "Do you have a recent photo of your husband?"

Didi looked around in confusion. Apart from the blown-up wedding portrait near the staircase in the hall, she and Oscar didn't have any photos in the house. "I think we—"

"Perhaps on Facebook?" asked the woman. "Or on your phone?"

"Of course!" Didi reached for her iPad on the table and opened Facebook with trembling fingers. None of the photos featuring Oscar were very clear, until she came across a picture of them together from last summer. Their cheeks were touching, and they were both smiling into the lens. Oscar's skin had been slightly burned by the Thai sun. She turned the iPad to show the police officers. "I think this one is the best."

"Please email it to this address." The man wrote on a card and handed it to her.

"What are you going to do now?" asked Nelly.

"Nothing yet," said the woman. "If your son-in-law still hasn't come home by tomorrow morning, we'll file an official report."

❦

The wooden stork was still in the front garden. It looked as if the orange stick representing a leg had sunk a little more lopsidedly into the white gravel. The colorful garland in the window was gone. Hennequin's black Alfa Romeo was in the driveway, gleaming under the carport—the exact same spot where the Audi driven by Oscar Stevens, the man of the house, had been parked last Wednesday. He'd probably gone back to work.

"Just as I thought," whispered Miriam. Her first instinct had been correct. Hennequin was indeed a maternity nurse. Just about the least appropriate job she could imagine for her brother's widow.

She drove slowly down the street and passed number 66 almost at a walking pace. The sheer curtains in the large, square window made it impossible to see what was going on inside.

She made a right at the end of the street and stopped her car in a turnout. On her iPhone, she googled "maternity nurse" and "working hours." She soon came across a forum where qualified maternity nurses gave advice to women who were still in training. Hours were apparently scheduled in consultation with the family, but on average, a maternity nurse worked six hours a day. What time did Hennequin start work? When Miriam had followed her here last week, it had been nine o'clock. But that seemed a little late to start the day with a young family—sometime between seven or eight o'clock would make much more sense. The forum confirmed this.

In that case, Hennequin would finish work at one or two o'clock this afternoon. Miriam looked at her iPhone. It was only quarter to ten.

She started the car and drove home.

❧

"Look at the state of your hands. I haven't been able to take my eyes off them all day," said Nelly Vos. She was standing beside Hennequin in the kitchen, helping her rinse out the bottles.

"I know, right?" Hennequin spread her fingers and examined them nonchalantly. Blisters. Cuts.

It had been quite a job to fill the hole last night. There'd been sand left over, which she'd spread over a large area. Then she'd covered the grave with leaves and branches until the ground looked perfectly undisturbed under the beam of her flashlight. She hadn't finished until around midnight. At home, she'd scrubbed away the sand and dirt that had gotten under her fingernails and in the folds of her skin. Her hands were clean now, but the blisters and cuts were still there. They couldn't be hidden.

"I had to dig a grave for your daughter's rabbits," said Hennequin, demonstratively stretching and bending her fingers. "The soil here is quite hard. I'm afraid my hands aren't used to that kind of work."

❧

Miriam's hair was still damp from the shower. After her drive to Baljuwstraat, she'd gone for a run, hoping that the monotonous movement would help her gather her thoughts. That hadn't happened. Miriam's own indecisiveness was driving her crazy.

On impulse, she grabbed her phone and dialed Arnold Kramer's number. The phone rang five times, then went to voice mail. "This is Miriam de Moor." She deliberately omitted her job title this time. "I'd really like to speak to you again. I've obtained new information about two people who were witnesses in the case against your daughter. One turns out to have died in August of alcohol poisoning, and the other was reported missing two months before that. If you think your daughter might have anything to do with this, could you please call me?" She gave him her personal number again and hung up.

Her heart was pounding in her rib cage. She was breathing rapidly. Why was she so worked up?

Did she seriously think that Arnold Kramer would call her back? He seemed to have done everything he could to cut his daughter out of his life and deny her existence—although on Miriam's departure, when she'd literally been standing on the doorstep, he'd suddenly become remarkably candid.

Certain things happened after the death of my first wife . . . Perhaps I was away from home too much . . . Didn't want to see it.

What had happened in Hennequin's childhood home after her mother's suicide? Had Hennequin done something to make her father send her away? Or had Kramer been referring to the murder at the boarding school?

Perhaps she would have to ask Hennequin herself. She looked at the clock. It was almost one p.m. There was a good chance the nurse had finished work for the day.

❧

The ginger troll from Norway had wheeled Didi's collapsible shopping cart out of the garage and taken it to the nearby supermarket.

Peace and quiet.

Nelly Vos was really starting to get on Hennequin's nerves. The woman glared at her, literally breathed down her neck. Sometimes, Hennequin got the impression that Didi's mother suspected something, but that couldn't be. If Nelly had any inkling of what she was planning, she would never leave her alone with her daughter and granddaughter. And a SWAT team would have swooped in to arrest her by now.

❧

Miriam had stopped her car in a small lot near the apartment block. The building was staggeringly tall. An impregnable fortress of glass, concrete, and metal that towered above the city. Hennequin lived in number 534. Miriam didn't know which floor that was on. It could be the fifth, but apartment numbers weren't always logical in buildings like these.

Miriam shifted in her seat and pulled her belt a little tighter around her hips. As always, it carried handcuffs, a small flashlight, and a baton. The holsters for her gun and pepper spray were empty—those weapons were in the safe at the station. For anyone in the know, the incomplete belt would be a clear sign that she wasn't officially on duty. She could only hope that Hennequin wouldn't notice.

Her phone rang. *Kramer?*

She grabbed the phone out of her pocket and stared at the screen. It wasn't Kramer.

"What time should I report for duty?" asked Boris.

It felt good to hear his voice. Really good. She waited a few seconds until her breathing was more under control and said, as nonchalantly as possible, "Be there at half past two to give us enough time to get you ready. The briefing starts at three o'clock."

"Get ready for what?"

"I'll have to find you a bulletproof vest, and there are some forms for you to read through and sign."

There was a brief silence on the other end of the line. "Could it get dangerous?"

"It's standard procedure. We all wear bulletproof vests on duty. But I'm not expecting any dangerous situations; otherwise I wouldn't take you with me."

"Er . . . expecting?" asked Boris.

She chuckled. "It can happen sometimes. That's why you have to sign a form before you get in my car."

"And I assume this form says that I'm of sound mind and I risk life and limb of my own free will? And that the police can't be held responsible if anything happens?"

"Exactly." She chuckled. "Are you getting cold feet?"

"I wouldn't miss it for the world."

Miriam explained to Boris the reason she had given her colleagues for his "work placement": he was a well-known artist hoping to find inspiration and do some research for a series of pieces on the theme of police work. He would, of course, have to stick to this story if her colleagues started interrogating him. Police officers were inherently nosy and thought nothing of bombarding complete strangers with blunt, direct questions. It was second nature.

"You paint a lot of urban scenes, so it's kind of true," she said, trying to justify her choice. "Are you looking forward to it?"

"I can't wait." There was a laugh in his voice.

"Great. By the way, what's your date of birth? I need it for the forms."

He turned out to be a year younger than she was.

"I have a thing for older women," he joked when she commented on it.

A few minutes later, she hung up. She'd left home all guns blazing. Now, she was here. The clouds had drifted away, and the sun was shining on the glass façade of the apartment block. A flock of geese flew across the clear blue sky in a V formation. After talking to Boris, she felt lighter. She didn't want to let Hennequin spoil her good mood.

There was plenty of time for that tomorrow. She'd had enough dark thoughts for one day.

She started her car and drove home.

❧

"Well, I'm off," said Hennequin to Didi. "I'll see you tomorrow."

Didi was sitting on a dining chair. She'd sat a lot today, Hennequin noticed. Didi had hardly spent any time in bed. She still moved like a drunken sailor, but there was no denying it was getting a little easier every day.

Good. Hennequin wanted Didi to be able to walk by herself. It would make everything so much better.

"You're crying," she remarked.

Didi stared into space and whispered, "You always think this kind of thing only happens to other people."

"And so you should. If you wasted all your time worrying about what might happen to you, you wouldn't have a life." *Whereas you should know better, Didi.* She leaned over Didi and lowered her voice. "You had your fair share of misfortune in your childhood; I just hope that was the last of it."

Didi's face fell.

Hennequin straightened up again. "Sorry. I shouldn't have said that. You don't want to be constantly reminded about your father and sister dying so young. Especially at a time like this." She paused to enjoy Didi's pained expression. All her words were hitting their target.

"I barely knew my father," said Didi softly. "I still feel guilty about that. I look at photos of him and think, Who were you? The only things I know about him are what my mother's told me. How proud of me he was and how I used to ask him for a piggyback ride and then start giggling. Apparently, that's what he called me: Giggles."

"You were only three. It's perfectly normal for you not to remember anything."

A shadow passed over Didi's face. "But I was six when my sister had that accident."

"Can't you remember her either?"

"I can, actually. All too well. She was always so cheerful and sweet." Didi clenched her jaw. "I was there when it happened. I saw it."

"What happened?"

"I was her big sister; she was so small. I should have . . ." She shook her head almost imperceptibly.

"So what happened exactly?" Hennequin persisted.

Didi said nothing, as if she could no longer hear Hennequin.

"Have you ever sought help? Had therapy?"

"No," whispered Didi.

Hennequin looked down at her with a smile. She absorbed every facial feature, every tiny movement. "Do you really not remember what you saw? Was it a car accident or something?"

"I—I really don't want to talk about it." Didi looked at her hesitantly, her head tilted. "I really don't. It's not you. I just . . ."

Hennequin put her hand on Didi's shoulder and stroked her. "You don't have to apologize to me. I'm here to lighten the load, remember?" She smiled. "I'll leave you in peace. Or would you prefer me to wait until your mother gets home?"

"No need." Didi's face broke into a cautious smile. "I can already walk a lot better than last week."

"I'm so glad. Chin up." Hennequin gave Didi's shoulder a squeeze. A little too hard. She felt Didi flinch.

❦

A soft murmur was coming through Miriam's earpiece. The lot where she'd just parked the police car was dark and quiet. A line of poplars between the parking lot and the road were blocking the moonlight and casting long shadows on the ground.

Miriam was waiting for two colleagues. They'd arrested a Romanian man who'd been loitering at a gas station. After briefly questioning him, they'd decided to search his car and had found a few bags of cannabis. Miriam's authorization was required before the man could be put in a cell at the station.

"I never realized how busy you are on weeknights," said Boris.

Miriam chuckled. "This is pretty quiet."

Boris raised an eyebrow. "Really?" He looked around, scanning the dark parking lot as if a thief might jump out at any moment. "That's not very reassuring."

"Thank you," she said dryly.

"You know what I mean. You're making a difference."

Miriam looked straight ahead. She could make out a light between the poplars. Her colleagues were approaching. "I'm afraid the people we catch on a night like this are the tip of the iceberg. The really dangerous ones are careful not to attract attention. They stay under the radar."

It wasn't her colleagues. The headlights of a solitary car cut through the night.

"It's one of my biggest frustrations," she continued. "That we're usually too late. Only rarely do we catch people in the act or arrest them before anything happens. Most of the time, we're one step behind. We don't get to the scene until after a theft has been committed, or after someone has been wounded or killed, and then all that my colleagues in the detective bureau can do is try to find out how it happened and who did it."

"That's still an important job," said Boris.

"Thank you. But recently it's been troubling me more than usual."

"Why?"

She paused.

"Because of something that happened to you?"

She nodded. Silently, she stared into the distance. She'd been so determined to enjoy Boris's company. To forget about Hennequin, Bart, her investigation . . . But she couldn't. She felt a tremendous urge to confide in Boris. It would be wonderful to be able to talk to someone about it, someone who would look at it from a fresh, dispassionate perspective. She'd been bottling it up for far too long.

But what if he didn't believe her? What if, like her colleagues, he thought she was just grieving, paranoid?

In the twilight, she sought his gaze. "My brother died six months ago," she said flatly. "He fell down the stairs in his own house. I suspect that his widow pushed him."

❦

Hennequin stood at the window and looked out over the city. Night had fallen. The wind was blowing around the building, a soft, low howl that she'd grown to appreciate. She clutched a glass of Brunello di Montalcino and took a sip. Keanu had always been fond of this ruby-red Italian liquid, which he considered the best in the world. A wine to drink on cold winter evenings with friends, if you had something to celebrate.

What a shame there was nothing to celebrate today.

She'd become a little melancholy in the hour she'd just spent in the bar of a five-star hotel, more out of habit than because she had any serious plans to find a new Mr. Money to sink her teeth into. On Thursday, she'd be out of here.

But first, Nelly Vos had to disappear, just like Oscar Stevens. In a few hours, Hennequin would have to return to where she'd left Oscar to prepare another grave. A task she had to complete in no more than two nights. Of course, she couldn't lure Nelly the same way as she'd lured Oscar. Nelly was a woman and didn't even like her. So she would have to use a different method.

A more violent one.

She was prepared for that.

Hennequin put her empty wineglass down on the kitchen island. She thought about tonight, about how she would come home from the hard labor that she sadly couldn't delegate to anyone else, exhausted, with aching muscles and torn-up hands. And alone.

Alone again.

On a whim, she grabbed her phone from the charger and called Mali.

The masseuse answered right away.

"I need you, Mali." Hennequin didn't mention her name. Mali knew who she was. There weren't many customers like her.

"I am on my way," said a voice with a heavy Thai accent.

"Not now, Mali. Later, two a.m." When she noticed a slight hesitation, she added, "I'll pay you double, sweetheart." Without waiting for an answer, she continued, "See you later," and hung up.

❦

Nelly Vos was sitting opposite her daughter at the dining table, drinking a glass of wine.

"I haven't always been the mother I wanted to be for you," she said.

"It's OK, Mom. You did your best." Didi had taken two sips from her mother's glass. Since the maternity nurse had said that a little bit of alcohol wouldn't affect her breast milk, she'd been less strict with herself. But she would have liked more than a few sips.

"I should have stayed single for a while after your father died. If I regret anything, it's that I rushed into a new relationship. I'm convinced that Claartje—"

"Mom, I don't want to talk about Claartje. Not now. OK?" She looked her mother straight in the eye.

Nelly paused, rotating her glass on the smooth tabletop. "You know, when you make such important decisions as having children and getting married, you're often still a child yourself. You're convinced that you're going to do everything better than your own parents and that you definitely won't make the same mistakes they did." Nelly looked up. "And that's often true. You don't make the same mistakes. You make different ones."

Didi took the glass from her mother and had another sip. "I can't stop worrying, Mom. What if Oscar really did run away? He didn't actually want children. And then I put on weight, and suddenly I couldn't walk. The arguments . . . It must have been too much for him."

"If he decides to run away, then that's his choice, darling." Nelly reached for the glass. "It's not easy being a parent. You have to learn to put yourself second. The moment your child is born, you don't have a minute to yourself because you've brought a living creature into the world, one who is wholly dependent on you. That bond is never broken, ever, no matter where you are. People often underestimate the constant sense of responsibility and worry you feel as a mother." She looked up.

"And maybe that's a good thing, because if people knew what they were getting themselves into, a lot fewer babies would be born."

Didi was only half listening. "I should have paid more attention to Oscar," she said. "It was all about me and Indy. I didn't think about anything else; I just expected him to support me."

"If a man can't even handle the stress of pregnancy and childbirth, what are the chances he'll be able to handle bringing up a child? Oscar's still so young and strong; he has buckets of energy. By the time Indy's a teenager, he'll be wearing reading glasses and struggling to shake off sports injuries. He'll have enough problems of his own on top of his daughter's." Nelly reached out for Didi's hand across the table. "Perhaps it's a good thing he ran away now. Better now, before Indy bonds with him and then starts asking the same questions you once did about her father being gone. Questions no child should have to ask."

Didi paused. "I keep hoping to hear his car pull up, that he'll come in and say that he's sorry and that he wants to make things work with me and Indy."

"I hope so too, for your sake, darling."

"What if he doesn't come home again tonight?"

"We'll worry about that in the morning."

❧

Miriam was back behind the wheel of her own car. It was half past eleven, the evening shift was over, and they were on their way home. Boris didn't think she was being paranoid. Not once had he hinted that she was stuck in the grieving process. He'd listened to the whole story about Hennequin and interjected lots of questions. Boris found the name change suspicious in itself. What was wrong with a name like Catharina Kramer? On hearing about her roommate's murder, and that Bart de Moor had also died by falling downstairs, he became very concerned. Boris fully understood why Miriam was so determined to pursue Hennequin Smith, but also why she was keeping her investigation from her colleagues.

"Now that I've reached a dead end, I think I'll pay her a visit tomorrow," said Miriam.

Boris looked at her sideways. "Isn't that dangerous?"

"It takes a lot to scare me." She smiled wearily. "And I'll stay away from the stairs."

"But especially the balcony. Promise?"

She chuckled.

"Shall I come with you?"

"I have to do this on my own." Miriam put her hand on his leg. It felt good to be able to touch him. She hadn't dared to all night, for fear that it would lead to even more touching.

Unexpectedly, he put his hand over hers. He stroked it with his thumb. She felt his thigh muscles tense up.

She didn't pull her hand away until she had to change gears. A few minutes later, she parked her car a block away from their apartments. The parking spots out front were all taken, as usual at this time of night.

"Well," she sighed. She looked at him. "So from now on, you won't be nervous when you see an officer in uniform?"

"No. But actually . . . Still a little bit. So . . ." He leaned over and kissed her softly. "You'd better take yours off."

❦

The sheer curtains and the long, thick drapes were both drawn. If anybody out there were still awake and had focused their telescope on this guest room out of boredom, or driven by a perverse interest, they wouldn't be able to see what was going on in here. The Peeping Tom wouldn't be able to see the candles—the flickering flames, their reflected light, and the shadows moving spookily across the white walls, the ceiling, and the shiny white resin floor. Nor would they be able to see

Hennequin sprawled on the double bed, naked, on her back, glistening with oil, while the small, delicate, equally naked Mali slid over her with a serene expression on her face, her eyes half-closed. Mali leaned on the mattress on her hands and feet and massaged Hennequin's body with hers: her small breasts, her buttocks, her weight. She did it well. She did it so well she could make Hennequin forget that she was alone.

With her body, and her almost ascetic devotion, Mali briefly took away Hennequin's bleak, gnawing loneliness, the cold but real awareness that there was no one in the world who felt a deep connection with her, no one to whom she could reveal herself in all her dark, obscene facets or her humor, sensuality, and insecurities. Nobody had been allowed behind the scenes of her play because she simply wasn't prepared to expose her vulnerability to anyone.

Except Mali.

Without words, Mali had penetrated her being, her soft core. She connected with her in a way so intense, it surprised Hennequin and moved her every time. Their bodies and minds were linked.

Hennequin wasn't alone.

She wept silently.

This was the last time she would see Mali. She wished she could take her with her.

She was going to miss her terribly.

"You want happy end, Henneken?" asked Mali softly. Her slender hand was already making its way down Hennequin's belly.

"Yes, please," whispered Hennequin, closing her eyes.

Day Nine

WEDNESDAY

Miriam held her mug of coffee with both hands as she listened to Chief van der Steen. Fewer than half of the forty chairs in the white-and-gray briefing room were occupied. The chief—a tall, gray-haired man she had rarely seen smile, even at parties—was rushing through the agenda, which covered everything that had happened last night and anything relevant for those on the upcoming day shift. Miriam and her colleagues were asked to look out for a family of Irish Travelers who'd stolen a trailer and managed to escape last night after a chase. The family had no fixed abode and couldn't speak Dutch, but since some members of the family had previously been arrested in Rotterdam for the same offense, it was suspected that they were staying in the area. A photo was then shown of a young, blonde woman who was wanted for unpaid fines.

Miriam's mind wandered for a moment. She felt good. A little languid, and content. A slight tingle went through her when she thought back to last night.

After the shift, she and Boris had had a few drinks in her apartment, and she'd indeed ended up taking off part of her uniform for him. Jokingly, teasingly, yet with a serious undertone. She was still extremely cautious, though now she felt much more comfortable cuddling up to him and allowing his hands to explore her body. It had gone further than she'd planned, but she had no regrets. Boris was a great kisser, and when he put his big, long arms around her, she felt nurtured and safe. And other things besides.

"We're also asking everybody to keep an eye out for this guy." Karel showed a photo of a dark-haired man. White, early thirties, slim, confident. He radiated success.

"His name is Oscar Stevens, married to Dineke Vos. Oscar was last seen at five o'clock on Monday afternoon on his way home from work. He'd told his wife that he had to work late, but that wasn't the case."

Male officers sniggered.

"I know what you're thinking," said Karel seriously, "but this man has no history of this sort of behavior, and he's also just become a father. He had, however, apparently been arguing with his wife."

Miriam stared at the address next to the photo of Oscar Stevens. She knew that address.

❧

"Leave it, Mom. Hennequin will do that later when she's finished changing the beds." Didi was sitting up in the bed in the living room, feeding Indy.

It was remarkably quiet in the house. Nelly had taken Didi's cell phone and put it away somewhere in the kitchen, with the sound off. "Let's take a break," she'd said, and when Didi began to protest, she'd added, "It's only for half an hour. Your baby needs attention too."

Nelly was right. Didi was a nervous wreck. Relatives, friends, and acquaintances were calling constantly to ask if Oscar had been found yet. The phone had started ringing at quarter to eight this morning. And every time she heard that sound, Didi's heart skipped a beat.

Nelly looked at Didi and then at the basket full of laundry in her hands. "I'll take care of this. We don't need Hanneke for this little bit of ironing."

"Her name is Hennequin, Mom, and she's done so much more than washing and cleaning. She's been a huge help with Indy."

"You still think so?" Her mother nodded to Indy, who was drinking greedily from the bottle. "She doesn't know much about breast pumps, at any rate."

Didi said nothing. Nelly was right. Since she'd started pumping with bigger flanges on her mother's advice, her nipples were looking less irritated, and the pain and burning sensation had subsided.

"I'm sure she's a lovely girl, but I think it's ridiculous that we still have a maternity nurse here. We can easily manage on our own."

"You don't have to do that work, Mom."

"It's work to her, but not me." She looked Didi straight in the eye. "To be honest, she's getting on my nerves."

"Why?"

"She never leaves you alone. Haven't you noticed that? When I'm trying to have a conversation with you, she's always there. Some things are simply private. Especially now, with Oscar. I don't think we need strangers around at a time like this."

"Mom, Hennequin has seen my stitches. She was right there when Oscar and I argued about Jip and Janneke, and she even dug a grave for them. She didn't have to do that. Do you understand?"

"That's not how I see it. But it doesn't matter. We have other things on our mind at the moment."

Didi took the nipple out of Indy's mouth, put the empty bottle on the table next to the bed, and held Indy to her chest to burp her. She wished she could just enjoy her baby, who was so wonderfully warm and smelled even more wonderful, but all she could think of was Oscar.

The house phone was on the dining table with the batteries pointedly beside it. "Mom, what if Oscar wants to contact me, his phone's almost dead, and—"

"Fine." With a sigh, Nelly put the batteries back in the phone. It started ringing right away.

"Who is it?"

Nelly looked at the tiny screen. "Your in-laws." She passed the handset to Didi. "I'll go and get the ironing board."

Didi took the phone and pressed the green button. "Hi, Henriette."

"Didi, hello," said an agitated voice. "Have you heard from him?"

"No, nothing."

"I didn't sleep a wink last night."

"Neither did we," said Didi.

"Have you heard anything from the police?"

"They said that Oscar's now officially a missing person. The man who called assured me that they're looking all over the country for him."

She heard her mother-in-law sigh deeply. "I'm worrying myself sick about what might have happened. Be honest. Were you not getting along? Or is there anything else we should know?"

"No, there was nothing wrong. Nothing serious, anyway."

She still couldn't bring herself to say it, even though she was screaming inside, *Your son didn't want this child!*

"Yesterday you said you'd had an argument."

"That was Sunday. He went to work on Monday as usual, and according to his colleagues, he got into his car at five o'clock to drive home. But anyway, you already know that. I told you that yesterday."

Her mother-in-law sighed again. "I know, I know. Let's hope they find him soon, whatever's going on. Hopefully we'll all be able to laugh about it one day."

"I hope so too, Henriette. I'll call you as soon as I hear anything," Didi promised, and hung up.

Nelly had been listening. "That poor woman. She's also worried out of her mind, of course."

Didi stared into space. "Mom," she said softly, "I had such a strange dream last night. I have a very strong feeling that Oscar will never come home. That we'll never find out what happened to him."

Nelly shook her head. "I wouldn't worry about that. He'll show up eventually."

Didi turned toward her mother. "You really think so?"

"Yes. That's men for you. You can never rely on them."

❦

There was no need to hire a moving company. She had no attachment to anything here. Her clothes could stay, as could the dishes, the bed, the plant. It was just stuff. Even the blown-up photo of the railway bridge would be left behind. She'd dragged it around with her for long enough to remind herself of the task at hand.

The owner wouldn't notice that she'd moved out and that the penthouse was empty until the lease ran out. That was still a long way off, since she'd paid for a year in advance.

What she was going to miss, was this place. The ever-changing, almost unfiltered daylight that flooded in through the enormous windowpanes. The sound of the wind and the views of the city and the harbors. The acoustics—she couldn't remember anywhere where her music had sounded better. And she was going to miss Mali. The only person in the world who could sense what she needed and gave it to her—in exchange for money, admittedly, but she didn't have to explain anything to Mali, and that was a rarity in this world, where everyone seemed self-absorbed and unable to relate to others. She herself had lost that trait long ago. Empathy was a weakness. It didn't get you anywhere; it kept you small and humble.

Tomorrow she would be done here. It would all be over, and she'd leave this rotten country, never to return. The tickets were booked. A wild goose chase covering three continents that, for her alone, would finally end in New York City. A bustling, overcrowded, megalomaniacal place full of skyscrapers, where it was a thousand times easier to disappear.

Miriam staggered down the stairs to the parking garage. She raised her hand and pressed the unlock button on the remote control. The hazard lights of one of the patrol cars, a small Volkswagen, started flashing. She walked toward it. He colleagues fanned out around her. They chatted, joked, and talked about a soccer match scheduled for this evening, which required extra officers from the riot police. Miriam only caught snatches of the conversation. It was as if she were walking through a transparent tunnel that let in light and images, but hardly any sound or wind. A soft whistling filled her ears.

What on earth had happened to that family on Baljuwstraat? What had Hennequin done there? Did those people know her—or vice versa? And where was the husband? She was desperate to drive straight to the young family's home and ask them all these questions.

But she couldn't. Her colleagues were already in contact with them.

Miriam got into the car, pushed the driver's seat forward, and adjusted the rearview mirror. She started the engine and drove slowly out of the parking garage.

She couldn't drive to Baljuwstraat, but she could go somewhere else. The fact that Oscar Stevens had gone missing would make the conversation she was planning to have with her brother's widow all the more interesting.

She hoped Hennequin would be at home.

Miriam ran her hand over her belt. She felt her cool, heavy service pistol in its holster, the pepper spray next to it. This morning she'd taken her weapons out of the safe at the station, as usual. Nobody on duty left the station without them. But it had felt different this time. Miriam was no fool. She was well aware that she couldn't use her weapons during her visit to Hennequin. If something went wrong, she was on her own.

❦

"Didi, look how well you're walking."

Didi smiled as she crept cautiously toward the bed in the living room. "It's a lot harder than it looks, Mom. I can feel every step."

"But it's less painful than it was before, isn't it?"

"Yes, definitely."

But it still hurt. And on top of that, Didi felt exhausted. She'd hardly slept last night. She pricked up her ears at every sound; every time a car turned onto the street, she thought it might be Oscar's Audi. Fortunately, Indy was sleeping well, probably because Didi was now producing enough milk. The amount had increased miraculously since her mother's arrival. Nelly's presence was having a positive effect on her and Indy.

But Oscar was still gone.

It felt so unreal.

Carefully, Didi sat down on the bed. It was virtually painless, which still came as a surprise.

"Come and sit at the table," she heard Nelly say. "You're not ill. We can get the bed out of here, don't you think?"

Didi stood up again and walked toward Nelly. Sitting down on a dining chair opposite her mother, she looked at Hennequin, who was humming to herself while ironing on the other side of the room. She wasn't doing a very good job of it. Thankfully, the maternity nurse was better at taking care of her and the baby. Although Didi had apparently overestimated her in that department too.

"Do you think I might have a relapse?" she asked Hennequin.

The maternity nurse looked up from her work. She held the iron upright in her hand. The steam shot out from the red-hot surface, and it struck Didi as somehow menacing. Perhaps it was the way Hennequin was looking at her. Her usual gentleness and compassion seemed to have disappeared.

"In what sense?" asked Hennequin.

"Walking is getting easier, and the pain is subsiding, but could it get worse again?"

Hennequin looked at her icily. The weak autumn sun streamed in through the sheer curtains and illuminated her emerald eyes like a spotlight. "I wouldn't worry about the future. You could get hit by a bus tomorrow."

What was that supposed to mean?

Didi looked at her mother, who was engrossed in a magazine and didn't seem to have been listening.

Hennequin put the stacks of ironed and folded laundry into the basket and picked it up. "I'll go and put this away. Then I'll bathe Indy and bring her downstairs for her bottle."

"I'd like to bathe her myself," said Didi.

Hennequin raised a thin dark eyebrow. The laundry basket was balancing on her hip. "I don't think that's a good idea."

"My mother will help me. Won't you, Mom?"

"Of course I will." Nelly had put the magazine down. After a quick glance at the clock, she turned to Hennequin. "In fact, as far as we're concerned, you don't need to come anymore. You've been a great help to Didi and Oscar, but now that I'm here, it's a bit pointless for you to be cooking and cleaning while I sit twiddling my thumbs."

Hennequin's eyes widened. "But I'm happy to help."

"So am I," said Nelly calmly. "I'm happy to help as well."

Hennequin seemed taken aback for a moment. "Tomorrow is my last day. It's already been allocated by the agency. I also factored it into my own schedule."

"Does it have to do with your hours?"

"That too."

"We don't have to tell the maternity agency that you didn't come for the full ten days," said Nelly, glancing at Didi. "Do we? Then she'll get paid anyway."

Hennequin put the laundry basket on the table and tried to make eye contact with Didi. "Have I done something to upset you?" she asked softly. "Are you not satisfied?"

Didi didn't know what to say. She could barely look her in the eye. "Oh, we are. Of course we are."

"I get the feeling that I've done something wrong, that I haven't helped you enough. Is that it?"

"No. It's got nothing to do with you. You've been a huge help. It's just—"

Hennequin sat down beside her with her hands in her lap. "Oh, I get it. You'd rather be by yourselves, of course. Especially at a time like this. How silly of me."

"It's not that," Didi heard herself say.

"Of course it is." Hennequin's face broke into a smile. "You know what? I'll go home now. But let me stop by tomorrow morning to tie up a few loose ends. OK?"

Dumbfounded, Didi agreed.

"Great!" Hennequin stood up, picked up her bags, and carried them into the hall. "I'll be here around eight."

❦

Hennequin's black Alfa was parked in pride of place in front of Baljuwstraat 66.

Miriam had stopped her patrol car along the curb and was sitting behind the wheel. She wished she could look through the wall, past the bricks and curtains, to see what was happening inside.

She heard her colleagues talking to one another in her earpiece. The sound was less reassuring than normal. The voices reminded her that she could be called away at any moment to deal with an arrest. She was optimistic that today would be uneventful; day shifts were usually quieter than evenings or nights. Still, there was a greater chance of finding dead bodies in the morning. Most suicidal people killed themselves in the evening or at night and usually weren't found until the following day. The same was true of those who died of natural causes.

A young woman walked past with a stroller. She ran her eyes anxiously over Miriam's car. Miriam sometimes forgot she was driving a marked patrol car that carried all kinds of associations for civilians. In the city center, it was perfectly common to see a police car. But not here.

She started the car and drove out of the neighborhood. On the outskirts, there was a roundabout with a carpool lot and a bus station. She parked there, with the nose of the car facing the road. She took out her personal phone and called Arnold Kramer. To her surprise, the man answered right away.

"This is Miriam de Moor, Rotterdam police."

"I have nothing to say to you."

"I'm very sorry to disturb you, but you really have to listen to me." Without waiting for his response, Miriam continued. "Your daughter is working as a maternity nurse for a young family here in Rotterdam, and the father of the baby was reported missing a few days ago."

The man said nothing. Miriam heard him start to breathe more heavily. At least he was still on the line.

"His name is Oscar Stevens. Does that name mean anything to you?"

"No. But I haven't seen my daughter for over twenty years. You should probably find someone who—"

"The mother of the newborn baby is called Dineke Vos."

The man was silent for a moment. Then, with a slight tremor in his voice, he asked, "Vos, you said?"

"Yes. Dineke Vos."

"Didi . . ."

"No, Dine—" Miriam gripped her phone with both hands. "Do you know her? Mr. Kramer, it's very important. A few days ago, her husband left work and never came home. We fear that something has happened to him and that Catharina is involved." She knew she sounded emotional, but no longer cared.

"This isn't a general investigation, is it?"

"You're right. It isn't. This is—" Her breath stopped short.

"Personal?" Arnold Kramer persisted. She could hear his breathing.

"Mr. Kramer . . ." She cleared her throat. "Your daughter's last husband, Bart de Moor, was my brother. He was quite wealthy, and after a brief marriage, he fell down the stairs and died in his own house."

"Fell down the stairs?" he whispered. "Oh my God."

Miriam heard a voice in the background—a woman's. "Who's that? What's wrong, Arnold?"

"Ms. De Moor? I'll call you back later."

"Today?"

"Yes, today. I promise."

He hung up. Miriam sat there with the phone in her hand. She stared vacantly ahead. *Arnold Kramer knows Dineke Vos.* She decided she would feign illness to get off work and drive to Arnhem if he didn't call back within an hour.

A black Alfa approached the roundabout from the direction of Baljuwstraat. It was driven by a woman with upswept blonde hair. She turned onto a wide road leading to the city center. Miriam started her car and followed at a discreet distance.

❦

"Why are you so attached to that maternity nurse?"

Didi looked at her mother. "Attached? That's a bit of an exaggeration, isn't it?"

"You treat her with kid gloves."

"I don't want to hurt her feelings, Mom. She doesn't deserve it. She's been really kind and good to us."

"You keep saying that, but that's the woman's job. If she were bad-tempered or incompetent, she'd be out of work."

"She was right there when Oscar and I argued, and after the rabbits—"

"I know. But you're taking it too personally. People in these sorts of caregiving professions are chameleons. They adapt to each situation. And they have to, because they move around so much."

"But I doubt she sees many fathers go missing just after the birth of their baby." Didi paused and clenched her jaw. Missing. Oscar was missing. She'd once read that disappearances were worse for those left behind than deaths or even murders, because you never gave up hope. There was no closure. What if Oscar never came home? What if he was gone for good?

Nelly had stood up. "Coffee?"

"Sure," she said flatly.

Didi was grateful that her mother had dropped the subject. She loved Nelly dearly, but she was simply wired differently on an emotional level. Some things that deeply affected Didi didn't seem to bother her mother. Didi was certain that Hennequin had been shocked to hear she was no longer needed.

Perhaps she should ask her mother to go and buy Hennequin a farewell gift.

❦

The hallway on the top floor of the apartment building was plain and completely white with a high ceiling. There were two doors opening onto it, so this big building had only two penthouses. One of the doors belonged to number 534. Miriam walked up to it. She examined the door, which was wide and white with a thick metal strip along the edge. There was an old-fashioned peephole at eye level, but a small, round camera had also been installed above it.

She was thankful that she'd been able to come up directly in the elevator. Here, she would be much harder to ignore than if she were pushing a buzzer by the mailboxes far down in the lobby. She'd considered doing that until a resident on his way out had opened the door to the elevator for her with a friendly nod. A uniform did wonders.

What was more, today she really was on duty. Not that that exactly helped matters. At the station, they could see exactly where she was; the location of all patrol cars was closely tracked. If anyone had a problem, her colleagues in the control room could see at a glance which officers were nearby. Miriam hoped that nobody was paying attention right now, wondering why she'd stopped on Baljuwstraat and then at the carpool lot near the roundabout before driving to the city center, where she'd parked the car a few minutes ago. She convinced herself that as long as she kept this brief, there'd be nothing to worry about.

She took another deep breath and rang the bell.

❦

Hennequin looked contentedly at her computer screen. The money she'd inherited from Bart and Keanu was neatly spread across various banks in and outside Europe. Wherever she went next, she would always be able to access her money. Still, she had to be careful. She was constantly mindful that people were trying to find her—she had been ever since she'd left the Netherlands to start a new life in America. It came with her lifestyle; she could never live in the same place for very long or grow attached to a neighborhood or its residents. That had always been a good thing. A great thing, even. It had suited her perfectly. But now that she was about to move on from this city, she didn't feel excited; she felt dejected. For the first time in her life, she was living somewhere she didn't want to leave. She hoped to find a similar penthouse soon after she arrived in New York.

The doorbell rang.

She closed her laptop in annoyance. The security in this building was a farce. Who kept letting visitors through to the elevator? She hurried to the door and looked through the peephole.

It took her a full second to recognize the person waiting on the other side, but less than a fraction of a second to decide that her curiosity outweighed her horror.

❧

Hennequin opened the door surprisingly quickly. Even up close, she was as beautiful as she'd been at Bart's funeral. Impeccably groomed, immaculately applied makeup. Shiny, auburn hair flowed down over her shoulders. She was wearing a black tracksuit that looked expensive. The upswept blonde hair that Miriam had seen before had to have been a wig.

Why did Hennequin wear a wig outside the home?

All kinds of thoughts crossed Miriam's mind. Hennequin was disguising herself. But from whom—Dineke Vos? Did they know each other? Did Hennequin not want Dineke to recognize *her*?

Miriam suddenly wished she'd postponed her surprise visit until after she'd spoken to Arnold Kramer.

"Well, look who's here," said Hennequin coolly. She peered at Miriam with her almond-shaped eyes. "Long time no see. To what do I owe the pleasure of your visit?"

"I saw your name pop up in our system."

"Parking fines? Oh no!"

"No idea why. And I'm not really worried about that. I just wondered how you were doing." Miriam's voice sounded higher than usual. This annoyed her. She always remained calm and could cope with any situation. But now that the object of her obsession was so close she could literally reach out and touch her, it had a strange effect on Miriam's voice and body. She realized she was shaking.

"Really? What a surprise."

"We both lost someone who meant a lot to us. I came across your name in our database and thought—"

"Well then, I'm going to arrest my brother's widow?" Hennequin scanned Miriam's uniform; her eyes briefly lingered on the pistol. Her lips then curled up. It was an unpleasant smile. Her eyes didn't change. They remained as cold and impassive as always.

"Arrest you? Do I have any reason to?"

Hennequin smirked. "Still as suspicious as ever. What a shame. Come in, Officer."

"Inspector," Miriam couldn't resist saying. She regretted it immediately.

Hennequin didn't even seem to hear. She went into a narrow white corridor leading to a spacious living room.

Miriam closed the door behind her and followed Hennequin. This apartment gave her the creeps. In her job, she'd visited hundreds of homes, from smelly, dirty student houses to detached mansions full of glitz and glamour, but no property she'd ever set foot in had been as cold and sterile as this. White floor, white walls—glass, concrete, metal.

The only soft furnishings in this futuristic space consisted of a gray rug and a single sofa that looked outrageously expensive. On the wall behind the kitchen island there was a photo of a railway bridge, which Miriam instantly recognized from her brother's house. But that seemed to be the only thing Hennequin had brought with her from the mansion. There was an overgrown potted palm in the corner, but despite its size, it barely obscured the view since the windows stretched from the floor to the high ceiling. Overawed, Miriam stood looking at the city, the harbors, the seagulls flying past, and the shimmering North Sea far beyond the city limits.

"A bit different from your brother's house, isn't it?" she heard a voice say behind her. It sounded taunting.

Miriam thought back to Bart's mansion, which had been large and luxurious, but not flashy. On the contrary, it had been warm, with lots of photographs and paintings on the walls, rugs everywhere, and sofas and chairs you could sink into. She'd never felt lost in that big house; it embraced you as affectionately as her brother himself.

She turned abruptly to Hennequin. "My brother loved cozy décor."

"Yes, it was so adorable; he was a man of simple tastes." Hennequin continued emotionlessly. "I still miss him. But anyway, what brings you here? In full regalia, no less. Gun, handcuffs . . ."

Miriam felt a flush of anger, but she controlled herself. "I was surprised to discover you're a maternity nurse. That doesn't strike me as your kind of job."

Hennequin's expression hardened. "Have you been keeping an eye on me or something?" She made a sweeping gesture across the city. "Isn't there enough crime for you to fight out there?"

"More than enough. But some crimes hit closer to home than others."

When Hennequin didn't respond, Miriam said, "Oscar Stevens is missing. But that won't be news to you. You know who I mean."

Hennequin raised an eyebrow. "Missing? Is that what they call it these days?"

"What do you call it, then?"

"That pathetic creature is probably fooling around with one of his mistresses. Is that why you're here? I'm not one of them, if that's what you're thinking."

"Not anymore, or never have been?"

Hennequin raised her chin. "What do you think? That I'd get involved with a man like that?"

Miriam said nothing. She had no idea how—or even if—Hennequin was connected to Oscar and Dineke. Hennequin could be telling the truth or just making this up. "How well do you know Dineke Vos?"

Hennequin looked at her inscrutably. "Last week she gave birth to a bouncing baby girl. A real cutie. Too bad the father doesn't seem very interested."

Miriam observed Hennequin's beautiful face. No trace of uncertainty. If she did have a history with Dineke and Oscar—which Miriam suspected, judging by Arnold Kramer's reaction—then she was a remarkable actor. Miriam's heart slammed against her ribs with anger and frustration.

Softly, but with a trembling voice, she asked, "What are you doing with those people, Hennequin? Why are you there?"

"Working. What else?" Hennequin looked past her to a point on the horizon. "I enjoy working with people. It's very rewarding too. I think I've found my vocation."

Miriam heard her call number in her earpiece. She listened intently, still looking at Hennequin. It was serious. A robbery at a jeweler's in the city center. A big one. Several wounded, a possible fatality. One of the robbers was thought to be still in the shop.

She couldn't ignore this.

"We'll talk more another time. I have to go," she said, hurrying to the door.

Hennequin followed her. Her footsteps echoed between the high white walls.

Miriam opened the door and stepped out into the hallway.

"Well, bye, then. Best of luck writing those tickets," said a voice behind her.

Miriam stopped abruptly and turned around.

Hennequin looked at her, her arms crossed. Her eyes sparkled, and a mocking smile played about her lips.

She was laughing at her.

This woman was clearly laughing at her!

Miriam looked Hennequin straight in the eye and then said quietly, but with an unmistakable threat in her voice, "You'd better watch out, Hennequin Smith. Or should I say Catharina Kramer?" She turned around and walked toward the elevator.

🌿

The phone rang. Didi felt her stomach clench at that sound. She grabbed the handset from the tabletop and looked at the screen, her heart pounding. A private number.

It wasn't Oscar.

It was the policeman who'd come to take her statement. "We've just found your husband's car."

"Where?"

"Behind the Ravensteijn Hotel in Ridderkerk. It had been left in the staff parking lot and had probably been there for a few days."

"Ridderkerk?" Didi wondered aloud.

Nelly came into the living room from the kitchen, carrying Indy. She had a bib over her shoulder and a bottle of milk in her hand.

She nodded to Didi and held up the bottle, silently asking her daughter if she wanted to feed Indy herself. Didi shook her head. "They found Oscar's car, Mom. In Ridderkerk. At a hotel."

"Do you know that hotel?" asked the policeman.

"By name, but I've never been there."

Nelly sat down to give Indy her bottle. She looked at Didi anxiously and listened.

"Are you sure your husband couldn't have arranged to meet someone after work?"

"I've already told you everything I know: that Oscar said he had to work late and I shouldn't expect him home before nine o'clock. I automatically assumed that he'd stay at the office, not that he had a meeting somewhere else."

"I'm not talking about a business meeting." He cleared his throat. "My colleague has probably already asked you, but is it possible your husband was having an affair?"

"I don't think so," murmured Didi. "But I don't know what to think anymore, I really don't. I'm not sure of anything anymore."

🌿

"And no one saw him leave his car there?" Miriam wedged her BlackBerry between her cheek and her shoulder as she opened her door. She'd just finished a very difficult, emotional shift. The jeweler had died from his wounds, his wife was in the hospital in critical condition, and their two young children were being looked after by relatives. On arrival at the scene, she'd encountered chaos: broken glass, blood, and terrified people, but no trace of the perpetrators. It still made her angry. It was shocking what some people were prepared to do to avoid working for a living.

On the way home, she'd heard that Oscar's Audi had been found and immediately called Rens. He'd been on duty all day at the station, so was likely to know more. That turned out to be the case.

"No, but the car is thought to have been there for a few days, probably since Monday evening."

"Surely a big hotel like that has security cameras?"

"They do. Just not around the back. Roel has checked it out. In any case, the guy wasn't booked in at the hotel, and he wasn't seen in the restaurant either. But that means nothing, of course."

"Was he meeting another woman in the parking lot?" Miriam wondered aloud. She climbed the narrow stairs to her apartment.

"Or another man. Or his dealer."

"Was he an addict?"

"We don't know. But it sounds sketchy, doesn't it? Tells his wife he has to work late, and his car is found at a hotel."

Miriam opened the door to the living room. "Hang on, Rens," she said, taking off her belt. She put it down on the breakfast bar in the kitchen and held the phone to her ear again. "No criminal record?"

"Nothing. Spotless. But what does that tell us? That he's a decent family man or that he's one step ahead of everybody and never gets caught? Roel suspects that this guy was mixed up in something illegal or got into his dealer's car and witnessed a few things he shouldn't have, with the result that his body will be found by an angler or hiker any day now."

Miriam looked inside her fridge. There were three chilled bottles of beer. She opened one of them. "Has Roel run a thorough check on his home life? Friends, acquaintances?"

There was a brief silence on the other end of the line. "Hey, I don't mean to pry, but why are you suddenly so interested in this case?" She heard Rens chuckle. "Is he one of your ex-boyfriends?"

"Yeah, the love of my life. Man, I don't even know the guy. But . . ." She thought for a moment. Rens was the only member of the force she still spoke to about Hennequin from time to time. She was desperate to talk to a colleague. But if Karel van der Steen got wind of this, she might as well hand in her uniform.

"But what?" Rens persisted.

"Nothing. Never mind."

"Come on, Miriam. How do you know this Oscar Stevens?"

She bit her lower lip. "Are you alone?"

"Yes. I'm in the car."

"Remember my brother's widow? She's working for them as a maternity nurse. For the Stevens family on Baljuwstraat."

It didn't take Rens long to figure out what that meant. His reaction was stronger than she'd expected. "For Christ's sake, Miriam. What are you playing at? Are you crazy?"

"Rens, she turns up here, starts working as a maternity nurse, and *bam*, the husband disappears. A respectable man who's just become a father, no criminal record. What do you think?"

Rens's voice suddenly sounded serious. "If they launch an investigation, I'm afraid you'll have to turn this over to Van der Steen. There's no other option."

"I can't."

"I get it. But please don't burden me with this, Mir. I think the world of you, but I don't like being asked to lie."

Ouch. "Understood," she said. "You're right, Rens. Sorry. Pretend I never called. Give my regards to your family."

"Likewise," he said. "And take care of yourself."

Miriam hung up. "Rens's family sends their regards," she whispered to the wall. She sipped her beer and took a portion of lasagna out of the freezer, put it on a plate, and placed it in the microwave.

What a dreadful day. A man shot dead, his wife seriously injured, and inconsolable children. She'd put her closest colleague in an awkward position by burdening him with information he couldn't discuss with anyone. And she'd played her trump card against Hennequin. What had possessed her to get so riled up and call her Catharina Kramer? It had achieved nothing.

To make matters worse, Arnold Kramer hadn't called her back.

She finished the bottle of beer, grabbed a second from the fridge, and dialed his number. The phone rang five times before going to voice mail. She tried it a few more times. Was he not in or just not picking up? She looked at the clock. Half past five. She could quickly eat her lasagna and then drive the ninety minutes to Arnhem, but in the evening traffic, that could easily take three hours. And perhaps he really wasn't at home.

It wouldn't surprise her after the day she'd had.

She heard something or someone whistling behind the building. Curious, she went back into the kitchen and looked out the window. Boris was down in his studio. He still had his fingers in his mouth. He started grinning broadly and waved at her. Then he grabbed a bottle of wine from his desk and held it up.

Miriam smiled back. She was amazed to feel the stress drain from her body. Nodding, she pointed downward, and mouthed, "Your place?"

He nodded.

She raised her hand and spread her fingers, her palm facing Boris. "Five minutes!" She turned away from the window and hurried to the bathroom for a quick shower.

Under the running water, she felt even more relaxed. It was as if the shower were washing her worries away. By the time she'd dried herself off and put on a pair of jeans and a hoodie, she felt much better, almost energetic. Tomorrow she had the day off, so she could sleep in before driving to Kramer's house. She was planning to keep knocking on his door until he told her everything he knew about Dineke Vos and her relationship with Hennequin.

But this evening she didn't want to think about it. She didn't want to think about anything; she just wanted to enjoy herself.

A silver-colored aluminum suitcase measuring thirty by twenty by eleven inches. It held everything she needed. Clothes, wigs, a few electronic devices, and external hard drives. A much smaller suitcase contained her laptops, and everything else fit into her handbag—ultimately, her passport and ticket were the most important things.

She'd worked out the route she would take in detail. She would travel partly by air and partly over land. It included illogical connections, which would give her a huge head start in the event that someone followed her. She didn't think that was very likely. Still, she'd planned this as if her life depended on it. Her plane left tomorrow evening from Charles de Gaulle Airport in Paris, headed for Beirut. From there, she would travel via three stops in the Far East and Central America to her final destination: New York. In two weeks, her new life would begin there.

She hummed softly as she wheeled the suitcases to the front door. They were due to be picked up any moment by Worldwide Baggage & Packages, which would take them ahead to Beirut.

Hennequin looked around in delight. There was nothing left in the entire penthouse that she needed. Earlier today, she'd put everything she valued into her car.

Tomorrow was going to be a wonderful day.

❧

"Stay."

"Better not," said Miriam, almost with a sigh. She shook her head, more to convince herself than Boris.

Boris kissed her, ran his fingers through her hair, and with his other hand pulled her hips closer to his. "I want you."

"I want you too, but I think it's too soon," she whispered.

He let go and looked down at her with a sad expression.

"I'm going now." She stood on tiptoe to kiss him on the mouth.

He leaned toward her. "If you're lying in bed alone later and change your mind, you have my number," he whispered, tucking a loose lock of her hair behind her ear. "I'm crazy about you, Miriam de Moor." He kissed her again.

"I'll never get away if you carry on like this," she said softly.

"That's exactly my intention."

"See you soon."

"Shall I come with you tomorrow when you go to see that guy in Arnhem?"

"No, that's something I have to do on my own, but we could meet tomorrow evening?"

"Deal," said Boris.

Miriam opened the gallery door and stepped out into the night. Cold wind circled around her warm body. Her own front door was scarcely ten steps away.

While she unlocked it, Boris stood on the doorstep, a big silhouette watching over her. "Sleep well," he whispered.

"You too."

Day Ten

THURSDAY

Miriam opened her eyes. It took her a while to realize that she was lying on her back in bed. It was still dark. According to the glowing numbers on her alarm clock, it was six a.m.

Something wasn't right.

There was a different smell in the bedroom. The space felt different. She couldn't see anything. It was pitch dark, as always, thanks to her blackout curtains.

She tried to move her arm to the right to turn on the lamp, but she couldn't. Her wrists were tied together. Very tightly, as if they'd been wound with a thin string. *That's not possible. You're dreaming.* She told herself not to panic. This was clearly a dream, like the sort where you tried to run, but couldn't move. A twilight state between sleeping and waking. She lifted her arms straight up in the air and tried to pull her wrists apart. From the force of the movement, they banged against something metallic. The pain was real.

Where was that smell coming from? A sweet, intoxicating, artificial odor that reminded her of auto repair shops and cleaning windows.

Finally, her eyes adjusted, and she saw the dark figure standing over her. The next thing she knew, she was blinded by a bluish-white flash of light, and a crackling noise filled her ears, like static electricity or a bolt of lightning. She screamed. Very briefly.

❧

Hennequin returned the stun gun to her back pocket. A handy device. Illegal in the Netherlands, but easy to buy over the border. She'd had years of enjoyment from this one. It had just shot half a million volts through Miriam de Moor's slender body. Hennequin hummed softly.

A few months ago, she'd surprised her old teacher the exact same way. Klaas de Vries, the loose-lipped drama queen. As a result of his testimony, and that of a classmate, she'd spent a year in juvenile detention, and her father had washed his hands of her. Fortunately, De Vries had had a remarkably well-stocked liquor cabinet. That had helped her create a convincing scene for the police, medical examiner, and next of kin. A thorough investigation was unlikely, so there was very little chance that the marks from the stun gun would be discovered. The symptoms of ethylene glycol poisoning and alcohol poisoning were very similar.

It had also worked beautifully with Keanu Smith.

Hennequin held a small flashlight between her teeth and pulled off the duvet. In the sweeping beam of light, Miriam looked like a teenager. Small and slight. She was wearing a tight black T-shirt and short gray marled underpants.

Her former sister-in-law was now partially paralyzed; her limbs were gently spasming, and her eyes were closed. Her mind was clouded, disoriented. She would remain in shock for at least another few minutes. Plenty of time to tie her ankles together.

Hennequin wrapped a plastic zip tie around Miriam's ankles and pulled them together. She looked down at her with satisfaction. She could finish the job right now. Quickly and virtually painlessly. She could also take the time to enjoy it. See what this arrogant bitch looked like on her knees, begging for her life. There was room for a bit of fun.

She wasn't due to start her last day with the Stevens-Vos family for another two hours.

Hennequin shined the light over Miriam, watching her face, her jerky breathing, her occasional muscle spasms. She didn't want this to end. It could go on another hour, as far as she was concerned. Miriam's comment had piqued her curiosity.

Catharina Kramer.

How had she found that out?

And who else knew about it?

Still, she had to temper her enthusiasm. That scream had been one too many. This place was hardly remote; dozens of people lived within earshot of this tiny apartment. At the same time, a little scream or two was unlikely to attract attention in a bustling working-class neighborhood. Living in a big city numbed your senses. But still. To be on the safe side, Hennequin tore off a piece of duct tape and stuck the silvery strip over Miriam's mouth.

❦

"If you scream, I'll kill you. The same goes if you talk back."

Miriam blinked against the bright light shining straight into her eyes. She was breathing rapidly and shallowly through her nose, and all her muscles ached. Her heart was pounding frenetically behind her ribs.

The beam of light revealed a hand holding a syringe. "This is ethylene glycol, better known as antifreeze. If this gets into your bloodstream, you'll fall into a coma and never wake up. But before that happens, you'll feel sick as a dog and be in so much pain that death won't seem like such a bad thing."

Miriam recognized that voice.

Hennequin. She was here, in her bedroom.

222

She had to alert Boris, make a noise somehow. But her bedroom was above his kitchen, and at this hour, he would be asleep two floors below in the basement. Even if he woke up, he would never realize what was happening up here.

She was on her own.

"OK," she heard Hennequin say. "I'm going to remove the tape because I have a few questions for you. I want you to answer them calmly. Nod if you understand."

Miriam nodded. She felt her skin becoming clammy.

Hennequin leaned toward her and ripped the tape off her lips.

"How did you find out my name?"

I can use my hands, thought Miriam. *And my legs. She has only bound my wrists and ankles together.* Very carefully, hoping that Hennequin wouldn't notice, she tried to move her legs. It worked. *I'm not tied to anything.*

She was blinded once again by the flashlight. "I asked you a question."

"Via a private investigator in Florida."

Hennequin paused. Then she asked, "Who else knows my name?"

"A couple of my colleagues at the station. If you do anything to me, they'll—"

"Silence."

"Hennequin, listen, you really have to—"

"I don't have to do anything," she heard her whisper.

Miriam tried to quell the panic surging through her so that she could think more clearly. Hennequin was standing somewhere in the dark at the foot of the bed, but perhaps she could lure her closer, swing her legs up, lock her fists together, and use them as a sledgehammer. And with her elbows . . . But it had to work the first time. She wouldn't get a second chance. With her wrists and ankles bound together, she would never be able to reach the door faster than Hennequin. And she wouldn't be able to walk down the stairs.

The stairs.

The narrow, steep staircase that led from her apartment down to the street. The floor at the bottom was made of stone.

"Who have you spoken to?" asked Hennequin.

"A couple of colleagues. If you kill me, they'll know exactly who to look for."

"Of course they will. But without a body, there's no murder, and no case. Aren't you supposed to know that sort of thing?" Miriam thought she could make out a suppressed giggle. Hennequin had total control, and she was clearly enjoying it.

Miriam didn't hold out any hope that Hennequin would let her live—she just wanted to prolong her suffering. She was threatening to inject her with poison, and there was no doubt she would follow through with it. But only after she'd found out everything she wanted to know.

With a quavering voice, Miriam said, "You did it. It was you who arranged to meet Oscar Stevens in that parking lot and abducted him, wasn't it?"

"I'm asking the questions here."

"Then you killed him, didn't you?" gasped Miriam. She struggled to get the words out. "Why, Hennequin? And why did you push Bart down the stairs? He never hurt anyone. He was my brother, my only true friend."

Hennequin was still shining the light squarely in Miriam's face. She said nothing.

"He gave you everything; he was crazy about you."

Hennequin started moving. Miriam heard her footsteps on the wooden floor. The boards creaked. "Bart was crazy about what I embodied for him: success," she hissed. "He wanted a trophy wife to show the world how successful he was. That was all that mattered to him. It wasn't about me; it was all about him."

Hennequin's voice sounded even closer now. Where exactly was she standing? That smell again. That sweetish smell.

Antifreeze.

Miriam rolled over, away from the light, and kept rolling, off the bed. Unable to break her fall, she landed flat on her back on the floor. She stretched her arms above her head, groping for something to use as a weapon. Was this the bedside table? She grabbed hold of it, but wasn't strong enough to lift the piece of furniture up from this low position. The table crashed to one side and the bedside lamp smashed on the floor. A few books brushed past her face.

The next moment, the light was back in her eyes. She turned her head away, rolled onto her side, struggled onto her knees, and tried to crawl away, but Hennequin's hands grasped her ankles like metal shackles. With a few angry jerks, she pulled Miriam toward her.

"I'm going to kill you, you bitch."

The flashlight had fallen out of her hands and rolled across the uneven old floor. The beam of light shone fleetingly on Hennequin. She was wearing black leggings and dark sneakers. Turning Miriam over, she swore under her breath.

Miriam tried to pull her legs loose. She had to keep moving, to stop the needle from being plunged into her ankle or leg. Her struggling provoked a vicious kick in her side. And another. A fierce stab of pain shot through her abdomen. Tears welled in her eyes.

Do something. Say something!

"I know everything about you, Hennequin," she gasped. "I know about your mother's death, the boarding school, and your conviction. I've talked to everyone. Walter and Liesbeth miss you terribly. They wonder what they did to make you cut them off. They loved you like their own daughter. They believed in—"

"Shut up! Shut the fuck up! You know nothing, absolutely nothing!" Miriam wasn't anticipating the kick to her stomach. She immediately curled up to protect herself, but Hennequin didn't stop. She kicked her lower back and her head, twice, three times, until Miriam lay still, groaning softly.

She could barely breathe; her body had never known such pain. No bone felt unbroken.

Somewhere on the edge of her consciousness, she registered Hennequin opening the bedroom door, letting in a faint gray light. The next moment, she heard a tearing sound near her head. She closed her eyes when Hennequin grabbed her face and taped up her mouth again.

"From now on, you'll keep your mouth shut. You're nobody. And as soon as I'm done with you, I'm going to finish something I've been looking forward to for twenty-three years."

❧

It was half past six. With Indy in her arms, Didi looked out the window. The street was dark; a solitary streetlamp glowed at the crosswalk. Nobody was awake across the road; there was no sign of life in any of the houses. Still, it was clearly morning. You could tell by the growing noise of traffic on the distant highway.

Could Oscar be driving along it right now? She'd once read about people who'd suffered temporary memory loss and sometimes didn't come home until years later. But she also knew other stories. Stories she preferred not to think about now.

Didi pressed her nose between the soft hairs that grew in all directions on Indy's head. Despite her anxiety, she delighted in the warm, contented little person who lay in her arms, so full of trust. "Thank goodness I've still got you," she said softly to Indy.

She turned away from the window. Indy's room was the nicest in the house. It smelled lovely, of baby oil and new clothes. Carefully, she put Indy back in her crib. She managed it. No nauseating stab of pain shooting through her back and lower legs. No feeling that her legs could give way at any moment. There *was* still a nagging ache, but it was bearable, and it was worth it. She'd taken Indy out of bed by herself for the first time and fed her. It might be a while before she could run or play tennis again, but at least she could look after her child.

As she settled Indy in, Didi realized that she'd reached a milestone. It was the first day that she truly felt like a mother.

Hennequin was panting. Her hands were clasped like bench vises around Miriam's ankles. She was furious. Her stun gun had fallen out of her pocket in the struggle, and there was no time to look for it. Miriam de Moor fought like a lioness. She was much faster, smarter, and stronger than Hennequin had expected such a petite little woman to be. A miscalculation. She should have injected Miriam while she was still paralyzed on the bed. It was too late now. The needle had broken off when she'd tried to stick it into Miriam's leg during the fight. So, the ethylene glycol was no longer an option, and that was a pity.

But what she was going to do now would be just as effective. And equally undetectable.

She preferred to keep her hands, clothes, and the trunk of her car clean.

Miriam felt as if all her bones had been shattered. She could see the faint outlines of her own kitchen and breakfast bar sliding past her. It was a strange sensation, until she realized that *she* was moving, not the kitchen.

Hennequin dragged her by the ankles into the living room.

Miriam tried to think. Where was Hennequin taking her? What was she planning to do? Suddenly, it dawned on her.

The stairs.

A wave of fear swept through her. In panic, Miriam drew up her knees and struggled to free herself from Hennequin's grip.

Once again, Hennequin kicked her fiercely in the stomach, twice in a row. Tears welled in Miriam's eyes, and a spurt of stomach acid shot up into her throat. She thought of the frighteningly steep stairs and the hard stone floor at the bottom. *I have to stay low, as low as possible.* She had to prevent Hennequin from pushing her from a standing position, as that would result in a dangerous free fall that could easily break her neck or back. Hennequin removed one hand to open the door. It was jammed. The grip on Miriam's ankle loosened.

With all her remaining strength, Miriam rolled to the side. It worked. Hennequin was forced to let go of her other ankle. Miriam heard her cursing as she quickly got up onto her elbows and knees and jumped up. She was dizzy and her whole body hurt, but she didn't stop. This was the last chance she would get. She fled backward toward the kitchen, jumping like a kangaroo with her ankles tied together, and used her arms as a rudder. *The knife block.* She had to get to it—before Hennequin did.

"Fucking bitch!"

The screams Miriam tried to let out sounded like muffled groans behind the sticky duct tape. The next moment, she was pushed hard. She collapsed forward, fell sideways against the window, and landed half sitting on the deep windowsill. Instinctively, she shrank back against the glass, pulled her knees up, and lifted her feet off the ground to use them as a thrust weapon. She snorted air in and out of her nostrils like a wild animal. Her lungs were about to burst.

Hennequin groped for her ankles and her arms. She moved around in a semicircle, as if she were dancing. Miriam kicked her hands away, tried to hit her, but Hennequin dodged every time and kept coming back, grinning, as though this were effortless, like a cat toying with its prey. Miriam was crying out inside. Hennequin was bigger and stronger, and Miriam's training wasn't worth much now that she could barely move. She pressed herself against the window, kept lifting her legs up and thrusting them forward. Her lungs were burning. *I can't keep this up for much longer.*

She felt cold glass on her back; the chilly night air was only kept out by the thin window now shaking in its frame with every blow. Impulsively, she turned her body 180 degrees, grabbed the handle of the window, and rammed it upward. The window burst open, and she almost lost her balance. Cool air flowed past her. The wind pulled at her hair.

"Hell no, you're staying here," she heard Hennequin growl. Miriam felt hands like cold hooks gripping one of her feet.

In a final attempt to escape, Miriam launched herself backward and pulled her legs away. She couldn't stop herself from falling. She tried to cling to the window frame, but couldn't get enough grip due to the unnatural position of her hands. Instinctively, she made herself as small as possible and squeezed her eyes shut.

❦

With a grim and determined expression, Hennequin looked down through the window. Panting through her teeth, she hissed with malice and gripped the window frame with her gloved fingers. In the soft moonlight, she saw Miriam lying below her, surrounded by glittering shards. She'd fallen through a glass roof. She didn't seem to be moving.

A light came on in the apartment downstairs. It illuminated Miriam's body. Hennequin couldn't see much blood, but Miriam was lying in a strange position, with her head to the side and her arms bent next to it, as if she were holding a baseball bat.

She heard a sound.

Hennequin's eyes flashed along the back walls of the adjacent buildings. More lights had come on. The breaking glass had caught people's attention. Even for jaded city dwellers, this was too much noise. She looked down once more and clenched her jaw.

She couldn't stay to make sure that Miriam was dead. Nor could she get rid of her body, as she'd planned, so that her death would be recorded as yet another disappearance. Somewhere behind those windows, someone had already called the police. And they could be here at any minute.

This would have consequences for the rest of her plans.

Hennequin ran into the bedroom, turned on the light, and scanned the floor. The stun gun was lying halfway under the bed. She grabbed it and put it in her pocket. Then she went back into the living room and hurried down the stairs. Once outside, she returned at a walking pace to her car, which was parked a block away.

On her way to Baljuwstraat, she would have enough time to think of an excuse for her early arrival. There was no time to lose. She had to improvise.

She'd had it all planned out. Nelly Vos and Miriam de Moor would go missing—two completely unconnected people. No team of detectives would link these two disappearances, unlike those of Oscar Stevens and Nelly Vos, of course, since they were family. And they'd rot away snugly beside one another on the same patch of woodland—but with any luck that wouldn't be discovered till years later, if ever. In any event, their disappearances would be blamed on Didi Vos, the new mother who killed herself shortly after her husband and mother went missing and, to the horror of the nation, dragged her newborn baby into her terrible, incomprehensible decision.

A family tragedy.

This was the plan.

It would be the talk of the town. Was this young woman responsible for the death of her husband and her mother? There would be dramatizations on TV. Heated debates. Shocked neighbors would be interviewed, telling the cameras that they would never have expected such a thing from someone like Didi Vos, who was always so cheerful and full of life, so friendly to everyone. Goodness personified.

Hennequin had thought it all out.

But perhaps the new plan forming in her head was even better. Fairer.

And she would still be able to get away with it, thanks to her perfectly mapped-out escape route. By the time her name came into the picture, she would have long since boarded the flight from Paris to Beirut.

But whatever happened, Hennequin would not drive to the airport before finishing what she'd moved here to do months ago. She wasn't going to wait another twenty-three years. There was too much at stake to stop now.

❦

"Hey, Hennequin, you're early. Did you visit the hairdresser's?"

Hennequin stroked her auburn hair that was tied in a casual knot at her neck. She smiled apologetically at Didi. "It's a pretty dramatic change, isn't it? This is actually my real color, but I'd gotten so used to that blonde. Do you like it?"

"It suits you." Didi put her mug back on the table. It was remarkable how much a new hair color could alter a person's appearance. Hennequin looked different this morning. Still as stylish as ever, to be sure, but her face seemed a little harder with the dark hair. It also had an effect on her eyes.

"Why are you so early?" Nelly had let Hennequin in and was standing by the kitchen with her arms crossed. She was wearing a velvet lounge suit. The purple fabric clashed with her red hair.

"I got the time mixed up. Would you believe it? So bizarre! But fortunately, you're awake." She put a bag on the floor and pulled out a wad of forms. "Where's Indy?"

"Upstairs. She's already had her bottle. This morning I was able to take her out of her crib for the first time." Didi beamed and pointed to her legs. "It's going well today."

"That's good news," said Hennequin softly. More to herself than in response to Didi.

"Isn't it? I was so happy."

"Didn't I tell you to take it one day at a time?"

"You were right." Didi looked at the maternity nurse again. That dark hair really did make a difference. "Gosh, Hennequin. Your hair. It'll take some getting used to."

Hennequin gave her a faint smile. She pushed the forms across the table and handed Didi a pen. "This is an evaluation form from the maternity agency. Dora wants to know how you rate my performance."

Nelly was still standing in the doorway. "I'll go and get the laundry out of the dryer," she said.

Didi watched her mother leave the room. She was slightly annoyed at her behavior. Why couldn't she just let Hennequin do her job? Today was her last day.

"Take your time," said Hennequin to Didi. "Give your honest opinion, OK?" She winked. "In the meantime, I'll go and help your mother."

❧

Squares of white with a dark outline, like school graph paper. Glowing plastic boxes—flickering light that seemed to increase and decrease in intensity, hurting her eyes.

Voices. Pain. An indescribable headache.

Cold.

It was so cold.

Hennequin went into the garage. The space smelled faintly of gasoline and the rabbits' straw. There was still a large unopened pack of it on the shelf against the wall. The fluorescent lamps cast a greenish light on the concrete floor. Since Oscar's disappearance, Didi's Corsa had been moved out of the garage and parked in the driveway in front of the house.

Nelly Vos straightened up when she heard Hennequin come in.

Hennequin looked the woman straight in the eye. She closed the door behind her.

"I can manage by myself," said Nelly.

"Why the hostility?" Hennequin took a step closer.

Nelly frowned. "Hey, didn't . . . didn't you have green eyes?" She scanned the other woman's face. "You remind me of someone," she whispered.

"Oh, do I?" Hennequin unzipped her bag and wrapped her hand around the stun gun. She took out the device and, without missing a beat, pushed the contact points against Nelly's shoulder.

Nelly immediately crumpled. It was an extraordinary sight, like a life-size marionette whose strings had been cut all at once. The woman lay at her feet on the concrete garage floor, spasming slightly.

Hennequin leaned over her. She whispered, "You should never have taken my father away from my mother. Now you'll see."

Humming contentedly, Hennequin put the weapon back in her bag. She grabbed Nelly by the armpits and pulled her body back slightly to straighten her out. With a plastic zip tie, she bound her wrists together and did the same to her ankles. She stuck three layers of duct tape over Nelly's mouth. Nelly was untrained and much less fit than Miriam, but Hennequin wasn't going to take any chances after Miriam's escape. With two extra zip ties, she bound her ankles to her wrists.

Hennequin stood up straight. Altogether, it had taken perhaps two minutes and required a minimum of effort, yet she was panting slightly. She felt her cheeks glowing with excitement.

❧

"Miriam? Miriam?"

She turned her head toward the voice. The blurred image came into focus. Boris was sitting beside her in a blue-and-gray tracksuit. Frowning, he took hold of her hand. There were more people standing around her. A nurse. And Rens, in uniform.

"Am I OK?" she asked.

"It could have been worse," said Boris. "You cracked your shoulder blade and broke your arm. You're in a cast."

"How did I get here?"

"By ambulance. You're the talk of the neighborhood. Our street was swarming with police earlier. What happened, Mir? Did you—"

Rens came forward and put his hand on Boris's shoulder. He leaned toward her and looked at her with a deadly serious expression. "Who was it?"

"Hennequin," whispered Miriam. "Hennequin Smith. She tried to murder me. And then . . ." She attempted to sit up, but a nurse sprang into action and held her back.

"Ms. De Moor, you must lie down. You've got a concussion."

Miriam barely heard her.

As soon as I'm done with you, I'm going to finish something I've been looking forward to for twenty-three years.

"What time is it?" she asked.

Boris looked at his watch. "Half past seven."

"We have to go to Baljuwstraat."

"What for?" asked Rens.

"That's where Didi Vos lives. Oscar Stevens's wife."

"The guy who went missing?"

Miriam nodded. "Hennequin and Didi Vos used to know each other."

"And why do we need to be there now?"

"Because I'm certain Hennequin killed Oscar, and now she's going back to finish the job." She sat up. "I have to go. There's a newborn baby in the house."

The nurse pushed her back against the pillows and leaned over her. "Ms. De Moor, you really must lie down."

"I feel fine!"

"You do now," said the nurse patiently. "And let's hope it stays that way, but that's not guaranteed. You've been unconscious. It's not a good idea to get out of bed."

Rens had made a note of the address on a piece of paper. He muttered goodbye and went out into the corridor.

"Go with him," said Miriam to Boris. She squeezed his hand. "He has to take me seriously. They need to send a unit to Baljuwstraat right now, and they mustn't underestimate the urgency of the situation there. Hennequin is highly dangerous. Do you believe me?"

"He is taking you seriously, Miriam. Everyone's taking you seriously. Look at you. It's a fucking miracle you survived that fall."

"Shall I give you something to calm you down?" asked the nurse.

"No, thank you. I'm OK."

"If there's anything I can do, just press this button." She pointed to a display attached to the left-hand side of the bed. Then she looked at Boris over the rim of her glasses. "You should probably go. Ms. De Moor needs to get some rest."

Boris nodded and watched the woman walk out of the room. He then turned back to Miriam. "You heard her."

"She's exaggerating. I feel fine."

"You don't look fine, Mir. It scared the life out of me." His eyes searched her face. "Honestly, I thought I was losing my mind when I saw you lying there. I thought you were dead."

"You can't get rid of me that easily," she whispered, holding his gaze. She paused, then said softly, "Thank you, Boris."

He raised an eyebrow and looked around in confusion. "For what? For coming to the hospital with you?"

"That's not what I meant."

"What, then?"

"For what you're about to do for me."

❧

Hennequin pulled Didi's Corsa out of the short driveway and parked it in front of the neighbors' house. She quickly got into her Alfa and reversed it into the garage in a single smooth maneuver. Then she shut the garage door.

She looked intently at the door connecting the garage to the kitchen. Didi had surely heard the drone of the engine. She was probably still engrossed in the extensive questionnaire that Hennequin had downloaded, customized, and printed out yesterday.

She got out, walked around to the back of her car, and opened the trunk. It contained a plastic sheet and a spade, which were no longer needed. Nelly would get the same treatment as Didi and the shrimp, in the same place. Hennequin had been there four times in the past few months to scout out the area. It was busier now than twenty-three years ago. Their appearance could cause a commotion. But it was a calculated risk, since the German border was only a ten-minute drive away. She would be driving through Germany long before the Dutch police even realized what was going on, and by the time the German police started looking for her, she would already be in Belgium. No one could stop her. Around this time tomorrow, she'd be drinking a well-deserved cocktail by the rooftop pool of the Four Seasons Hotel in Beirut.

But first things first.

Hennequin kept an eye on the door. Had Didi really not heard anything, or was she just not curious enough to come and take a look?

The troll had regained consciousness. She stared at Hennequin fearfully and tried to say something, but couldn't due to the thick layers of tape.

Hennequin wished she had more time to savor this. Nelly Vos, gagged, and terrified; it was a beautiful sight.

She crouched down. "Listen carefully," she said softly. "In a moment you're going to do exactly as I say. First, I'll untie your ankles, and then you'll get into the trunk of my car." She took out the stun gun, and Nelly flinched. "If you don't listen to me, I'll have to force you. You now know how it feels. And it can get even worse."

Tears welled in Nelly's eyes; she shook her head in panic.

A click.

Hennequin turned around with a jerk.

Didi was standing in the doorway, holding Indy and staring at the scene with a dazed expression on her face. She still hadn't realized what was happening.

Hennequin rushed at her and tore Indy out of her arms. The next moment, she thrust the weapon forward and fired it.

Once Didi had collapsed at her feet, she turned to Nelly. "We're going for a drive. You, your daughter, your granddaughter, and me. It's going to be a wild ride, but if you do what I say, no one will get hurt."

❧

"I must be crazy," said Boris.

"I'll make it up to you."

"Any minute now, your brain will swell up, and you'll drop dead, and it'll be my fault. Lift your foot."

She did as he asked. "There's nothing wrong with my brain."

A pedestrian walked past the idling car and looked curiously inside. When he saw that there was no cause for alarm, he walked on.

Less than fifteen minutes ago, Miriam had snuck out of the hospital in a pair of shorts and a very baggy T-shirt she'd taken from another patient's locker. Now, Boris was helping her put on her tracksuit, which was gray with white stripes down the legs. "The stripes match your sling," he said. Miriam pretended it didn't hurt, but she broke into a sweat with every movement. The headache wasn't too bad; her skull was pounding slightly, but it was bearable. Her shoulder and her back were what hurt the most. She had so much adrenaline coursing through her, it barely registered that she'd survived a fall out of a window mere hours ago.

She'd instructed Boris to bring clothes from her apartment, along with her phones. Just as Miriam had expected, the police had already left her apartment. After all, the suspect was known, and there wasn't much evidence to collect.

"Please, Boris, let's go."

He shifted into first gear and steered his Volkswagen Caddy off the service road and onto the thoroughfare.

Miriam looked at her feet. She was wearing a pair of fake pink UGGs that she'd always used as slippers. This was Boris's interpretation of "a pair of comfortable shoes."

If the situation hadn't been so serious, she could have laughed about it.

🌿

Didi was trembling all over. Her hands were clenched around the wheel of the Alfa Romeo so tightly, her knuckles had turned white. She tried to focus on the road ahead. She had no idea where Catharina was making her drive to. Her tears had dried on her cheeks.

"You're doing well," she heard Catharina say behind her. "Very well."

She couldn't understand how she hadn't recognized her in all the days that she'd posed as a maternity nurse and talked to her about her sadness and her insecurities—they'd even spoken about Claartje! She'd trusted her implicitly.

But how could she have recognized her? The woman sitting in the back seat with Indy on her lap didn't look anything like the Catharina Kramer she'd once known. She'd only been six at the time, Catharina twelve. The most terrible year of her life.

Now she'd returned, like in a horrible nightmare.

❦

Boris drove his van into the residential neighborhood. Miriam sat impatiently beside him. Her colleagues were sure to be there already. Still, it looked quiet. No sign of any disturbance. No streets cordoned off.

"Here it is, on the left."

There were three police cars on the street. They were unoccupied, and there were no officers outside either.

"Drive past slowly."

Boris did as she asked. Miriam shifted in her seat and tried to look through the window, but the curtains were closed.

"And now?" asked Boris.

"Park. I'm going to call Rens."

Boris spotted a small turnout at the end of the street and reversed into it so that they could see the house.

Miriam took her work BlackBerry out of her pocket and phoned Rens.

He answered right away.

"Where are you?" she asked.

"Baljuwstraat. Hey, why aren't you resting?"

If only you knew. "What's the situation like there?"

"Quiet." He paused. "Very quiet, I think it's safe to say."

She clenched her fist. *Too late.* "Are they—they aren't, are they?"

"No, calm down. There's no one here."

"That's not possible!"

"I'm not making this up, Miriam. There's nobody home. No sign of forced entry or a struggle, nothing. The Opel Corsa at the curb next door is registered in the name of Dineke Stevens-Vos. Perhaps she went for a walk with the baby."

"Or she got into somebody else's car." *Just like Oscar.*

"What did you say?"

"I was thinking out loud. Hennequin Smith drives a black Alfa Romeo. Are you looking out for it?"

"Of course."

"OK, thank goodness. Please don't underestimate how serious this."

"Relax. We're not underestimating anything here. You could have died; everyone is well aware of that."

"What are you going to do now?"

"Mieke's going to wait here until this woman comes home. We'll head back to the station in a minute. Hey, wait . . . How did you get your work phone?"

"Somebody was kind enough to fetch it for me. Will you please let me know if anything happens?"

"Sure. If you promise me you'll go to sleep now."

"Will do." She hung up.

Boris looked at her. "Well?"

Miriam stared at the house. "Nobody home. They think that mother and daughter have gone for a walk."

"What now? She could be anywhere."

"Not anywhere. She had a plan." Miriam leaned against the headrest. Perhaps she was mistaken, and Hennequin wasn't intending to harm Didi. Did she have a score to settle with anyone else?

As soon as I'm done with you, I'm going to finish something I've been looking forward to for twenty-three years.

"1990," she said aloud.

"What about it?"

"Something must have happened in 1990, something serious. If so, her father must know." She grabbed her iPhone and called Arnold Kramer.

Voice mail.

"Damn!" She threw the phone. The device ricocheted off the dashboard and landed on the floor between her feet. She suddenly noticed that her whole body was trembling. Her shoulder started to hurt again. *Don't think about it.*

"Maybe he's just not at home?"

"He's pretending he's not at home," she said, grimacing with pain as she picked up the phone and returned it to her pocket. "He promised to call me back yesterday."

"Where does this guy live?"

"Arnhem."

Boris started his car.

❧

Didi felt a slight rocking motion in the car. It had to be her mother. Her dear mother, who'd traveled all the way from Norway and stayed to help her, was bound and gagged and locked up like a wild animal in the trunk.

Nelly had warned her about Hennequin.

"Where are we going?" Her voice sounded squeaky. She looked in the rearview mirror.

Catharina's cold eyes were fixed on her. She was stroking Indy's arm nonchalantly with a syringe, humming a song. When she caught her eye, the corners of Catharina's mouth curled up into an icy smile. "You'll see."

❦

"Can't you drive any faster?"

"We don't all have a fancy car with a flashing blue light on the roof!" cried Boris. He stared feverishly ahead. The wheels were racing along the road.

"I'll get the speeding tickets thrown out."

"If you still have your job after this. Try calling that guy again."

Miriam took out her iPhone and redialed. To her surprise, her call was answered this time. It startled her. "Mr. Kramer? This is Miriam de Moor, Rotterdam police."

She heard him mumble something.

"Please don't hang up! An urgent search has been launched for your daughter."

"By who?"

She closed her eyes for a moment. He was listening, thank God. "My colleagues," she said. "An arrest warrant has been issued. Yesterday, I confronted your daughter about her past, and in response, she broke into my apartment and tried to kill me."

Arnold Kramer didn't answer. Miriam could picture his strained expression.

"I need you to tell me something," she said. "Last night your daughter mentioned something that she had to finish, something she'd been looking forward to for twenty-three years. We have good reason to believe that that is what she's doing right now." She paused. "Do you know what Catharina was referring to? What happened in 1990?"

Kramer still said nothing.

"Does it have anything to do with Oscar Stevens or Didi Vos?" There was a tremor in her voice. "Please, if you know something, tell me now. Several lives are at stake!"

She heard the man sigh deeply. It was not a sigh of exasperation, but of someone who was overcome by emotion and struggling to find the words.

"I don't know Oscar Stevens, but Didi was Catharina's stepsister," he said.

Miriam heard the man take another deep breath. Just as she began to worry he would hang up, he continued. "A year after my first wife died, I married Nelly Vos. She had two daughters from a previous marriage, Claartje and Didi, both much younger than Catharina. I then sold the house and went to live with my new wife in Lent, near Nijmegen."

"And sent your daughter to a boarding school," Miriam concluded.

"No, not at all. That didn't happen till later. Catharina and I moved in with Nelly and her two daughters. We hoped we could be a family. But we had trouble with Catharina. Terrible trouble."

"Why?"

The man paused. "I don't know. After all these years, I'm still not sure what came over her. Maybe I was blind to who my daughter really was. She wasn't an easy child; she had a lot of anger in her. You know, she was badly bullied at school. My wife told me about it, and that it was serious, but I couldn't do much to help. I was away from home a lot. Nowadays, you often hear how bullied young people are prone to suicide and how they direct that sort of anger inward. But I don't think I took it very seriously at the time, just as I didn't take my wife's illness seriously enough."

"What illness did your wife have?"

"She suffered from depression."

Miriam paused. She thought back to her visit to the house in that peculiar little village. "Did Catharina find her mother's body?" she asked softly.

"No, she didn't. Thank goodness. She was found by the cleaner while Catharina was at school."

"Where were you at that time? Abroad?"

"No, I was in the Netherlands, but later that week, I was due to go away again for several months."

Miriam was so absorbed in the conversation that she hadn't noticed Boris slow down. She looked at him pleadingly, and he nodded to the phone as if to say, *What's the rush? You've got the man on the line, don't you?*

Miriam gestured for him to keep driving. If Kramer hung up, she would be at his door soon afterward to drag the rest of the story out of him.

"How did it affect Catharina?" she asked.

"She went quiet. Shut herself off. I could barely get through to her. I took a sort of sabbatical and stayed at home for a year to look after her. That was practically unheard of at the time. I was there for her every day; she couldn't stand it when I went out."

"What did she do?"

"She was inconsolable; she clung to me and became physically ill, to the point of vomiting. But eventually I had to go back to work, which meant I was often away from home for several months at a time. I'd known Nelly for a while; she was a good friend of my wife's, and we grew close very quickly after her death. We thought that we could give Catharina a fresh start in a different place, far away from our old village. A completely new life, with two sisters, so she wouldn't be alone anymore, and with Nelly to look after her." He cleared his throat. "But Nelly struggled to keep her in line."

"In what way?"

"Catharina was twelve, an adolescent. She didn't listen to Nelly; she'd talk back, swear at her . . . Nelly wasn't used to that. Perhaps there was too much of an age gap with her own daughters; they were so young."

"Where is Claartje now?"

"You don't know?"

"No."

"Claartje is dead." He was breathing heavily. Miriam heard him swallow. "A dreadful accident."

"What kind of accident?"

For a moment, it seemed as if Kramer could no longer hear her. There was silence on the other end of the line.

"Hello? Mr. Kramer, are you still there?" said Miriam.

"We'd only been living in Lent for a few months," she heard him say suddenly, to her relief. "The three girls were together when it happened. Claartje was four years old; her sister was six."

Miriam began to count. Catharina was now thirty-five. At the time of the accident, she'd been twelve. *Twenty-three years ago.* "That was in 1990, I take it?"

"Yes, correct. My marriage to Nelly broke down after that, because she was convinced it wasn't an accident. Didi had said something along those lines to her mother, things about Catharina. She was very confused. The girl was very young, deeply traumatized; she had no idea what she'd witnessed. I didn't think Nelly should trust her daughter's recollection."

Miriam sat hunched forward. The car shook and vibrated from the speed, but she could barely feel the pain in her shoulder and back anymore. "What exactly happened?"

"Nobody knows the precise circumstances. Catharina often went for walks with her stepsisters. Despite our problems with her, she took care of them like a big sister. And those girls looked up to her. But that day—"

"Yes?"

"That day Catharina came home without Claartje. They'd been playing near the railway bridge. At some point, Catharina decided to take the girls onto the bridge. That was off limits. The bridge is high, and the currents of the Waal are very strong. Desperate people sometimes jumped from there, and—" He coughed. "Catharina said that Claartje had tripped and fallen into the water. The fire brigade and the police launched a search right away, but they didn't find her till the next day. Far downriver. Dreadfully sad. An accident. It was declared an accident."

"By the police?"

"Yes. And that was how it was reported in the newspaper."

"Some people had doubts, you mean?"

"Nelly did. Didi had told her that Claartje had been pushed by Catharina. Nelly believed her daughter."

"And you? What did you think?"

"Catharina was my child. She was all I had left. She insisted that it was an accident. She said she felt terrible for taking the girls onto the bridge."

"Did you believe her?"

"I . . . wanted to believe her, but Catharina wasn't always truthful. And even though Didi was young, her distress was real; it ran deep. It's easy to point the finger at others, to judge other people's decisions, but I was going through an extremely tough time, was often working away from home, and Nelly was grieving. She couldn't cope with Catharina anymore. Only then did I send my daughter to a boarding school."

"Where you exposed other children to your daughter." It sounded reproachful. Why on earth had she said that? She'd gotten carried away.

"If you'll excuse me," she heard Kramer say, "I have to go. Good luck with your investigation."

He hung up.

Miriam called back, but it went straight to voice mail. "He turned his phone off!" She searched frantically in her iPhone for his landline number, but there was no answer.

"Damn it! Damn it!" When she tried to put her fingers to her temples to think more clearly, she got a painful reminder of her cracked shoulder blade and broken arm. She groaned softly and then looked gloomily ahead. "Where are we now?"

Boris pointed forward with his chin. "Ressen junction. We're almost there." He glanced at her and then back at the road. "Well?"

"In 1990, Didi Vos was Hennequin's stepsister." Miriam did her best to summarize Arnold Kramer's story.

"What now?" asked Boris.

Miriam clenched her jaw. Her head was spinning. She was convinced that her brother's widow was planning to murder Didi, and perhaps the baby as well. She wouldn't put it past a woman who'd probably committed her first murder at the age of twelve and her next three years later. If all the mysterious deaths and disappearances linked to Hennequin turned out to be well-disguised murders . . .

Miriam stared out of the car window at the pastureland and windmills. They passed a small bridge. She thought back to the blown-up photo she'd seen on Hennequin's wall in Rotterdam. Hennequin's penthouse was cold and sterile, with no decoration or personal touch, except for that one picture on the wall. She'd recognized the print from her brother's mansion; it had hung in Hennequin's study.

A photo of a railway bridge.

As soon as I'm done with you, I'm going to finish something I've been looking forward to for twenty-three years.

Of course. That was it.

"We have to go to Nijmegen," she said. "That's where it's going to happen. Hennequin is in Nijmegen."

❦

Didi looked up at Hennequin. "I can't do this. It hurts too much," she wailed. Her face was contorted; her hands clawed the weeds above her head as she tried to keep her footing in the low bushes. She was halfway up the high, steep embankment. At the top was the railway line that ran toward the water and over the steel bridge.

Hennequin simply smiled and held Indy tighter. The shrimp was cold. Her lip was quivering. As much of a crybaby as her mother.

"Hennequin, Catharina, please . . . My pelvis still isn't—"

"Stop whining, sis," hissed Hennequin. "There's something up here I want to show you."

Nelly crawled up the embankment beside her daughter. She inched along on her hands and feet. "Come on, lean on me."

Hennequin saw Didi put her hand on her mother's shoulder. The woman tried frantically to keep climbing; her face had turned a deeper red than her hair. Didi grimaced. She suddenly let go of her mother, as if she'd gotten an electric shock. Hennequin could see that it was more a question of balance than strength. The muscles around that unstable pelvis would now be cracking and zinging from exertion; they would be making a sound as soft and melodious as the railway line behind her.

"I have to do it by myself," Didi whimpered and doggedly continued to climb. *What a tear-jerking scene,* thought Hennequin. But she didn't shed a tear. The two women down there had ruined her life.

And now they were going to pay the price.

❧

"Shouldn't you have alerted your colleagues by now?" asked Boris. They were almost in Nijmegen. "I don't know what you're planning to do when we get to the bridge, but there's no way you can handle this on your own, and it sounds fucking dangerous."

She shook her head. "What if I'm wrong? What if Didi went for a walk after all, or she was picked up by a friend or relative? I just can't guarantee there'll be anyone on the bridge."

"But I still think—"

"I know. But I have to deal with this myself. Don't worry. I can call in my colleagues at a moment's notice if it turns out to be serious. And believe me, I will."

Hennequin looked back. A small bicycle bridge ran alongside the track, separated from it by a kind of windbreak or noise barrier. Every now and then, someone rode past. None of the riders looked in this direction; from there, the track was largely hidden from view. The bike bridge hadn't been here in 1990. Back then, this area had been much quieter.

She straightened up and stared fixedly into the distance at the meandering river lined by a desolate stretch of road. Beyond that was her car, behind the barn of an abandoned farm. Close to the bank, but out of sight of passersby. There was also a sandy path off the farmyard that led between half-withered cornfields to a back road. From there, it was only four miles to the German border. Hennequin would hold on to the shrimp in case anyone tried to block her escape route. And shortly, when they were on the bridge, Didi and Nelly wouldn't dream of pushing her off, because if they did, she would take Indy down with her.

Brilliant.

"Over there! Can you see them? Are those people, there on the railway bridge? Damn, I knew it! I knew it!"

"Calm down! I have to keep my eyes on the road," grunted Boris. "How the hell do I get there? How about you tell me if I—"

"Turn off here!"

"Where?"

"Here!" Her voice cracked.

Boris jerked the steering wheel. His Caddy lurched dangerously as he changed lanes and maneuvered diagonally to take the turn. Drivers honked their horns around them, and one man flashed his lights in frustration.

Miriam looked back at her iPhone. She peered intently at the moving dot in the maze of roads. "Take a right at the end and then a left at the turn."

She sat hunched forward in her seat, as if that might help her reach the railway bridge faster. "And then—yes, there! Look! Stop, stop near the bank."

Boris brought his car to a halt on a patch of wasteland. Miriam jumped out and stood in the sand, looking up at a metal staircase that led up to a kind of bicycle bridge. "I can't see them anymore."

"On the other side," she heard Boris say beside her. He grabbed her good arm and led her to a brick arch. They ran under a short tunnel built right through the high embankment.

"There! There they are," she panted.

"Damn," muttered Boris.

Miriam squinted hard at the tiny figures on the bridge. She recognized Hennequin immediately. Two other people were walking in front of her.

Two?

Hennequin seemed to be carrying something in her arms, but Miriam was too far away to see what it was.

"Mir? Call the police."

"I *am* the police."

"You know what I mean," he said. "I know you deal with this kind of thing every day, but I . . ."

Miriam's heart was throbbing, and she couldn't catch her breath. "You're scared."

He kissed her on the forehead. "For you. I'm scared something will happen to you, OK?"

Without a word, she looked at him, and then her eyes darted back to the figures on the bridge. She took her work BlackBerry out of her pocket and dialed the control room.

Boris ran his fingers through his long hair and breathed a sigh of relief.

"I'm calling for backup," she explained. "Let's hope for both our sakes that my colleagues get a move on, because I'm going onto that bridge."

❧

"Why?" Didi asked Hennequin. "I've never done anything to you."

"You'd better think harder," snarled Hennequin.

They were standing in the middle of the bridge. It had turned cold. The sky was gray, and the air was damp. The wind pulled at Didi's hair. Just like that day. It had been windy then too.

It began to dawn on her.

Catharina was walking in front of her on the bridge. She was wearing a red windbreaker and yellow pants. Her dark curls were blowing in all directions. She was holding Claartje's hand. She kept stopping and turning around. "Be careful, Didi. Stay right behind us, OK?"

"I want to hold your hand too," said Didi.

"You can't; it's not wide enough here." Catharina turned away from her again and kept walking. She wanted to go to the city, which was on the other side.

Mommy had told them not to do this. They weren't even allowed to go near the railway bridge. That was dangerous—highly dangerous. But they were doing it anyway. "We're going on an adventure," Catharina had said. Since she was there, she and Claartje were allowed to play farther from home than usual. But they'd never been this far. Didi was sure that Mommy wouldn't be happy about this. She really wanted to go back.

The iron bridge seemed to be moving slightly. Didi looked down. It was terribly high. The river looked like a sea; it was flowing fast, and she could see waves. She felt the wind pulling at her body. What if it started blowing even harder? She'd be blown away, swept off the bridge like a piece of paper, straight into the water.

"And then you'll die," Catharina had said. "Because you'll fall very fast, and it's a long way down, so the water won't be soft, but very hard, as hard as this bridge." She'd stamped her foot on the bridge with a proud look on her face. Catharina knew a lot. She'd learned it all from her father. Didi was still getting used to the idea that he was now her father too. She also had to get used to not being the eldest at home anymore. A lot had changed since Catharina and that man—"Daddy Arnold," as she had to call him—had moved into their house. Mommy wouldn't let her sleep in her bed at night anymore, because that man slept there now. And Catharina bossed her and Claartje around, sort of like a mother. But a mother who took you on adventures.

"Look around you. Can you see it now? Do you remember it now?" Hennequin nudged Didi.

"I was *six*," said Didi, crying. She stumbled and grimaced with pain. The climb had strained her healing pelvis. She grabbed hold of the railing to stay upright. It was dangerously low. In her childhood, it had looked much higher.

"Please, Catharina, give Indy to my mother." She looked at Nelly. Her face, which had been flushed with exertion, now appeared ashen. Didi had never seen her mother like this, almost paralyzed with fear.

"It was here," snarled Hennequin. "Right here." She clasped the baby in her arms. Her expression flickered between triumph and despair.

"Stay right behind me," said Catharina. "We're almost in the middle, see?"

Didi nodded and saw Catharina turn away from her again. It wasn't nice to have to walk alone the whole time. Claartje was allowed to hold her hand. She always got a lot more attention. From Mommy, but also from people in shops or on the street. They leaned over her and petted her like a dog. Claartje was only four, and everyone thought she was so cute with her blonde pigtails. Didi had stopped being cute a long time ago. She was already in primary school, so she was a big girl. And now she was even starting to get grown-up teeth. In the gap where her front teeth had been, an ugly white ridge was growing out of her gums. "Now you're becoming a big girl," Mommy had said. She didn't want to be a big girl.

She didn't dare to look down anymore, so she looked straight ahead, at Catharina and Claartje's backs. Claartje had brought Dolly with her. A ghost made of terrycloth, which she took everywhere with her. When she was watching TV, she stuck her thumb in her mouth and pressed Dolly against her nose. She would sit like that for hours. But she was always losing it. She'd leave it in a restaurant or in the car, or drop it in the supermarket, and then Didi and Mommy would have to look for Dolly or else Claartje wouldn't stop crying. Claartje was holding Dolly in her right hand. It looked like there were three people walking ahead of her: Catharina, Claartje, and Dolly. Why did she have to walk on her own?

"This is the middle," said Catharina, squeezing her eyes shut as the wind blew a few locks of long brown hair into her face. She tucked them behind her ear. "The exact middle. Over there is our house, and there is the city." She didn't look at Didi. She focused on Claartje, bent her knees slightly, and pointed to the city in the distance.

"I want you to tell your mother what happened. What really happened that day. And if you lie . . ."

Indy was stirring. She stuck a hand out of the swaddle.

Didi took a step forward. "Don't hurt her, Catharina, please."

Hennequin gave her a cold look. "I'll take good care of her when you're gone."

❧

"It's the baby," she said to Boris. "She's got the baby."

Miriam stood still. They were now almost within earshot of the three women. She didn't dare go any closer, for fear that Hennequin would threaten to throw the baby into the river.

Boris was standing behind her. He hadn't said a word since helping her up the embankment. He was scared, worried, or angry, or perhaps all three, but she didn't care. Her colleagues could be there at any moment.

Later, at the station, she would have to explain how she'd gotten mixed up in this. But for now, only one thing mattered: stopping Hennequin from killing three innocent people.

The powerful Waal swirled beneath her feet. It was as gray as the sky. She could imagine that it was possible to survive a fall from this height, but very unlikely. Most people would be knocked unconscious on impact, then caught up in the icy current.

Miriam looked at the sky. Hopefully a helicopter was on its way.

"Hey, do you see that?" she heard Boris say behind her. "What's that guy doing?"

She looked up. From the other bank, a man stepped onto the railway bridge. He was tall, with wide cheekbones, and his dark hair was thick and short. Bolt upright, and with a slow but confident gait, he walked toward the women.

"That's Arnold Kramer," she gasped.

❧

Hennequin's eyes lit up. "Dad? Is it really you?"

Her father didn't even look that much older than the last time she'd seen him. She'd expected him to be gray after all these years, like most men of his age. Wrinkled, tired. But she should have known better. She'd always thought she had the most handsome father in the world. And he still was.

A few steps away from her, he came to a halt. He looked at her sternly. "This has to stop, Catharina."

She looked back at Didi and Nelly, who were holding each other, their faces stained with tears, and then at her father. "I didn't do it, Dad."

"Do what?"

Indy stirred again under the swaddle. She began to cry softly. Her weak voice was almost completely drowned out by the strong wind.

"I didn't push Claartje. Didi made it up. It was an accident."

Her father looked at her in silence, his face tense, his jaw clenched as if he were in pain. His bloodshot eyes glistened.

"You sent me away, Dad! Because you didn't believe me. You believed *them*!" She turned her head once more to Didi and Nelly, her face twisted with anger. Then she looked back at her father and became a little calmer. "You got rid of me."

"Sorry, darling." Her father made soothing gestures. "It's OK. I'm truly sorry."

"I felt so alone." Her eyes filled with tears.

How many times had she thought those words? Oddly enough, now that she'd spoken them aloud, she felt lighter, less burdened.

"Not anymore, darling," he whispered. "You're not alone anymore. I'm with you."

"Are we back together now?"

He nodded slowly. "Yes. We're back together now. I love you. I never stopped loving you. Go on, give that baby to Nelly." Kramer gradually spread his arms. "I want to hug you, darling."

Hesitantly, she handed the baby to Nelly, who sobbed and clasped her to her chest. Hennequin walked toward her father, paused, and then put her arms around him. She pressed herself against his windbreaker. He smelled the same as before. "You didn't believe me," she whispered. "You sent me away."

"I never wanted to send you away," he whispered in her ear. "You were all I had. When I stopped seeing you, it ripped a hole in my soul."

"I want to stay with you."

"You *will* stay with me. From now on, we will stay together. I love you. I've always loved you."

Hennequin nodded. Her eyes watered.

"Sorry, sweetheart," he whispered, tightening his grip. "But it has to stop now."

❧

Miriam watched breathlessly as Arnold Kramer embraced his daughter. It was an intimate moment, almost too intimate to observe as an outsider. And too painful. There was so much sadness written on that man's face. Untold sorrow covered him like a gray blanket.

Miriam realized that Hennequin was his only daughter. She remembered all too well what he'd said: *She was all I had left.*

Suddenly, she saw Kramer make a strange, unexpected movement. A sidestep toward the railing. And another.

He whispered something in his daughter's ear.

"No!" Miriam lunged forward.

The next moment, Kramer fell sideways over the low railing, clasping Hennequin tightly in his arms.

There was a scream. More screams.

"No!" Miriam ran to the edge of the bridge. She leaned over the railing and watched in horror as two figures, limp as rag dolls, were swept away by the river below.

She barely noticed Boris holding her back. He pulled her away from the edge. "Are you out of your mind?" he shouted, but it sounded very far away.

As if in slow motion, she saw her colleagues come running from either direction; some had drawn their guns. The bridge was cordoned off on both banks. Flashing blue lights, police tape.

She heard a helicopter in the distance.

❦

Didi collapsed. She was shaking so violently she could no longer stand up. Someone put a warm coat over her. It had a police badge on it.

"Indy," she cried. "Where's Indy?"

"Here. I've got her." Nelly came and sat beside her with the baby in her arms. Indy was crying. Her wails were barely audible above the wind and the shouting of the police officers who'd gathered on both sides of the bridge.

"Poor Arnold," Didi heard her mother say. "He sacrificed himself."

"That Catharina is no loss," remarked a policeman behind her, "if what I've heard is true."

"I'm not sorry either," said her mother to a woman in a tracksuit who was standing nearby. Her arm was in a cast, held up by a sling, and she had a pair of dirty pink UGGs on her feet. She'd introduced herself as an assistant prosecutor. "She pushed my other daughter off this bridge."

The policeman looked down at Nelly and Didi in horror. "What? When?"

"A long time ago. After that, her father sent her to boarding school, but he should have reported her to you there and then; it would have spared us no end of trouble. She was a horrible, evil child."

The louder the commotion grew around her, the calmer Didi felt. She stared at the railing. It had looked much higher back then.

Didi gripped the railing, the thin iron tube at eye level. It felt very cold and also slightly rough. "Are we going back now, Catharina? Mommy said we're not allowed up here."

"That's what makes it an adventure. We won't tell Mommy Nelly."
Catharina's hair blew forward again; dark strands snaked around her face. "Don't move," she said to Claartje, letting go of her hand. She unzipped one of her jacket pockets and took out an elastic hair band.

"See that boat, Claartje?" said Didi. "Look, over there."

Claartje looked around dreamily, her thumb in her mouth, pressing Dolly against her nose with a curled forefinger. Always that stupid Dolly.

Catharina turned her head so that the wind blew her hair out of her face. She was trying to fasten her unruly locks into a ponytail.

"Over there!" said Didi, but Claartje didn't listen. She just gazed at Dolly, holding the toy with an outstretched arm, swinging it back and forth.

On a whim, Didi snatched Dolly out of her hand and dropped it. The dirty white object was caught by the wind and whirled down from the bridge like an oversized snowflake.

"Dolly!" cried Claartje.

She reached out her hands and stepped off the bridge.

Acknowledgments

Maternity care and midwifery: Anne, Sietske, Maartje, Liesbeth, Anke, and Daphne. Extra thanks to Mieke, an old hand, and to the parents of newborn Eva, who let me shadow them for a day as a maternity nurse.

Police: Debby, an assistant prosecutor at Rotterdam police, who, among other things, allowed me to accompany her on a night shift, and Edwin.

Rotterdam: Vincent, Lobke, and Elvin.

Readers: Berry, Annelies, and Monique.

Extra thanks to Renate, Liesbeth, and Sabine for their constructive remarks, and to Sanne.

About the Author

Photo © Noortje Dalhuijsen

Nova Lee Maier is a pseudonym of Dutch bestselling author Esther Verhoef, whose psychological thrillers and novels have sold more than 2.5 million copies in the Netherlands. Verhoef has received more nominations and awards than any other thriller writer in the Netherlands, including the NS Publieksprijs (NS Audience Award/Prix Public), the Diamanten Kogel (Diamond Bullet), the Hebban Thriller Award for best crime thriller of the year for *Close to the Cradle*, and the prestigious Gouden Strop (Golden Noose) Award for best crime thriller of the year for *Mother Dear*, which is available in English. Her books *Close-Up* and *Rendezvous* are also available in English. For more information, visit www.novaleemaier.com and www.estherverhoef.com.

About the Translator

Photo © 2019 David Smith

Alexander Smith studied modern and medieval languages at Cambridge University and has lived and worked in the Netherlands, Japan, and South Korea. He won the Royal Netherlands Embassy Prize, and his previous translations include Esther Verhoef's *Rendezvous*. His work has also been published in the *International Herald Tribune*, the *Observer*, and the *Art Newspaper*.